Port Starbird

A Storm Ketchum Adventure

by

Garrett Dennis

Garrett Dennis

TBD Press, Binghamton NY

This book is a work of fiction. The Kinnakeet Boatyard, HatterasMann Realty, the Sea Dog Scuba Center, Tibbleson Construction, Hurricane Ernesto, and all named modern-day characters and events are fictitious. Other businesses and organizations, locales, scientific and religious references, and historical figures and events are real, but may be used fictitiously.

PORT STARBIRD
Storm Ketchum Adventure #1
ISBN: 978-1496145727

Cover by Tatiana of Vila Design
http://www.viladesign.net/

Author's Note

This book can be read independently of the other books in the series, but for a more satisfying experience, I recommend reading the books in order. *Port Starbird* is the first book in the series

To my wife, my biggest fan and promoter.

~ One ~

He was an old man who fished alone in a canal, and he'd gone almost his entire life without taking a fish.

Almost, because he wasn't dead yet, though that was probably due more to plain stubbornness than to healthy living. And he wasn't really such an old man; the graying hair, though short, and close-cropped salt-and-pepper beard made him look older than he actually was. But he was in tolerable shape and the beard, the gnarled walking stick, and his sun-faded attire combined to create an oddly distinguished effect in a washed-out, island sort of way – perhaps on the order of the Cuban Hemingway (whom he admired), with maybe a dash of grizzled Crocodile Dundee given the wide-brimmed tarp hat he generally favored on bright warm days at sea; though he was considering losing the beard now that it was June.

And he didn't fish; he was no Santiago. But he was in fact standing on a canal bulkhead. The dog was the one interested in the fish, which was why they'd paused here. When he was a child back North, he and some friends had occasionally tried to fish at a pond, using earthworms if they could find some and assorted kitchen scraps if they couldn't, but it didn't take. There was too much waiting and too much work and not enough of a return to justify the effort. It tasted better to him when it came ready-to-cook from the local seafood market, or better yet already cooked by someone else. Though he anachronistically happened to be living near a renowned fishing mecca, the sporting aspect of it didn't enter into the equation for him, as fishing didn't qualify as a sport to him.

But it did to most of the Captain's charters and the Captain needed a first mate, so Ketch and the dog continued on to the boatyard. It was a short walk from where they lived and the dog, accustomed to the route, was unleashed as usual but obedient as usual and didn't stray too far. It was safe here on the quiet soundside back streets, far enough away from the summer traffic on Route 12; and it was a Monday, not a turnover day for the weekly vacation rentals.

The town of Avon's Kinnakeet Boatyard wasn't really a boatyard anymore, since nothing got built or repaired there, nor was it a true marina. It had rather become more like a floating trailer park, an eclectic collection of structures that largely served as an economical refuge for transient seasonal workers, itinerant wind worshipers, and ersatz hippies. A handful of smaller commercial vessels berthed there out of convenience or frugality, but they were outnumbered by houseboats in various states of disrepair, some mobile and some not. There were also three weather-beaten cabins not much bigger than gardening sheds, and sometimes a camping tent or two or three, dotting the shoreline, plus lately a wheel-less laundry truck resting on cinderblocks, with an attached cable siphoning electricity from a nearby utility pole. And there was a small treehouse, which currently appeared to be uninhabited.

Ketch wondered where these people would end up when they all got evicted, which could happen by the end of the summer. He knew where he himself would be going, or thought he did; the logistics of it all were still a bit hazy, but he'd work them out eventually. The devil is indeed in the details – twenty-five of which, at close to a hundred pounds each and with all the associated hardware, had arrived on Saturday and were now stacked behind his house.

He paused for a moment to visually survey the boatyard when he and the dog rounded the bend and it came into view. Despite his relatively advanced age compared to most of the free-spirited residents, he felt an illicit affinity with this place – the boats gently bobbing on the sound in the early morning light, the why-don't-we-get-drunk-and-screw spirit that prevailed, the whole salty bohemian scene. If he ended up having to leave his house before the boatyard was cleared out, he guessed he might try to crash here for a while if he could.

The 'Kinnakeet' part of the boatyard's moniker was an old Original American, or perhaps Indigenous American, name. Ketch preferred these terms over the misnomer 'Indian', which had arisen simply because Columbus hadn't known where he was going, and over the insufficiently specific 'Native American' – everyone who was ever born in the Americas was technically a native American, it seemed to him. Avon was located on Hatteras Island, one of a series of narrow barrier islands along the Atlantic coast that comprised North Carolina's Outer Banks region, and the town itself had originally been called Kinnakeet.

He wished it still was. For reasons that continue to remain largely obscure, when postal service was established on Hatteras Island in the late eighteen hundreds, the government decided to rename most of the island's settlements, and Kinnakeet became Avon. North of Avon there was Salvo, once called Clarks; during the Civil War a passing Union ship had spotted the settlement, which was unmarked on its map, fired a salvo of cannonballs at it which missed their target, and marked 'Salvo' on their map. That one made a modicum of sense. But north of Salvo was Chicamacomico, which inexplicably became Rodanthe; and similarly south of Avon, Cape became Buxton, Trent became Frisco, and Hatteras somehow retained its name – all for no good reason that he knew of. The village of Waves, a relative newcomer, was originally South Rodanthe.

There was some fascinatingly quirky history to be had around these parts, to be sure, and the island was still quirky today in many small and delightful ways. Ketch liked quirky, especially if he could find it by the sea. At one time he'd favored Key West, which was arguably the King of Quirky – but in recent years that island had devolved into largely just another cruise stop, as far as he was concerned.

People and events still generally tended to move more slowly here and Hatteras Island, in addition to its unique background and a modern persona that still often enough leaned pleasantly toward quaint, to his mind projected an aura of tranquility and a sense of sanctuary, especially here in Avon. He'd come to realize that he valued this more than anything else, and in fact had pretty much required it after the breakdown (if that's what it had been), now that he thought back on it; and that was what had finally lured him here for good.

But all good things must end someday; or so he'd heard it said and sung.

The Captain interrupted his preparations for the morning's charter when he spotted Ketch and the dog approaching the dock. "Hey, lookee, there's a Storm a-comin'!" the old mariner bellowed.

A boy and girl configuring a kiteboard near one of the shore cabins anxiously glanced up at the sky. Maybe later they'd trek on down to Canadian Hole, a premier location for wind sports in Pamlico Sound just south of town between Avon and Buxton; or maybe not if the Captain had spooked them, Ketch thought. But then he realized that wind zealots like those two probably knew a lot more about the weather than most people did.

A disheveled, golden-skinned young man with a mop of unruly black hair emerged from the cabin of a docked trawler that had plainly seen better days. He stretched, yawned, and smiled. "Jeez, Don, you know what time it is?" he softly inquired in the Captain's direction. He silently waved to Ketch, and Ketch waved back.

Was Mario living on his boat now? Maybe he

couldn't handle rent at the moment beyond the cost of his boatyard berth, which owning the boat obligated him for. Ketch knew there were precious few conventional rentals that were affordable to locals like Mario in this town, especially during tourist season. He also knew the boat was an inheritance. He wondered why Mario didn't just sell it, and if maybe he should stop back by with a twelve-pack and a pizza later.

Mario didn't often fish, and never chartered. He took on odd jobs around town, a little of this and a little of that, everything aboveboard to the casual observer. But obviously not always, on closer inspection – for one thing, Ketch knew he could invariably produce some primo square grouper when called upon, not just your backyard variety. So, there was one possible reason for him keeping the boat. But Mario was always cheerful, and was generous with what little he had. Ketch knew he'd give you the shirt off his back if you really needed it; though he might have stolen it.

Ketch redirected his attention to the Captain when he'd gotten close enough to avoid raising his voice. "You know I hate that name," he mock-grumbled.

"Well, good mornin' to you too!" the Captain thundered back at him with a big grin. Ketch tipped his hat with a grudging hint of a smile in return. What else could one do? The old salt may be irrepressible, but he was a good man, and possibly the last best friend Ketch would ever have.

"That's better!" the Captain said. "How's my

Jacky-boy doin' today? That ole son-of-a-gun takin' good care a you?" The dog wagged enthusiastically. "Okay, so what are you loungin' around for? Come on aboard and make yourself useful, my back's barkin' already!"

The Captain and his *My Minnow* were both semi-retired. Though somewhat elderly, the boat was meticulously maintained – not unlike the Captain himself, who was not only a fan of the old *Gilligan's Island* TV series but also coincidentally resembled the husky, genial, garrulous Skipper of the original *Minnow*, down to the stereotypical cap he wore for the tourists; though he was somewhat fitter and trimmer than that actor had been. Others generally called him by his name, but Ketch just called him 'Captain'.

Ketch stepped onto the warped and decomposing planks of the dock and carefully made his way to the Captain's slip, the dog following eagerly. "First things first, boy, you know the drill," he said as he removed the dog's life jacket from his canvas backpack and fastened it around the dog. The dog waited patiently for Ketch to board and set up the ramp, then trotted onto the deck of the boat.

It felt good to be back on the boat again, after three weeks away. Ketch still didn't know as much about boats as he'd like, having always admired them but mostly from a distance until recent years, but he was learning. He knew the *Minnow* was a thirty-five-foot Bertram flybridge with twin inboards, which provided plenty of oceangoing horsepower; and he knew it had less than a three-foot draft, which was important because the sound could sometimes be that shallow in places.

Pamlico Sound, the estuarine buffer between the island and the mainland, was almost eighty miles long and thirty miles across at its widest point; but Ketch knew its depth seldom exceeded fifteen feet, and there were numerous shoals throughout that anything other than a flat-bottomed skiff could run aground on. There were navigable paths through the maze for boats with deeper drafts, but they sometimes weren't very wide and often weren't marked as well as they could be. The Captain's inboards were advantageous at sea, but despite the improved maneuverability they provided, they were still a net liability in the sound; outboards that could be lifted to cross a shoal without damaging props and rudders were more practical. But both Ketch and the Captain were familiar with their habitual routes, and it was a good boat.

Ketch also knew it would take some additional dredging and filling to convert this boatyard into a serious marina for the playthings of the privileged few, and probably some more dredging in the sound itself. Good news for the silver spooners, since one thing this town lacked was a real marina; bad news for the crabs, mollusks, terrapins, and juvenile fish and shrimp that needed the adjacent marshes to survive.

"So how are you, and how was your trip?" Ketch asked.

"How am I? The usual, another day older'n closer to death," the Captain grunted. "It was good to see everybody again and all that, a lotta yakkin' and so on. I'd rather've stayed right here, truth be told. Gotta do the family thing now'n again, though."

"I hear you."

"Say, you'd best stow that stick a yours inside so's it don't get to rollin' around like that one time," the Captain reminded Ketch. "How come you're carryin' that dang thing all over now anyways? Don't look like you really need it."

"Well... I like the way it looks, like it just fell out of a tree, and I like the way it feels in my hand. And it has a built-in compass in case I get lost, and a whistle in case someone tries to mug me, and it's handy when the footing is treacherous, like on that wretched dock. Why don't you tie up down at Hatteras like the other charters? You live there, after all. You could run aground up here one of these days."

The Captain chuckled and continued with his work. "Muggin', right. When's the last time you heard a somebody gettin' mugged around here? Anyways, my condo ain't waterfront, and it's cheaper here even with drivin' the boat and the truck back'n forth, you know that, and I know my way around. I don't have no money tree like some folks, though I guess I'll be bitin' the bullet soon enough. Speakin' of, you hear any more from that developer?"

"Ingram? Yes," Ketch answered as he pitched in and helped set up the gear. Today's outing would be a half-day inshore and nearshore charter, in and around the sound and Hatteras Inlet for a vacationing family group, nothing fancy. They likely wouldn't be catching anything extraordinary – the game fish Hatteras Island was famous for, like marlin, sailfish, tuna, dolphin, king mackerel, grouper, snapper, and wahoo, were generally found farther offshore than they'd be going today – but these folks were bound to make out better than they would on a head boat. They'd certainly get more personalized attention with this particular captain, Ketch knew from experience. These days a low-key charter like this now and then provided enough supplemental income for the Captain and enough adventure for Ketch, who wasn't motivated to work full-time at this occupation and was neither qualified nor inclined to mate on the big-game offshore charters anyway.

"He sent me another 'final offer' in the mail," Ketch elaborated, neglecting to specify just how final it really was. "It said I should respond immediately."

"Hey, let's use some a the bigger rigs today, I'm feelin' lucky," the Captain directed. "Another offer, you say? When was that?"

"A couple of weeks ago, right after you left for your vacation."

"Well, what'd you tell 'em?"

Ketch shrugged and kept working. The Captain turned toward him and grabbed a rag to wipe his hands. "Maybe you ought to take it this time. It's gonna happen, you know, no matter what them tree-huggers do, now he's done with his legal troubles. You don't wanna end up livin' smack in the middle a his mess, right?"

"Oh, I know it's going to happen." Ketch shook his

head. "But what he's offering is still less than what I could get for it on my own. Or could have, before all this damned foolishness. Also it's just what they decided is fair market value for the house, no moving expenses or anything." He snorted disgustedly. "Besides, I'm settled there now, and it's my home. I don't want to move, and I shouldn't have to just so some damn rich cracker can line his pockets some more and play king of the damn hill."

"Well, at least he ain't a damn yankee. Oh, sorry, forgot you was a yankee," the Captain jibed.

"Forgot you was a cracker," Ketch replied despite his agitation, completing his part of their standing joke.

"Anyhow, I hear most everybody's agreed to sell. I heard that fella with the horses finally give up."

"I don't care, and I don't care how much money he offers." Ketch scowled. "It just isn't right. And you should see the way that cocky bastard talks down to people."

"You talked with him direct?"

"No, but I have letters."

"Well, that might just be legalese, you know. God knows that's enough to piss off most folks, tryin' to read that crap."

"No, it isn't that, he dictated them. And anyway, what about the environment, and what about ruining what's left of this town? And what about probably getting away with murder, for Pete's sake, what about *that*? I know they haven't been able to prove it so far, but he may well have killed off not one, but two wives for their money. How can people just let that slide and go along with someone like that, like nothing happened? I don't understand..."

"I know, I know," the Captain interrupted. "But hey, come on now, don't go gettin' all worked up so early in the mornin', that ain't no good for us old folks." He stowed the rag and started climbing up to the flying bridge. "We can jaw some more later. Let's get goin', we got to be down to Oden's by eight."

Ketch took a deep breath. "Aye-aye, Captain," he exhaled. He didn't feel quite ready to spill the rest of his story just now anyway. There would come a time soon enough. Never mind the tree huggers... It might not pan out in the long run – in fact, would most probably not – but he had a plan that would hopefully enable him to at least make a truly unique statement on his way out, the essence of said plan being to basically make enough of a highly visible nuisance of himself to cause certain people in high places some public embarrassment and get folks talking.

He wished he could do more – like somehow prove that Ingram was guilty of murder; now *that* would surely stop him in his tracks, certainly more effectively than anything the environmentalists had done or could do – but he was no detective and thus by extension no Sherlock Holmes as well, which was what might be needed here in that regard since everyone else had failed to convict the man. But that was just a pipedream, and he had some work to do now.

While the Captain started the engines, Ketch

released the mooring lines. He took in the breast line to starboard and the forward and aft spring lines from the bollards to port, and then the stern line. At the Captain's signal he pulled in the bow line, and once they were clear of the boatyard he took in the fenders. While the Captain carefully guided the boat out into the sound, Ketch removed the lines from their cleats and coiled them and stowed them where they wouldn't get underfoot later. Then he set out the dog's blanket and water dish in the cabin.

He ordinarily did much of the piloting on their fishing charters, but for now he opted to settle in the cabin with the dog instead of joining the Captain on the flying bridge. It was hard to talk over the engines and the wind anyway. He gave the dog a hug to reassure the animal, who had started panting when he'd raised his voice earlier.

As they steamed south toward the village of Hatteras, Ketch thought about how Avon had changed since he'd first started vacationing here years ago, and throughout its existence. Though Hatteras Island was about fifty miles long, most of it was just a wisp of beach and marsh in width. It was wider at Cape Hatteras and some of the settlements, and maybe a mile wide at best through most of Avon; so Avon was basically a road town, really, most of its business district straddling the one and only two-lane highway that ran the length of the island. And though its beaches were clean and undeveloped, and there was no unsightly industry of any consequence, he had to admit it was largely ruined already, at least to his way of thinking.

Waste disposal, water pollution, and loss of natural habitat were always problematic on an island nowadays, especially if it was a tourist destination; and architecturally, there was precious little of historic value left in the town. No one had had the foresight or the wherewithal to preserve for the public the old lifesaving stations that had once existed along the Atlantic coast of Hatteras Island, except for the Chicamacomico station and museum thirty miles up the road; the Big Kinnakeet station on the south end of Avon, damaged by a hurricane in the Forties, had been demolished, and the remnants of the Little Kinnakeet station buildings on the north end were still in a state of restoration limbo and not open to the public.

And he'd lost count of the ostentatious new beach houses and soundside developments that had sprung up here in the last twenty years or so, often at the expense of older dwellings and other legacy structures. They, along with a plethora of associated realty offices that reminded him of remoras on a whale shark, were now nearly as ubiquitous as the cordgrass in the salt marshes and the sea oats on the dunes. And of course it was vastly different than it had been in earlier times, when this part of the island had been wider before the erosion that resulted from the decimation of the expansive stands of live oak and cedar harvested for boat building and other commerce, and from the now-nonexistent cattle devouring just about everything else they could get at back then.

But to the town's credit, there was less of the blatant commercialism and cultural homogenization here that he knew had infected other popular coastal areas like a plague. Yes, there were some small, touristy strip malls here and there along Route 12, and scads of vacation rentals – but there were no fancy resorts or even hotels, just the retro but trim Avon Motel; no chain restaurants nor fast-food abominations unless one counted the Subway and the Dairy Queen, neither of which bothered Ketch much since he happened to be fond of subs and ice cream; and no department stores, golf courses, apartment complexes, cheap boarding houses, or boardwalks stocked with carnival rides and arcades and other tacky amusements – yet. One would have to go off-island an hour's drive or so north past Oregon Inlet to the Nags Head / Kill Devil Hills / Kitty Hawk sprawl to start enjoying some of those fruits of so-called progress, or several hours farther south. Well, except for the mini-golf down in Frisco, and the go-karts and water slide and such up around Rodanthe, now that he thought about it – but there was nothing like that here in Avon so far.

Though radically changed in many ways, the town still retained some tenuous bits of character and individuality, some sense of history, and some meager traces of its original old-time flavor – but for how much longer? Who needed a state-of-the-art marina with upscale condos and a luxury hotel, for crying out loud, in Avon? And then what else would start sprouting up after that – Outbacks, Targets, amusement parks? And why would any of the bigger boats want to be based here in the first place? If there wasn't room enough in Hatteras, expanding between there and Frisco would make more sense. But Avon was Ingram's turf, and he guessed that might be reason enough.

Fishing and other water sports were indeed the main attractions on this stretch of the Banks, but due to its mid-island location sport fishing in Avon mostly meant surf fishing, either directly from the beach or from the venerable Avon Pier. You couldn't berth nor launch yachts and head boats in the breakers on the ocean side of the island, so from Avon their closest access to the Atlantic and its Gulf Stream would be via Hatteras Inlet to the south, where the *Minnow* was headed right now; and many of those bigger boats might also be unable to navigate the shallow sound between here and there. Were there definite plans in place to do more dredging in the sound between Avon and Hatteras? Ketch didn't know, but there would have to be; again, more bad news for the sound's ecosystems.

There was also Oregon Inlet on the north end of the island, but that was twice as far, and for Oregon Inlet it would make more sense to build around Rodanthe – though it wouldn't make much sense there either, since the Oregon Inlet Fishing Center, a full-service marina just across the bridge, was both close to the more populous and developed Nags Head area, and not appreciably closer to Rodanthe than

Hatteras was to Avon.

Ocracoke Island, farther south down the Banks across Hatteras Inlet, and its historic namesake fishing village seemed to have settled into a tolerable if uneasy truce between the old and the new, and the fact that Hatteras Island had the Cape Hatteras National Seashore along its Atlantic coast and the Pea Island National Wildlife Refuge at the north end of the island would thankfully limit some excesses; but probably not all. Ketch knew that the people who cared here had increasingly had to fight to preserve their free and open spaces, despite their supposedly protected status.

In spite of everything, Ketch believed that at this late stage of his life he was finally where his soul or essence or whatever needed to be, and he'd thought he'd be able to pretty much settle in for the duration when he'd taken the leap and moved here almost three years ago – but now he felt like maybe the lingering ambience of this place, still able to charm despite its imperfections, had lulled him into a false sense of security. Maybe he should have paid more attention and gotten more involved in local affairs, even though such activities ordinarily bored him. But what could just one man have accomplished anyway, especially a less-than-wealthy one these days?

Regardless, that was over his shoulder now; and here he was, reduced to ineffectually complaining about some of the undesirable aspects of the tourism that like it or not was now undeniably the lifeblood of the town, while admittedly offering no viable alternatives. There were no longer any lifesaving stations here, the Hatterasman was long gone, and the modern residents no longer salvaged shipwrecks or hauled lumber or built boats or milled anything or sold yaupon tea for a living. Though it galled him to stand by and watch the future steamroll what little was left of the town's invaluable past, the fact was without tourism this town would quickly fade into oblivion and wither away; and yet, like many of the locals he knew, he'd bite the hand that fed them all if he could. Ketch guessed that attitude might make him, too, a local now despite his short full-time tenure here, a thought he found perversely satisfying.

But that changed nothing, including the fact that, through no fault of his own, this issue had now become painfully personal to him. He didn't know exactly how it would all unfold; all he knew for sure was, things were going all to hell for him once again – pretty much the way they always had sooner or later, pretty much wherever the hell he'd been, pretty much all along the way.

~ T w o ~

But real men are not built for defeat.

*A*nd it was a hell of a fine morning for cruising, and cruising invariably put Ketch in a mystic frame of mind even after all these years, so his disposition had markedly improved by the time they reached Oden's Dock in Hatteras. You should only worry about things you can change, he told himself, and he couldn't change anything at this particular moment.

As they made their approach, Ketch was pleased to see there was a dockside helper today. Sometimes there was none, which made his job harder. He hung the fenders on the stern and each side of the boat and went to the bow. When they'd backed in close enough, he tossed the bow line to the helper. As soon as the helper's end was secure, he snubbed his own end to a cleat, made sure it was set into the chock, and quickly moved to the stern via the starboard side deck to repeat the process, which they completed today without the boat bumping the dock or the neighboring charter. The dog remained in the cabin as he'd learned was expected of him. Ketch did one quick, loose spring line before sparing a wave for the helper.

"Thanks, Ronnie Wayne, I appreciate it."

"No problem, Ketch, have a good trip!"

Ketch resumed tying up the boat, tightening the initial lines as he went. The Captain killed the engines and descended from the flying bridge. "Classic mornin', absolutely classic!" he proclaimed, stretching his arms to the sky. Spying his party approaching along the dock from the ship's store and shifting into what passed for his formal mode, he said, "Mister Ketchum, if you'll make sure they load the ice and bait as usual, I'll tend to bidness." He gathered his materials, disembarked, and intercepted the party halfway down the dock.

"Ahoy there, Doc, and good mornin' to y'all!" he brayed. A gull standing atop a piling slipped and nearly fell from its perch. "Cap'n Don and *My Minnow* at your service, folks!" He shook hands all around. "How's about we all set right down here'n get the paperwork out a the way before we board?" he said, motioning to a nearby picnic table.

Ketch helped the dog up to the dock and they made their way to the ship's store to arrange for the supplies. "Good morning, Roger, " he said as they entered the store. "We're ready for our usual for an inshore halfer for six, if you don't mind."

"Sure thing, Ketch. Hey, Jack!"

The dog wagged contentedly. They were regulars here now and the dog knew it was permissible for him to enter the store; and he also knew they'd pick up something to snack on later, generally a sausage biscuit and a package of little doughnuts, both of which Ketch would share with him.

As they returned to the boat Ketch overheard the Captain saying, "I'm real sorry Doc, I most surely am, but I'm only allowed by law to carry six passengers besides my crew, which is me'n my mate. It's a matter a safety, see..." Uh-oh, a spot of trouble in Paradise; looked like they'd brought more people than they'd said they would. But that was the Captain's business and he was good at it, and he'd find a way to satisfy them. Meanwhile he himself had better see to the ice and bait. "But hey, I got an idea, tell you what we might could do...," was the last thing Ketch heard.

Everything was in place and everyone seemed happy by the time the party boarded. Ketch got the dog settled in the cabin after they'd both been introduced to the Captain's party. Ketch chuckled inwardly; the Captain could certainly be charming when he wanted to be.

He again cast off while the Captain guided them out, and then he assumed his customary post at the cabin controls. He might go up top later if things were quiet, but he'd stay down below for now. This was the easy part of his job as mate; the Captain would do most of what Ketch considered the dirty work from here on while Ketch did the driving, which suited Ketch as he'd rather read than watch people fish.

He'd brought along a book, but he always enjoyed looking at the charts as well on these excursions. He was not formally trained in marine navigation, but he found the Captain's charts fascinating. At first glance an apparently unintelligible mass of shadings, numbers, graphic symbols, varying type styles, arcane abbreviations, solid and broken lines and geographic features, they were much more than road maps, and in their conciseness concealed a wealth of detail on such things as depth variations, shoreline features and surveys where available, and locations of lights, harbors, marinas, underwater obstacles, wrecks, navigational markers, dredged and undredged basins and channels, dredge dumping areas, and known artillery drops. Ketch thought of ordering a set of local charts just for his own personal perusal every time he saw them on the boat, but he'd somehow not gotten around to it yet.

"Mister Ketchum, let's head northwest, see if we can get us some flounder," the Captain called. "But watch the shoals!"

"Roger that," Ketch replied. Though the Captain had a good GPS, he intended to also reference the charts along the way. Technology has its advantages, but he thought it was a shame that the old methods had to drop by the wayside. Navigational techniques had of course been changing and advancing since the era of sail, but still...

Most recently, he'd just missed out on LORAN-C. Since World War II the LORAN network, a radio-based geo-location system, had been a reliable albeit complex way for sailors and pilots around the world to locate their position. But with the advent of GPS the decision had been made to shut down the broadcast towers, and the Coast Guard had taken the last U.S. tower off-line about three years ago. Ketch hoped the satellites didn't somehow become disabled someday, by terrorists or a war or even just the sun misbehaving – then everyone would be blind again, electronically speaking. He wondered how many people still knew how to navigate by the sun, moon, and stars.

His reveries were interrupted by the thumping of the dog's tail on the deck. The youngest member of the party had entered the cabin and was petting the dog and staring at Ketch. The Captain followed the boy in.

"Ahoy, Mister Ketchum, this young 'un here is called Henry," the Captain said, resting a hand on the boy's shoulder. The normally blustery skipper seemed atypically trepidatious, which Ketch found interesting. "See, we got us too many passengers today, legally speakin'," he continued, "so I'm thinkin' we might need to have two mates on this charter, if you catch my drift." Ketch did and nodded amiably, to the Captain's visible relief. "So, young Henry will be our second mate today," the Captain concluded. "Now Henry, Mister Ketchum here is our first mate, and I'm the captain – so he takes his orders from me, and you take your orders from him. You got that, son?"

"Yes sir," the boy replied deferentially, his head bowed. He looked up at Ketch. "Where'd you get that hat, sir?" he inquired.

Ketch gave the boy a friendly smile. Though it had been a long time and he hadn't seen much of his son even then, he remembered when that boy had been this one's age. "Do you like it?" he asked, and the boy shyly nodded. "Well, Indiana Jones gave it to me. Do you know who he is?" The boy nodded again, wide-eyed. "It's made from recycled truck tarps from South America. He wore this hat one time when we explored some ruins down there. He got a new hat after that, the one he wears in the movies, so he gave me this one."

The Captain guffawed, startling the boy. "Don't fall for his malarkey, son! He got that hat at Nag's Head Hammocks up in Avon, I was there when he bought it!"

The boy looked back at Ketch in confusion. "He's right," Ketch said. "I told you a tall tale. You know what that is, right? Anyway, it's a good hat, isn't it? Okay, come over here." He motioned for the boy to join him at the controls. "Have you ever driven a boat?" The boy shook his head. "Well here, take the wheel for a little while. I need a break." The boy's eyes grew even wider. "Really, it's okay. Here you go, two hands, that's right. Now do you see this mark on the compass? You have to try to make the needle stay close to that mark. That's good, now turn left, just a little, and wait for the boat to catch up with you. She responds slowly, so you don't want to oversteer..."

The Captain quietly exited the cabin, and the boy's face glowed as Ketch continued to coach him. When it appeared he'd more or less gotten the hang of it, Ketch left him at the wheel and went to fetch a bottle of water from the Captain's cooler. They were advancing slowly enough that it wouldn't much matter if they went a bit off-course, at least for a short time in this particular area. They had to be always mindful of the shoals in these waters. It would be embarrassing to run aground at any time, but especially so during a charter.

Ketch settled in the cabin behind the boy where he

could see the compass and the GPS, drank his water, and shared his breakfast with the dog. Then he rejoined the boy at the wheel.

"Good job, Henry! Really, not bad for your first time," he said. "Okay now, keep one hand on the wheel and put your other one here, on the throttles. We're almost where we want to be, so we have to start slowing down now. Remember, a boat doesn't have brakes..."

When it was time to stop, Ketch relieved the boy at the controls. "You can go out and fish for a while now, Henry, if you like," he said. "I'll call you back when I need you. Okay?" The boy left the cabin then, as did the dog who was curious as always about what these people might drag up from below the surface.

They'd idle and fish for a while here and see what developed. Ketch retrieved a battered paperback book from his backpack. He generally preferred his electronic-book reader these days, but exposing it to salt and spray was probably not a wise thing to do. The dog wandered back in and Ketch gave him a bone to gnaw on, then climbed up to the flying bridge. It would be comfortable there under the awning with the brisk sea breeze that was blowing today, and he'd have the controls there in case he was needed.

Meanwhile he'd see if he could remember what was going to happen to Harry Morgan next in *To Have and Have Not*. He'd read this book before, but it had been a long time. He reminded himself to revisit *The Old Man and the Sea* soon; though he'd read that one several times through the years, it was by far his favorite. Re-reading it periodically was almost like a religious obligation for him, and he'd lately been feeling drawn to it again.

But for now, back to Harry. He knew the adventures of pirates and smugglers, even the more modern kind like Harry, struck most people as romantic, but in reality it had always been a brutal and unforgiving way of life. But then again, nowadays there was the Wall Street crowd, for example, many of whom could be viewed as simply more sophisticated technology-based pirates, couldn't they? Their lives were usually longer and richer, but perhaps not any less difficult than the lives of the pirates of old, at least in terms of stress, especially for the ones who lived on the edge of the law or slightly beyond. And then there were people like Bob Ingram, the owner of HatterasMann Realty and the main depositor in Ketch's current bank of misery.

'HatterasMann' – a clever bit of wordplay, he supposed, but he wasn't amused by it. The Hatterasman was the noblest figure in Hatteras Island lore. He was a rugged, proud, unpretentious and self-sufficient abstraction, making his living from fishing, whaling, boat building, wreck salvaging, farming whatever he could get to grow in this harsh environment, doing whatever it took to survive back in the wild old days.

The Hatterasman was epitomized by the surfmen employed by the old U.S. Lifesaving Service and later the U.S. Coast Guard. At grave personal risk, these men attempted to rescue mariners from offshore shipwrecks, starting in the time before internal combustion engines and reliable charts. There'd been lighthouses along this coast since the late seventeen hundreds, but they weren't always adequate; and a combination of strong currents, frequent storms, and deadly shifting shoals had earned the coastal shipping lanes off Cape Hatteras the well-known epithet 'Graveyard of the Atlantic'.

Beginning in the mid-eighteen hundreds, crews of these courageous men would launch sturdy wooden surfboats into the breakers and row out when a wreck was sighted, often at night and regardless of the season, and even during the fiercest of storms. Their regulations required them to go out, but didn't require them to return. Numerous members of several crews had over the years been awarded Gold and Silver Lifesaving Medals of Honor for their efforts, the highest honors that can be given for saving lives in peacetime. There'd been seven official lifesaving stations along the Atlantic coast of the island from 1874 well into the next century, two of them in the Kinnakeet area.

Whereas 'Mann' was simply the maiden name of Ingram's first wife, the founder of the realty he'd simply inherited from her.

"Good work, Mister Ketchum!" the Captain called after Ketch had been reading a while, oblivious to the activity below. "We got enough flounder and spots to fill a cooler! How's about takin' us through the inlet?"

"Will do," Ketch called back. He summoned the boy up to the flying bridge and they got the boat underway again. Ketch knew the buoys and markers, such as they were in this changeable inlet, and when they reached the entrance of the inlet he pointed them out to the boy as he helped him navigate them through, giving a wide berth to other traffic and keeping a special eye out for the ferryboats that regularly traversed the roughly two-mile-wide inlet between Hatteras and Ocracoke Island to the southwest.

Ketch noted the boy's obvious exuberance at being permitted to pilot the boat from the flying bridge, and at the same time the boy's continued self-discipline. This must seem like a wild ride to him, Ketch thought, yet he's still paying attention and keeping himself under control. He also didn't appear to be getting sick from the pitching, rolling, and yawing of the boat, which were all exaggerated at this height. Ketch, too, had always been lucky in that regard; he'd never been seasick a day in his life, no matter the conditions.

When they were about to exit the inlet, Ketch realized the Captain hadn't specified which direction to proceed in from there. Before he could call down to ask, he spotted a pelican gliding by. He wondered if it was one of the regulars that had started showing up at the docks to claim some of the culls from the fishermen's daily catches. There were still not that many of them in this area, but they'd recovered from the DDT debacle of a few decades back and were no longer considered endangered, though it wasn't until the mid-Eighties that they'd begun nesting along this coast in earnest. They'd originally mostly lived farther south, notably in Texas and Louisiana, where the use of pesticides laden with DDT had decimated their populations in the Fifties and Sixties. As with other carnivorous birds, like the ospreys and the peregrines, the chemical had caused them to lay thin-shelled eggs. But now they were making a comeback, so much so that they were expanding up the east coast.

Ketch saw the pelican go into a steep dive straight into the water some distance up ahead. It appeared to be feeding on something, so he had the boy turn the boat in that direction. He focused and saw there were gulls and terns congregating there as well, and he thought he could see fish jumping at the surface. They throttled back some and when they got close he idled the engines, sent the boy back down to fish, and allowed the boat to drift along the fringe of the feeding area.

He checked the fish finder as they drifted. It looked like there might be two schools in the area, maybe Spanish mackerel and menhaden. Maybe they were being driven together by predators. This could be a hot spot. Whatever they were, this conglomeration of fish would soon be undergoing a three-pronged attack – the schooling ones on the outskirts of the swimming masses would be picked off by bigger fish, those that ventured too near the surface or above it were fair game for the birds, and the fishing hooks would hopefully soon prey in turn on the school's predators. The fishermen below wouldn't be targeting the menhaden if that's what they were, as they were filter feeders, but the mackerel and whatever else was after all of them below the surface might keep the party busy for a while.

It would probably be a little while before they caught much, so he allowed his mind to wander and considered Ingram again as those below started casting their lines. He remembered reading that Ingram's first wife had died under somewhat questionable circumstances, sometime before Ketch had moved here. A boat drowning, he now recalled, but there had been drinking and recreational drugs and a well-documented argument during a nighttime party on a yacht – which had been docked, not under sail; and there had been an inquiry. But it had been ruled an accidental drowning. At least they'd had a body to examine that time, unlike in the case of the disappearance of Ingram's second wife.

After a while Ketch heard a commotion from below. "Hey, you got somethin' there for sure, son!" the Captain exclaimed. "Lemme give you a hand with that!"

Ketch decided to go below in case he was needed, and also to tend to the safety of the dog. He'd leash the dog to something in the cabin until he knew whether they had a fighter on the line. If the dog got too close to the wrong fish while it thrashed its last life out on the deck, he could be injured by errant teeth or spines or bills.

By the time Ketch got the dog leashed there was a jack flopping on the deck. It looked to be at least a ten-pounder, which was noteworthy for a jack as it was a fighter, but he knew this fish shouldn't be eaten due to the possibility of ciguatera poisoning. If it were a pompano, okay, but not amberjack. But this wouldn't matter to the boy, who looked about as happy as a boy could look. He appeared to be having an excellent day, Ketch thought; good for him.

It looked like a couple of the others were reeling in mackerel – Spanish, smaller cousins of the king mackerel, but decent eating – and someone had hooked what looked to be a puppy drum, and another was struggling to bring in a thrashing bluefish. He'd been right to follow that pelican.

Before anyone could do anything with the jack, one of the men announced he had something really big, and the Captain hurried over to assist. Ketch considered releasing the jack, but it looked like it might be too late for that now, and they might want to mount it or something for the boy anyway. He found some gloves and showed the boy how to remove the hook and stow the fish.

An epic struggle appeared to be taking shape near the stern. "I don't know if this line is strong enough to hold 'im!" the Captain declared. "Don't yank on it Doc, we don't want 'im to throw the hook! Don't try to reel 'im in yet, if he runs let 'im take some line, hope there's enough! Everybody else reel in your fish and get your lines out a the water, we don't want to get tangled. *Now*! And you there, watch out for that blue, he's got razor teeth!"

Without being told, Ketch herded the boy back up to the flying bridge, where the view would be better. They prepared to throttle up. He'd use the boat to make up for any deficiency in the line. If the fish took out a lot of line, he'd make the boat follow it so they could reel in the excess and reuse it for the next run.

After several strong runs the fish finally began to tire, and they were eventually able to reel it in closer to the boat. When it got close enough, Ketch left the boy at the helm and went down and helped the Captain gaff it and haul it aboard.

It was a cobia. The Captain made everyone stand back while he put the creature out of its misery before it could hurt anyone. The cobia's horizontal pectoral fins can enable it to remain upright and thrash vigorously on a boat deck, making its sharp spines a hazard to bystanders.

Ketch called the boy down, then went into the cabin and released the dog so it could investigate. He heard his cell phone beep and retrieved it from his backpack. It looked like there were a couple more missed calls like the other day, but again the caller ID wasn't showing the number. Probably some charity or other; it had better not be telemarketers, since he was on the do-not-call list and he could and would report them. When he noticed the time on the phone's display, he was surprised to see it had been almost three hours since they'd left Oden's.

"Well, will y'all look at that – a cobia! I bet he's fifty pounds!" the Captain announced. "That's damn respectable for cobia. You did good, Doc – that there is a good eatin' fish! We better pack it in some ice, and then you can have 'em cut it up for you back at the dock. Here, you guys can stick it right in here, you're younger'n me and my arms are tired..."

When the fish was secure, the Captain went into the cabin to get a drink, and Ketch followed him in. "Ain't that the damnedest thing!" the Captain exclaimed, plopping down on a bench to rest. "Cobia's hard to find in the first place, never mind hard to catch, and we weren't even tryin', didn't even have the best bait. Just shit-all dumb luck, that's all. Good thing we had the heavier line on." He briefly grinned. "Well, they're happy now. Bet I'll be gettin' a good review on my website for this trip!"

"I wouldn't be surprised," Ketch replied. "It's a good fish, and it's been a good morning." The dog joined them and Ketch also sat, and scratched its ears. "Thank you again for having us, as always."

"No no, thank *you*-all for helpin' out! Especially with that boy like you done, I appreciate that. I didn't want to have to leave somebody behind, and I figured they'd let us slide with the second mate thing if anybody asked about it. Sorry 'bout springin' it on you like that."

"No problem. It's been fun, he's a good kid."

The Captain took a final pull on his water bottle and stood up. "Okay. Well, I think we might could start headin' back now, let 'em troll along the way if they want. I sure hope we don't have no more dumb luck though, or we could be out here all dang day. Don't stop unless you have to!"

"I hear you. If I see another pelican, I'll go the other way this time."

The rest of the trip was relatively uneventful.

Someone hooked a striper, and someone else added a trout to their cache. A pretty good haul overall for a half-day trip. He supposed he shouldn't be surprised. Pamlico Sound and the nearshore Atlantic here were said to offer a world-class variety of fishing opportunities; one didn't necessarily have to go all the way out to the Gulf Stream for a good time. But the Captain's charters hadn't been this lucky in a while.

Ketch called the boy in and let him steer again toward the end. After they docked back at Oden's, he thanked the boy and shook his hand, then removed the dog's life jacket and got the dog off the boat.

The dog lifted his leg on the first piling he encountered. Ketch figured he'd walk the dog for a bit, let him relax and do whatever else he needed to do while the others dealt with the fish, and then they'd clean up and ride back to the boatyard with the Captain. He leashed the dog and checked to make sure his doggy-waste disposal bag dispenser was clipped to his belt.

He was a bit fatigued, but he felt good; it had indeed been an enjoyable trip, with the boy's interest and enthusiasm an invigorating bonus. He stepped lightly as he regained his land legs. He felt like he could do anything. Nothing of course could reverse time, but days like this made him feel younger, like maybe he could keep up with just about anyone. And he could, he thought, if he stayed in shape; he could still occasionally defeat those two divers he played tennis with now and then, despite being almost twenty-five years their senior.

They meandered for a while along the patches of grass over by the inn. The dog squatted, Ketch cleaned up after him, and they started to head back across the parking lot. As they approached the restaurant, Ketch heard someone behind him call his name.

"Mister Ketchum? Storm? Hey, Storm Ketchum!"

When he turned and saw who it was, he remained rooted to the spot, his buoyancy dissipating like dry ice sublimating in the summer sun.

~ Three ~

Make them think you're more man than you are, and you might be so.

A jambalaya sweat broke out on Ketch's forehead, and he became momentarily light-headed and his mouth went dry. But he remained rational. His scientific training (and not the lame attempts at therapy he'd fleetingly tolerated until replacing them with the dog), allowed him to recognize these changes for what they were, simply symptoms of the 'fight-or-flight' or acute stress response, or what most people referred to as an adrenalin rush. Catecholamine hormones, including adrenalin, were flooding his system in preparation for violent muscle action in a primeval attempt to ensure his survival. Just survival of the fittest, that was all; a caveman thing.

"Mister Ketchum, I'm glad I ran into you," the man said as he drew up with Ketch and the dog. "My secretary's been tryin' to reach you by phone, but she hadn't had any luck so far."

Ketch didn't reply. He remembered being virtually incapacitated by this physiological response at various times in the past, and especially of course during his 'difficult' time, but he was over that now – wasn't he? You're fifty-eight years old, he told himself; don't panic, man-up and control it.

The interloper soldiered on with what seemed to Ketch an obviously insincere smile. "Sorry for the bother. I was gonna send someone out to pay you a visit, but my secretary showed me a picture of you on the computer just the other day, and then I saw you walkin' here, and I figured it'd be a good chance for us to talk. Anyway, I don't believe we've ever met." He stuck a hand out. "Bob Ingram."

Ketch didn't immediately respond to the proffered handshake. Surrender was of course out of the question, and technically wasn't a component of the fight-or-flight response anyway; and fleeing wasn't an option, it would be childish and embarrassing, and lashing out physically would be even more so. Thus though the 'fight' part of the response appeared to be biologically obligatory in this case, it would have to be muted.

He kept his hands to himself and coldly replied, "I know who you are." The dog, attuned to Ketch's tone and body language and extraordinarily sensitive to pheromonal signals as most dogs were, positioned himself between Ketch and the perceived threat and emitted a guttural growl.

"Jack, be quiet. Down!" Ketch commanded. The dog obeyed, but continued to keep a wary eye on the situation. Ketch tautened the dog's retractable leash and pressed the lock button just in case.

"Thank you," Ingram said, withdrawing his hand but still retaining the smile. "That's a fine-lookin' animal you got there. What's his name again? Loyal too, I can see – "

"What can I do for you?" Ketch curtly interrupted.

"Well," Ingram said, momentarily nonplussed.

Then he slapped another smile onto his face, the way politicians can when it might be expedient to do so. "Say Storm, mind if I call you Storm? I was just about to meet some folks for lunch, but how about we get us a cold drink and have a little chat first? They have an outdoor deck right over there at the Breakwater, and I know they wouldn't mind if your little friend joined us. My pleasure, of course."

Ketch focused and took the measure of the developer. Around forty maybe; average height, casually but impeccably and expensively dressed, hair well-styled, tanned but smooth skin, a gentleman's hands, well-fed. A good old boy, confident and condescending. "That's Doctor Ketchum to you, and I'm pressed for time. Please make your point now if you have one."

Ingram measured Ketch back for a moment. "Okay, I guess you won't be makin' this easy for me. I heard about you, I should've known." Ketch mimed absently checking the watch he wasn't wearing.

"All right then, *Doctor* Ketchum, here's how it is, short and sweet if that's how you want it." Ingram's smile faded. "We've reached out to you several times and got no answer. Assumin' you've been readin' our communications, you know what the situation is. You're one of the last holdouts, and we need to move on with our project." He held both hands up. "Now I know we said we'd proceed with the eminent domain thing if we hadn't heard from you by last Friday. Well, the paperwork's ready, but I hadn't turned it in just yet, and I'm still willin' to give you one more chance to sell before I do that, and I'm willin' to work with you on a timetable. And I'm still willin' to give you a little more money if you sell, since I'll save on legal expenses. So I'll give you one more week – but I'll be needin' a firm commitment from you no later than this comin' Friday." He paused to allow a response; when none came, he continued, "I believe that's more'n reasonable on my part, since this has been goin' on for quite some time now. Sellin' is the best deal for you, sir, no question, and I hope you'll come to see that by Friday. Otherwise I'll submit the paperwork next Monday for sure, and we'll move forward with acquirin' your property the hard way."

Ketch's shoulders drooped and his spirit flagged like a rapidly deflating balloon, but he tried not to let it show. So it was really going to happen, then, and rather soon from the sound of it. In his conscious mind, he'd known he was going to have to face it eventually, of course, though he'd hoped it would actually take a little longer; that was why he'd gone ahead and ordered the foam block floats (which he'd better hustle to install) that now sat behind his house. But subconsciously he'd hoped otherwise, a consequence he supposed of his former lifelong habit of avoiding thinking about unpleasant things and hoping they'd go away. But he was older and he knew better now, so it was good he'd acted with at least a little foresight this time.

Why did eminent domain even exist here in The Land Of The Free, and why was it allowed to not only continue but expand beyond its original intent, which it seemed to constantly be doing? He knew some of the answers to those questions, of course, because he'd Googled the subject after he'd received Ingram's last letter. Good old Google – where would we all be without it these days? He'd entered 'EMINENT DOMAIN NORTH CAROLINA' and braced for the onslaught. 'About 852,000 results (0.18 seconds)' – very impressive, and daunting. He'd shopped around on the first page and chosen a link, as most people end up doing, and started reading.

He remembered being initially bombarded with discourses on riparian rights, due process, adverse possession, inter vivos trust, primogeniture, easement, covenants and restrictions, preferential assessment, zoning, condemnation, and so on and so forth seemingly ad nauseum. And all of them intertwined throughout with innumerable ifs, ands, buts, and howevers. No wonder he'd never been inclined to study law – what a pointless morass it all seemed, not at all like his former profession nor the ecology of this barrier island, both of those being more or less contained ecosystems and thus more appealing to his brand of intellect. How did the law get so complicated? Whatever happened to good old-fashioned common sense?

One link had led to another, and he'd eventually found some friendlier text, the first being the one about land trusts. Now *there* was a clever idea, one he'd been able to wrap his mind around. You solicit small monetary contributions from a large number of people and apply them toward a land purchase. Each contributor becomes a joint owner of the land, and if someone wants to condemn the land and seize it, legal proceedings have to be initiated individually against each and every owner, so the cost and court time become prohibitive. However, to attempt that kind of undertaking on his own behalf would require lawyers and other support personnel, not to mention time and money, both of which he had too little of. So he'd gone on to another link, and another...

And finally found a small treatise on eminent domain that normal human beings could read and understand. He'd read that eminent domain in general is the power a state has to seize private property without the consent of the owner. This power has traditionally (since the eighteenth century) been used for large public construction projects, like roads, bridges, railroads, fortifications, and various other public facilities. He'd already known that much.

But then he'd been educated on *Kelo v. City of New London*, a U.S. Supreme Court decision from a few years back that had opened the floodgates to allowing eminent domain to expand from 'public use' to 'public benefit' by setting a precedent for a state to transfer property to a private individual or company for economic development. This had originally been intended to expedite redevelopment of blighted urban areas, but not surprisingly it had also enabled other kinds of development, especially in states that didn't further restrict it or set clear limits on it, which many did not.

So that was probably why Ingram thought he could

get away with taking his house – development of the Kinnakeet Boatyard locale could be interpreted as being for the benefit of the public; and perhaps the boatyard area could also be legally viewed as blighted, everything being relative and the boatyard being the closest thing to a slum in Avon.

He'd also read that the North Carolina General Assembly, to which the North Carolina Supreme Court tends to defer eminent domain authorizations, doesn't generally authorize it for Kelo-type economic development – but although some states had passed constitutional amendments to protect property owners against Kelo-related abuses, North Carolina was not one of them; and in fact, North Carolina was the only state whose constitution didn't expressly address eminent domain at all. He learned that such abuses had in fact occurred since that court ruling, and not just here in North Carolina but nationally as well, often based on intentional misuse of the legal term 'blight', to the extent that the terms 'blight' and 'public use' were now being so broadly interpreted that they'd lost their originally intended meanings.

Ketch was no longer as naive as he'd been at times in his younger days. Regardless of the legal logic (an oxymoron if he'd ever seen one) behind it, he was certain Ingram must have friends in the Assembly, or he wouldn't be so sure of himself. Or was he? Sure of himself, that is. Why would he still be practically begging Ketch to sell, when he'd said he could and would seize the property? Why not just do it? Could he be afraid of his application being rejected? Or were there other complications that Ketch wouldn't be aware of, such as a need for bribes or other deals that would make seizure more costly for Ingram? Maybe there were simply added legal expenses, as Ingram had said. He wondered whether Ingram had actually gone through this process with any of the other properties he needed to acquire, or if they'd all just agreed to sell under duress.

"Mister Ketchum? Storm?"

Ketch took a deep breath and tried to stand up straighter. "What you're doing should be against the law," he said. "You shouldn't be allowed to threaten people with eminent domain. The government is supposed to use it for the public good, for building highways and such. You're perverting it for personal gain. You're not the government, and what you want to do is for your own good, not the public good."

"Well, as it turns out, the law does allow what I'm doin'," Ingram quickly replied, "and like it or not, I'm doin' it. You're just gonna have to face up to that, sir."

Ketch supposed he could maybe make himself feel better by circulating petitions and trying to organize public protests, activities that some people he'd known had occupied their spare time with back in the Sixties and Seventies – but he knew others had already taken those routes here with about the same degree of success those people had experienced in stopping the war back then...

"And what I'm doin' *is* for the good of this town, and there's enough folks agree with me on that," Ingram added.

...But heritage be damned, and the environment as well – after all, progress is growth, right? Resources are infinite. It's man's destiny to subdue nature, and the loss of species is simply an inevitable byproduct of progress, just the way of the world...

"Mister Ketchum?"

...Too many people still believed these things. That was the heart of the problem, there were too many people now, and more than ever before with too much discretionary income...

"Storm?"

...Like those fruit flies in their little vials back in the lab, they'd shortsightedly gorge themselves on as much as they could get and wantonly multiply until all the food was gone, until the planet was drained, and then they'd all die. But all that would happen later, not in our lifetime, so screw it, let's just make as much money as we can right now...

"Doctor Ketchum? Storm? Hey Storm! You okay?" Ingram glanced toward a nearby bench. "Maybe you should set for a minute? Here, let me help you."

When Ingram reached for Ketch's arm, the dog leapt up to intercept, snarling and snapping menacingly. Ketch woke from his reverie and yanked back on the fortunately locked leash. "Jack! No! Down!" The dog desisted and sat, but continued to complain in a lower tone and continued to stare directly at the developer with trembling lips. Ketch tightened his grip on the leash. He noted that the dog's teeth didn't appear to have made any contact so far – which was good, as this dog was a power chewer and he surely didn't need that kind of trouble on top of everything else.

"Whoa, that was close!" Ingram exclaimed. He'd staggered backward during the near-attack and almost lost his balance, and was now steadying himself. "You're lucky you had that stupid mutt on a leash!" His eyes flashed while he fished a handkerchief from a pocket of his sport coat and mopped his brow.

Stupid mutt? He probably thinks I'm stupid, too, Ketch thought. "I'm not lucky," he replied in a surprisingly (to him) strong voice. "You're the lucky one. You're lucky you found two wealthy women you could exploit, you're lucky they're out of your way now, you're lucky they couldn't prove anything, and you're lucky you're not in jail. That's what I call *lucky*." He snapped the leash. "Let's go, Jack."

"What?" Ingram spluttered in indignation. "What did you say to me?"

"Stop bothering me and do whatever you have to do, if you really can. We're done here," Ketch said. He got the dog turned around and they started walking back down to the dock.

"Well, I'll be goddamned – you got some nerve mister, I'll tell you that! You better watch your mouth, sir!" Ingram called after him. Ketch didn't respond. "You ever hear of slander? God damn it!" Ketch kept his back to the developer and kept walking.

When they turned the corner at the dock Ketch steered the dog toward a wooden bin resting along the outside wall of the building and sat down hard on it.

45

The dog sat facing Ketch and pressed his muzzle into Ketch's abdomen, which was his way of hugging. The dog moaned, and Ketch put his arms around him and massaged his flanks. "It's okay, buddy, all done now. You're a good boy," he said. When the dog had been sufficiently consoled, Ketch pulled back and slumped against the wall.

The 'insolence of power', indeed – old Shakespeare had nailed that one right on the head. People like Ingram truly believed they were powerful enough to get away with just about anything, didn't they? And they didn't usually care who knew it, and they often enjoyed flaunting it. Like that rich heir who got himself killed a while back by skiing into a tree while playing a forbidden game of football on a slope that was only off-limits to commoners, like that ex-presidential hopeful preaching family values who challenged reporters to try to catch him cheating on his wife and then got caught doing just that... Rules were irrelevant – they were just for the rabble, they didn't apply to the golden ones.

But maybe they were right more often than not, come to think of it. Ketch of course didn't definitively know what had happened to Ingram's wives, any more than the police did, but something certainly smelled fishy in both cases – and yet here was Ingram, prancing around free and clear and carrying on with business as usual.

Nonetheless, it was true that Ingram hadn't been convicted of anything. Ketch wondered if Ingram was in fact innocent, and he'd just been inexcusably rude and insensitive to the man – but he seriously doubted it. As he had in his former profession, Ketch usually tended to draw his conclusions from empirical evidence, not from what some media talking heads conjectured and the sheeple in their audiences subsequently believed; innocent until proven guilty, it was the basis of the legal system, and he agreed that to do it any other way would be wrong. But in this case, knowing what he did about the man, there were just too many convenient coincidences and too many bells that didn't ring quite right.

A grand jury had decided the evidence didn't warrant prosecuting in the drowning of the first wife. The second wife's disappearance had led to a locally sensationalized murder trial, due mostly to investigators finding some minute traces of her blood around the couple's in-ground pool. There'd been evidence of some public rancor between the two that the prosecution had claimed established intent; the wife had supposedly spoken with a friend about the possibility of divorce, which was claimed to provide motive; and everyone knew Ingram wasn't the model husband his defense tried to portray him as.

But there was no record of a divorce motion nor a consultation with any divorce attorney, the physical evidence was scanty and circumstantial, and there was no murder weapon, no timeline, no witnesses – and most importantly, no body. They couldn't even prove she was dead, and the evidence hadn't been sufficient to obtain a conviction. To the general dismay of most Dare County residents, a hung jury had resulted in a mistrial, and the district attorney had declined to retry the case.

From what he'd read and heard, though, Ketch believed Ingram hadn't mourned much after either of his alleged losses, and all of Ketch's acquaintances thought Ingram was probably guilty of something. He'd heard the stories about Ingram's volatile temper, and about him hooking up with the second wife before the first one drowned; the trial hadn't slowed him down much once he'd made bail, from what he'd seen in the papers; and he remembered hearing about there being other women during the trial, though he'd never seen them named. And finally, his business ethics were suspect, at least from Ketch's perspective. About the only good thing he could think of to say about the man was that he wasn't a bad father – there were no kids from either marriage.

Granted Ingram had seemed genuinely upset just now, but that was most likely just a reaction to being crossed, something men like him didn't take kindly to. Ketch concluded he didn't need to worry about it. In the extremely unlikely event he had in fact made a mistake, if it someday somehow turned out he owed the man an apology, he'd give him one. Maybe. If.

Meanwhile, he had a bag of dog poop to dispose of, and they should be getting back to the boat. Ketch patted the dog's rump and stood up. "All right boy, come on, time to go."

They walked past a row of vending boxes in front of the ship's store, the kind that dispensed newspapers and such. There was one for the daily paper, then one for a free tourist magazine, then one for free real estate guides from HatterasMann Realty... Ketch opened the door of that last one, dropped the bag in, and proceeded on to the boat.

"Hey, what took you two so long?" the Captain inquired as they boarded. Ketch shrugged, all he had energy left to do at the moment. "Well, the boy said to thank you again," the Captain continued, "and a couple of the guys are over there at the table gettin' their catch squared away. The rest of 'em already took off." He patted a cooler. "They gave us some cobia, and some pretty fair tips. Here's yours."

"Thanks," Ketch said. He took the bills and stuffed them into a zippered pocket of his cargo shorts. He'd tally them up later. The Captain didn't pay him for serving as mate, he worked for tips, and that was fine with him. Though the Social Security wouldn't kick in for a while yet and he did have to pay for flood insurance, he had his pension and a halfway respectable investment account that provided him with another income stream, and his house was paid off. *His* house! Anyway, he didn't really need the money and was happy to just go along for the ride, but it did feel good to be appreciated once in a while. And of course having some extra cash handy was never a bad thing – just ask Ingram.

"You're lookin' kinda beat," the Captain observed. "You okay?" Ketch nodded. "Well, let's don't worry 'bout cleanin' up just now, I can hose 'er down back at the boatyard. I'll just top 'er off at the pump on the way out is all."

"Okay," Ketch said. "Thanks, I am a little tired."

When they took the boat back out into the sound and he had a stiff salt breeze in his face once again, Ketch started to feel a little better. This day had certainly had its share of up and downs so far and it was nowhere near over yet, but it was still a beautiful day nonetheless.

On impulse he invited the Captain to bring the cobia to the house later for an evening cookout. He had two cases of beer and some wine, and he could pick up some sides at the market. What the heck, he'd invite Mario too if he was around, and maybe whoever else he happened to run into between now and then. He could use some company tonight.

~ **Four** ~

Everyone takes a beating now and then, one way or another.

*K*etch was still physically fatigued when he and the dog arrived back at the house, but he was too restless to sleep. He also hadn't had lunch, but he didn't feel like taking time for that either. Aftereffects of the adrenalin overdose, he guessed.

He supposed some would agree that a few beers might be justifiable considering his situation, but he disliked drinking alone and this town lacked the kind of dive bar that would be apropos of the situation, and besides he was no longer inclined these days to waste time sitting in a bar doing nothing constructive. He'd have a couple tonight at the cookout; for now he'd just run some errands. He nudged the air conditioning up a notch, filled the dog's water dish, and scanned the mail he'd brought in from the mailbox.

No more bad news there at least, just a bill and two pieces of junk mail. He dropped the bill into the in-box on his desk and considered the other two items. The first one was yet another credit card offer. He opened it and stuffed the contents of that envelope and the envelope itself into the enclosed postage-paid return envelope. The other one, a special offer for some kind of home security system, didn't have a postage-paid return envelope, so he crammed everything from that one into the postage-paid envelope from the credit card company as well. Recycling was a virtue after all, was it not? The postage-paid envelope was now too fat to seal properly, so he taped the flap.

He considered taking the pickup, then decided he needed to pedal. The dog appeared ready for his afternoon nap anyway. If they don't get their eighteen hours a day they get cranky, he thought, but with affection. "Jack, I'm going out. I'll be right back, you be good," he said. The dog, settled in on his designated end of the couch, wagged once without picking up his head and closed his eyes.

The bike had saddlebags mounted over the rear wheel, so he wouldn't need his backpack. He stuck the envelope in the mailbox, flipped the red flag up, and headed out, with the open shirt he still wore over his tee shirt flapping behind him in the breeze and an OBX ball cap in place of the tarp hat. His twenty-one-speed Schwinn all-terrain bike was overkill on this mostly flat part of the island; a balloon-tire island bike would have sufficed. He couldn't recall the last time he'd had to shift out of whatever gear it was currently in, but he'd brought the bike with him when he moved and he liked it.

He pedaled south down North End Road, enjoying the sunlit scenery along the way. This was a pretty drive. The grounds of most of the soundside properties bordering the narrow paved road were grassy and often attractively landscaped as well, with various kinds of trees and interesting semitropical foliage providing a soothing contrast to the sand and rocks and stock plantings that predominated on many of the oceanside properties on the other side of Route 12; though a lot of those were also impressive in their way.

He passed the Sands of Time campground, cheery-looking and well-kempt as always, and the Baskins Gallery, probably his favorite place to impulse-shop on the infrequent occasions he indulged in that quintessential American pastime. He briefly considered stopping there today, but decided against it. They'd undoubtedly have some new piece of nautical bric-a-brac or artwork that he'd have to find a place for in the house, and he should save the saddlebag space for the food he needed to buy. He should also watch his time, he supposed.

The houses in this part of town varied in size and age, and most were not new – including his own, which had begun its life as essentially a four-room bungalow on stilts. The living room and dining area in the front, and a galley kitchen in the back behind the dining area, were now open. One of the two adjacent back bedrooms included a full bath, and there was a half-bath with a washer-dryer stack along the inside wall of the kitchen. The flooring was rustic wood plank throughout.

Wooden riser steps led up from the front yard to a covered deck that ran the length of the front of the house and continued down both sides, where it was screened-in; and a set of open wooden steps led down to the back yard from the kitchen door at the end of that side deck. The tan-stained decks and deep brown cedar shake siding were in fair shape all around.

There was no shed, but he had a sizeable though low-ceilinged enclosed storage area under the house that served the same purpose. Since it was an older property that predated the recent building boom, he had a relatively large lot irregularly bounded by lush wild scrub on both sides, which provided some privacy; and he had some grass, which he kept neatly mowed. There was no garage, but he could park a car on the gravel driveway under the kitchen-side deck; also no pool, but he didn't need one since his back yard abutted the sound and he had a small boat dock he could swim from.

With its simple design and about a thousand square feet of living space on its single floor, it was nowhere near as impressive as the newer places around town – but still, it had cost him about half of the savings he'd managed to accumulate over the years, which included the proceeds from the sale of the last house he'd owned. A similar place on a lake where he'd lived back North would have cost him half as much or less – but a similarly aged oceanfront bungalow, if any still existed here, would cost twice as much or more, and then he wouldn't be able to keep a boat. In any event, he was on the water and he felt it was worth it. It wasn't fancy and it wasn't huge, but it was all he needed – and it was *his*, damn it.

He turned onto Harbor Road and proceeded east toward Route 12. As he passed the firehouse, he decided to take a little time out after all and stop at the dive shop before hitting the market. He didn't enjoy biking along the highway as a rule, but the shop wasn't too far up the road and it wasn't a freeway, just a two-laner; but it was that time of year and there would definitely be traffic.

The Sea Dog Scuba Center sported a colorful sign on its roof, complete with the traditional American red and white diver-down flag and a pirate dog inspired by an unfortunately deceased pet, but that was its only notable feature. Otherwise it was a nondescript unpainted wooden building that was completely incongruous with its more modern strip mall neighbor. It did however house something special that made it another of Ketch's favorite places.

She was no Miss America, nor that young if truth be told; but she was attractive and perky and in good shape, and though Ketch had figured he was pretty much done with women now, something about her just rubbed him the right way, and her agreeable nature and pleasant voice with its classically seductive Carolinian cadence affected him more than he'd voluntarily admit. And her shoulder-length auburn hair, which perfectly framed her lightly freckled face when it wasn't tied back in a ponytail.

"Hello? Kari? Anyone home?" he called as he entered the shop and glanced around the interior. After his ride the air inside was invitingly cool, and so was all the shiny and neatly displayed gear. And it was the middle of the day during tourist season and the place was deserted. Ketch hoped she was making ends meet. She might do better in a better location, which would probably mean Hatteras on this island, but maybe not as there was already competition down there. Or better yet somewhere else entirely perhaps, but Ketch didn't like to think about that.

Not that he was in a position to help a lot, and not that she'd be likely to take charity from him or anyone else anyway, but he wished he could do something for her. He could buy some new gear, maybe a buoyancy compensator since his was starting to get a little raggedy – but she'd unfortunately probably insist on giving it to him at cost as she often did. That and free tank rentals were the only rewards he got (or wanted) for occasionally assisting with her certification classes and dive charters, and he didn't think he could forgo even those without getting her hackles up.

"Well hey, Ketch!" she said as she emerged from a room in the back. "Long time no see! What brings you round today?" It was funny how he sometimes bristled at Southern accents and idioms when they were coming from a man; depending on the man, of course – Ingram's manner of speaking being especially irritating to him, for example. But her voice had quite the opposite effect on him.

"Oh, hello." Looked like today was a ponytail day. Ketch unconsciously stood a little straighter and brightened visibly. "Well, I was thinking of picking up a tank, for one thing." After he'd said it, he supposed he had thought of doing that sometime recently; but that wasn't really why he was here.

"Okay, no problem. Hey, where's my Jacky?"

"I'm on my bike. Jack's sacked out back at the ranch. We went out with the Captain this morning."

"Bike, huh? What are you gonna do, strap that bad boy on your back and pedal it on home?" she asked with a grin. "You remember those tanks weigh about forty pounds full out of the water, right?" Seeing Ketch's look of consternation, she added, "Hey, you look hot. You want a Co-Cola with some ice?"

Ketch cleared his throat. "Well, I can come back with the truck later or tomorrow, you don't have to fill one for me right this minute. And yes, a cold drink would be nice, thanks." What was the matter with him? She'd been over to the house at least a couple of times before. He felt like an awkward teenager.

"Come on back here to the kitchen and I'll pour us a couple," she said with a follow-me wave. While she set them up she remarked, "I hope you're not fixin' to dive solo. It's not sanctioned and you ought to know better, bein' a divemaster and all."

"Not really, I just want to clean the bottom of my boat," Ketch replied. That would be the used seventeen-foot Whaler he'd picked up for a song a while back. Though the boat was ancient, the outboard wasn't, and he'd gotten a great deal on it. "Besides, it was only unsanctioned until they found a way to make money on it. As I imagine you know, PADI started offering what they call a 'distinctive specialty course' on diving without a buddy, and I heard SDI has a class like that too."

"Yeah, they did, but that doesn't mean they advocate solo divin'. It's to teach experienced divers how to take care of themselves in an emergency in case you get separated from your buddy, or when you might not have a competent buddy, or can't have one. You know, like if you're takin' pictures, or buddied with a stranger, or tec divin', and even just when you're teachin' students, if you think about it. *And when you're cleanin' boats,*" she pointedly added. "They're not just doin' it for money, it's so you can dive safer. And I know *you*, sir, haven't taken that course."

Ketch ruefully shook his head, his awkwardness gone now. These certification agencies... From the Fifties on, they'd admittedly done a lot to advance the sport and make it safer – certainly orders of magnitude safer than when Cousteau pioneered his prototype Aqua-Lung in the Forties – but it seemed to him that nowadays they always had a hand out, trying to nickel-and-dime everyone with innumerable 'specialty' classes and unnecessary certification levels and always looking for new ways to make money. They put him in mind of car dealers at times; or maybe labor unions, another institution perhaps outliving its usefulness.

"Always the instructor, eh? What could a course like that teach me that I don't already know? I'm a divemaster, I can take care of myself, I carry a Spare Air. Me diving solo has to be safer than diving with the eight-year-olds they've started trying to suck in. What do they call that silliness, 'Bubble Blowers' or something like that?" Then, as he paused to catch his breath, a light bulb suddenly came on and he quickly backtracked. "But you're probably right," he said, sheepishly enough he hoped. "It's probably a sensible thing to do, especially at my age, and I should probably carry more redundant gear if I go solo. Are you qualified to teach that course, by any chance?"

She looked up at him in surprise. "I think so. I could check into what I'd have to do."

"Well then, how about if you do that and tell me when? I'll pay the going rate, whatever it is."

"Really? You're serious, right? You're not funnin' with me?" Ketch shook his head and she continued. "Well, I know there's some classroom material, of course, and three dives. And I know you'll need some more gear. You sure about this?"

Ketch nodded. "I am."

"Well then, will you put off cleanin' your ole boat 'til after?" she inquired mischievously. "Never mind, I think you'll be okay this one time. But you can't get the tank tomorrow, I'll be closed. It's my day off and I'm supposed to go see my mama."

"Oh, that's right, I forgot," Ketch said. "You know how it is with us retired folks. Like Mister Buffett said, the days drift by and they don't have names. Oh well, another time then. Now that I think about it, I might not be able to get back here before you close today. I have to prepare for a cookout at my place tonight."

"Oh yeah? What's the occasion?"

"No occasion, I just felt like it. We got some cobia today and I thought we could grill it up, that's all. The Captain's coming, and maybe some folks from the boatyard. No one was around when we docked, but I left notes for Mario and Len." He paused for a moment and took another drink. "Are you doing anything after work?" he casually inquired.

"I don't know – why, is that an invitation? I can't tell," she teased. "Sure, why not? Mick won't be around anyway. And hey, I could carry a tank over with me. What time?"

Kari attending would be good; Kari without that layabout Mick would be even better. He hadn't explicitly invited Mick anyway, but he wouldn't point that out. "Thanks, that's good of you. You close at five today, right? I'll start grilling at six if that's okay."

"Okay, sounds good! I could do with some partyin', I've been so busy here," she said. Ketch doubted that, but he didn't say so. "Can I bring somethin'?" she asked.

"No, you don't have time for that. I already have the kind of wine you like."

"You remember what I like? I'm impressed. Okay, I'll see you then, and I'll bring you a tank."

"Good," Ketch said with relief. Mission accomplished. He glanced at the wall clock. "Well, I should be going, I have another stop to make. Thanks for the drink."

"Anytime, Han Solo," she said as he hastened to make his exit. "See you later!"

Well – back to the business at hand. Ketch adjusted his cap, mounted the bike, and allowed himself a deep breath before he started pedaling again. He'd noticed he was finally starting to seriously tire in there; he felt a bit spryer now, but it was probably temporary. Maybe he'd have time for a power nap later if he hustled.

He headed back down Route 12. He'd intended to pick up something to go along with the fish at the Village Grocery, the town's homier alternative to the Food Lion supermarket at the south end, but he decided to quickly try his luck at the Barefoot Station first. It was located right at the Harbor Road turnoff, and if they didn't have anything suitable on the shelves they might sell him some lunch counter leftovers.

The Barefoot Station was yet another of Ketch's favorite places. It was no coincidence that both his house and most of the places he favored were on the north end of town – he'd already gotten the lay of the land during his periodic vacations before the move, and he'd only house-hunted here at the north end.

At first glance the Station looked like just another convenience store with gas pumps out front, but it harbored a few surprises inside that weren't obvious from the road. There was a breakfast and lunch counter in one corner, a room in the back where friends could drink some beer and shoot some pool, and via a side door inside the store the rest of the building housed a theater, with a stage and screen and at least a hundred seats it seemed to him, where old and second-run movies were shown periodically and an occasional inexpensive concert or show with regional performers was presented. He'd attended a memorable one not too long ago featuring an older country musician who called himself 'Gene the Plumber' – because his name was Gene and he was a plumber, he'd explained – whose daughter also sang and who'd sounded like Norah Jones.

He got lucky and came out in short order with a container of pasta salad, a bag of tossed garden salad, and a box of chocolate chip cookies, all of which he managed to pack into the saddlebags. He sprinkled some ice he'd also bought over the contents of the saddlebags before closing them. Once again these good people hadn't let him down. There were a lot of good people in this town, he reflected; in fact, at the moment he could think of only one truly bad one that he'd personally met in recent memory.

He supposed he'd have to start buckling down soon regarding that one – but not tonight, there'd be time enough to think about that tomorrow. He'd been beaten up enough for one day.

~ **F i v e** ~

A man shouldn't be alone in his old age if it can be avoided.

*K*etch had his second wind now. He had one of those small refrigerators that are popular on college campuses, and he'd moved it out to the front deck and stocked it as full of beer and wine as possible (but not *the* wine, which he'd stashed in the back of the kitchen fridge), along with a couple of sodas and water bottles in case it turned out anyone wanted those instead. There was more of everything in the kitchen if needed. The white plastic chairs and tables scattered around the decks were wiped down, and the dog had been fed.

Four tiki torches were in place out front, one each at either side of the steps and each corner of the front deck; they'd have those and the screened side decks if the bugs got bad later. That was one drawback of living on the sound, but it was manageable; and that and not being closer to the beach at least helped keep the prices around here down some.

He'd managed a shave and shower and a catnap in the hammock as well, and now he and the dog were relaxing on the front deck waiting for their guests to arrive, he in a fresh Hawaiian shirt and shorts, and the dog in one of his snazzier bandanas. Reggae music emanated at an inoffensive level from the satellite radio in the corner.

The sun wouldn't set until later at this time of year, but this was still a pleasant time of day for him and always had been, going way back to his college days when this had been Happy Hour time. Old habits die hard – he still preferred to stay up late, rise early, and nap at some point during the day, a routine he'd first established out of necessity while living in the dorms. Advancing age had if anything reinforced this tendency rather than diminishing it, perhaps because older folks, at least the ones who are still vital, are loath to waste time sleeping when the end is nearer, he thought. Plenty of time to sleep when you're dead – there was truth in that adage.

"So Jack, pretty soon we'll have some company. You'll like that," he said as he stroked the dog lying next to him on a throw rug. The dog had already inferred this from Ketch's recent activities, of course, and though he appeared calm he was in fact vigilant and slightly tensed in anticipation. He got more attention at parties, as well as a tasty tidbit now and then, and he did indeed like that.

This dog was a smart one, probably the smartest one Ketch had ever had. He couldn't speak, of course, but his listening vocabulary was prodigious for a dog, and he knew his way around and how things worked. He was a handsome five-year-old brown and white beagle/labrador mix, bigger and heavier than a beagle but smaller than a large lab – or to look at it another way, small enough to be manageable but big enough to be a factor to be reckoned with in a confrontation, as Ingram had learned earlier today. And emotionally, the dog had probably done more for Ketch than any high-priced therapist could have, in Ketch's opinion. Ketch figured he could maybe have another ten years with this one if they were both lucky.

Regarding longevity, it had once amused him to measure his life in terms of the number of dogs he'd had instead of in calendar years, but it was less amusing now that he might be a last-dog man, or at least a penultimate-dog man. There had always been dogs in his life, as far back as he could remember; and they'd always been loved; but as always he loved this last one the most.

The dog abruptly rose up and started wagging excitedly. Ketch didn't restrain him, as the dog wouldn't leave the deck without permission. Ketch hadn't himself seen, heard, or smelled anything out of the ordinary, but he knew the dog was right and someone they knew was on the way. Sure enough, a minute later the Captain's pickup pulled into the graveled drive and parked next to Ketch's.

"Hey, I see you finally got a date!" the Captain's voice blasted from his open window, flushing some small birds from the underbrush. He hopped down from the cab and lowered the tailgate. "Gimme a hand with this cooler. Len and Mario loaded 'er for me, and she's a heavy ole bitch even with nothin' in her."

Ketch obliged while the dog waited on the deck. "So, are they coming then?" he asked.

"Said so," the Captain replied. "Them and a couple beach bunnies that was hangin' around the boatyard, didn't know 'em offhand. Hope you don't mind." He made a show of squinting at Ketch. "There's somethin' different about you tonight, but I can't pin it down." He snapped his fingers. "I know! Did you get some action this afternoon?"

"I guess we know what's on *your* mind this evening," Ketch observed with a tolerant smile. "No, that's fine if they all come. But maybe I should order some pizza? I don't know if we'll have enough fish." He grunted. "Why is this cooler so heavy? Let's just leave it down here by the grill."

"I stuck some beer and flounder I had layin' around in there along with the cobia, brung some chips an' such too by the way. We'll have enough to eat. Think we should fire it up?"

"I guess so. I told Kari we'd start grilling at six, and it must be about that time now." Ketch remembered the poor dog patiently waiting on the deck. "Jack, you can come!" he called, and the dog raced down the steps to greet the Captain. "I probably already have enough beer, you know."

"Well, you never know, we'll have it if we need it. Besides, I like mine better. Hey, Jacky-boy!" The Captain gave the dog a brisk two-handed rubdown. "Kari's comin'? So you did get busy this afternoon after all, you dawg!" he grinned.

"Knock it off," Ketch said, but good-naturedly. "Jack, you stay in the yard."

"Hey, y'all!" Len walked into view, followed by Mario and not two, but three girls, a blond and two brunettes. Ketch had seen a couple of them around the boatyard now and again, but he didn't remember their names, if he'd ever known them. They looked to be in their mid-to-late twenties like their escorts, and were not hard on the eyes. The dog barked once, then trotted into the front yard to greet them.

Mario pushed ahead of the others. "Ketch, this here is Barb, Joette, and Diana," he said, pointing them out as he named them. "Hope it was okay to bring 'em, Don said he thought it'd be okay," he added in a lower tone.

"Of course," Ketch replied, "no problem, the more the merrier. We have plenty of everything." He stepped past Mario into the yard. "Ladies, welcome, it's nice to meet you. There are drinks in the fridge up on the deck there, and the door's open if you need anything else. Make yourselves at home."

"Thank you kindly, Mister Ketchum, and thanks for havin' us," the blond one (Barb?) said. "Oh, and you too, Captain Manolin," she added – since he'd brought the fish, Ketch assumed. The other two muttered similar sentiments and headed for the steps.

"You can call me Ketch."

"And Don!" the Captain called from behind the grill. "We're skippin' the black ties tonight! Though we do serve fine wine here – y'all bring any?" he cawed. "Well, I see I got a pan and a kit. Hey Ketch, get me some tinfoil and butter when you get a chance, and I'll get these babies started. And you ladies, make yourselves useful in the kitchen! Remember, you don't have to be crazy to work here, we'll train ya! And you there, Len, grab me a beer out a that cooler!"

"Aye-aye Cap'n!" Len grinned and saluted, cutting

a somewhat comical figure in bib overalls with no shirt, and his scraggly beard, straw hat and glasses.

"What's with you tonight? You look like a dang farmer – all you need's a corncob pipe!" the Captain said to Len.

"I got one, right here in my pocket!" Len replied, producing said object. "It ain't my fault, I ain't got to the laundrymat yet this week. Besides, I *am* a farmer." He passed a beer to the Captain and opened one for himself. "My daddy's got a tobacco farm back home in Tar Heel..."

"Here you go, amigo," Mario said, dragging a lawn chair closer to the grill and handing Ketch a beer. "You take a load off, I'll go help the girls in the kitchen." Amigo, indeed – although Mario could speak Spanish and one of his parents had been born in Mexico, Ketch knew Mario had never been there.

"Tinfoil and butter!" the Captain called after him.

"There's tossed salad, pasta salad, and cookies in the fridge," Ketch added. One kept most everything that was edible in the refrigerator in these parts, to deter what the locals variously and euphemistically referred to as 'palmetto bugs', 'water bugs', and so on – cockroaches, in other words, which thrived in sultry environments. He hadn't yet seen any in his house, knock on wood, but he still fumigated periodically.

Ketch eased into the lawn chair and twisted the cap off his bottle. This turned out to be a fine idea, he thought amidst the pleasant babble of voices. It was usually pretty quiet around here, which he also enjoyed, but sometimes too quiet. The dog settled next to him to wait for something good to happen with the grill, but then bounded up again as a weathered Outback pulled into the yard and popped its liftgate. He waited for Kari to start crossing the yard before sauntering out to meet her. "Kari, over here," Ketch called contentedly. Now that the best part of this day had arrived, the party was complete.

"Jacky, I missed you this afternoon," she said, giving the dog a quick hug. "Ketch, here's your tank, I'll just set it down over here." She leaned it up against a post in a shady spot under the house. "Hey, Don," she said as she joined the group at the grill. "And you are?"

"I'm Len. Nice to meet you, Kari."

"Ketch, you shaved!" she exclaimed when she finally looked more closely at Ketch, who rose and motioned to the chair.

"Here, have a seat and I'll get you some wine," Ketch directed. "Yes, I was getting tired of the beard, and I figured I'd better do it now before I got too burned."

"You look ten years younger!" she marveled.

"If you say so. But even if I were ten years younger, I'd still be twenty years older than you."

"Ha! Flattery will get you – well, maybe *somewhere*, who knows?" she grinned. "But really, I'm older'n dirt already, and I've got the big four-oh comin' up next time around."

"I'll have to teach you how to count in hexadecimal – then you could tell me you were twenty-eight and my math would be technically correct."

"Huh? What's that?" Len asked.

"Never mind, I'll explain later – or never," Ketch waved as he walked away. "First the wine."

"And tinfoil and butter, dammit!" the Captain yelled.

Ketch returned momentarily with a bottle, a wineglass, and a corkscrew (and foil and butter) and pulled up another lawn chair. Kari took the bottle from him and inspected it. "Is this the kind I like?" she asked. "I can't even read this label. What language is that? It doesn't look like anythin' I've ever seen." She removed the wrapper from the neck. "Huh – can't open it neither!"

"The language is Euskara Batua. It's from the Basque regions of Spain and France. I think you'll like it," Ketch said, taking the bottle back from her and working the corkscrew. "I tasted it. It's not exactly the same as what you're used to, but it's close – and better, I think." He was glad he'd thought to remove the price tag.

He poured her a glass. "Ooh, this is divine!" she shortly exclaimed. "I needed this! Where'd you find it? I'm gonna have to get me some of this!"

"Hey Ketch," Len interrupted. "I been wonderin' about that life ring you got hangin' out front, and I keep forgettin' to ask. Why's it say 'Port Starbird' on it?"

Thank you Len, Ketch thought. Kari couldn't afford to shop where he'd found that bottle – and neither could he really, other than for special occasions. "That's what I named my house," Ketch

70

answered. Almost all of the houses in this town had names – the only thing that was unusual about the white life preserver with red lettering hanging on a nail next to the steps was the spelling, which Len had noticed.

"Well, I know that, but I hate to tell you, it's spelt wrong, did you know that?"

"No it ain't," the Captain said, and Kari concurred.

Ketch explained. "The 'starboard' part is spelled the way it's supposed to be pronounced – and yes, it's also the way people often misspell it, and it's the basis of an old joke I know. I also wrote a song based on that joke."

"No shit? I got to hear that!" Len declared.

"If you mean the joke, okay. If you mean the song, I'll play it for you sometime – but not tonight."

"Aw, come on, why not? What's the matter, you shy or somethin'? You don't have to be shy with us."

"Well, we'll see," Ketch relented. "Maybe after we eat, if I've had enough to drink. I'm not used to playing in front of strange people."

"What, them girls up there? They ain't *too* strange. They'll think it's cool you wrote a song. Somebody get this man another beer!"

The fish didn't take too long to cook, and when Mario called down that the table was set, the Captain carried the pan upstairs and the others trailed behind with the wine, the Captain's chips, and some of the Captain's beer (at his direction). The sides Ketch had bought earlier were laid out on a table on the screened deck off the kitchen. Everyone filled their plates and carried them out to the front deck to eat. The dog followed the food.

As it turned out, they didn't have to wait until after dinner for their entertainment.

"Well dang!" the Captain exploded after they'd all sat down. "Must a cut myself on somethin'! Gimme another napkin," he demanded, the one he'd wrapped around his finger already turning red.

The younger girls all got up and rushed over to him. Joette took the Captain's hand in hers. "Huh, that's a good one," she said as the others looked on.

"Let me see that," Kari said. She took his hand and removed the napkin. "It's not that bad, you don't need stitches. Go wash it off and I'll find you a band-aid."

The Captain pulled his hand away. "Now you ladies quit your fussin', this ain't but a scratch," he protested. "See, it's slowin' down already." He wrapped a new napkin around the finger. "I never knowed a woman wouldn't worry herself to death over the silliest little thing," he complained with a wink at Ketch, obviously enjoying the attention nonetheless. He turned back to the women and continued, "Why, you should a seen some of the scrapes I got into back in the day, you'd like to had a heart attack! There was this one time back at the Turtle House, that's a place we used to go when I was stationed in Florida with the Coast Guard..."

Here we go, Ketch thought.

"This fella come in with a fish knife hangin' off his belt, with a blade 'bout as long as your forearm. Big ole coot, drunk as a skunk'n mean as a wild hog..."

72

"Now you've done it," Ketch said to Kari.

"Hush now, I don't think I've heard this one yet," she replied as she ate. "And pour me some more of that good stuff, if you please."

The sky was starting to turn dusky now, and where the Captain was sitting the glow from the torches illuminated his face like a primitive spotlight as he hit his stride. "I knowed right off it was me he was after, and I'll admit I had it comin' after that night I spent with his woman. I never said I was no saint," he grinned. "Well, he come right up to me at the bar, and there was plenty a room, everybody else backed right off, I guess they knew too."

"'I figgered I'd find you here', he says. 'I ought to just kill you flat out, but I ain't about to spend the rest a my days in jail over the likes a you.' Then he lays that blade up on the bar, and he leans his elbow on the bar and puts his arm up."

The Captain paused to spear some fish and take a drink. No one spoke and he took his time. He had their undivided attention now, and he knew it. Ketch had heard this one before, but the art was in the telling, and he was enjoying it just as much as everyone else.

"And then he says, with poison in his voice, 'We're gonna do this civilized-like. I'm gonna wrestle you. If you win, you walk – and if I win I get to take one a your fingers, right here and now.'" The Captain stopped for another drink, and this time there were audible gasps from the women.

"Well, I guess you didn't lose," Mario observed

after doing a quick head count. "That's just crazy," Diana said, and Barb asked wide-eyed, "You didn't really do it, did you?"

"Well, listen," the Captain said, and continued with his tale.

Ketch noticed that both he and the Captain had just about finished their current beers, so he went below to fetch a couple more, of the kind the Captain preferred. He'd miss a bit of the story, but not too much. He was pretty sure it was going to go on a little longer than it had the last time he'd heard it anyway. He returned in time to catch the end of the epic arm-wrestling match.

"You *lost*?" Joette squealed.

"Now hang on! Well I was damned if I was gonna let 'im get the best a me in front a all them people, so I called his bluff. I laid my left pinky on the bar and looked him straight in the eye. It was my bum hand a course, I wouldn't give him my right no matter what anybody thought, just in case. Well he looked right back at me, and the veins was still poppin' out a his head. And I never looked away, not even when he picked up that knife and raised it up to do the deed."

The Captain looked around with satisfaction at his captive audience. He tipped his bottle up, then frowned and turned it upside-down. Joette glanced around frantically and saw the bottle Ketch was holding out for her. She grabbed it and gave it to the Captain, who leisurely twisted the cap off. "Well, what happened then?" she demanded, biting at a nail.

The Captain took a long pull, then went on. "Well,

like I said, I looked 'im straight in the eye. Just like I figured, he hesitated, and then he starts goin' green around the gills. Pretty soon he looks away and lowers his arm. 'I can't do it', he says."

The tension had been eased as planned, and Ketch watched with interest as the Captain allowed everyone to let out a collective breath and start to relax.

"But then he blows hisself up and he says, 'But if I ever hear tell a you and her again, next time you won't be so lucky, you dirty son of a bitch', and then he slings somebody's beer in my face, turns his back, and starts walkin' away." Here the Captain paused again to ingest some more fish. "Well, I couldn't let that go by, not in them days. 'Gutless', I says loud and clear. He stops dead at that. 'What did you say?' he says, and he turns back around. So I says it again, still lookin' right at 'im – 'Gutless'! And then I added on 'Pussy!', for good measure. Next thing I know, that blade comes flyin' 'cross the room, straight at me."

"What happened? Did he cut you? What happened then?" The Captain let the agitated chorus run its course and winked at Ketch again as he slowly took another sip.

"Well, I saw that blade comin' and I didn't move a inch, never even flinched. My eyes were pretty good back then and I figured it'd miss, but even so I figured it a little too close as it turned out." He took another quick chug. "Whenever we was out to sea they always give me midnight watch, you know, on account a my eyes, 'cause they knew what a good lookout I was. Why, one time I spotted a -"

"What happened? What happened with the knife? What did you do then?" the chorus started again, protesting the turn the story was taking.

"Okay, okay," the Captain said with a grin. "Well, like I said, I figured it a mite close, and I should a ducked, 'cause I damn near got myself kilt that night. 'Course, I was pretty well lickered up, but still. Anyway, I sat there, still lookin' right at 'im, and I heard that blade go singin' past right under my ear, and right after I felt the blood runnin' down my neck. See, it nicked me, and it opened up pretty near a two-inch gash right here on the side a my neck." He tilted his head and displayed the scar for Joette, who now sat spellbound next to him.

"Oh, it's true, look at this, y'all come look!" she said. There was some murmuring, whether the impressed kind or the merely polite kind Ketch couldn't tell for sure, though with this crew he strongly suspected the former. Then Len asked, "So what happened to that ole boy? Did he just leave after that?"

"Oh, he left all right," the Captain emphatically answered. "I threw the sumbitch through the front window, and they called a doc to come stitch me up down at the precinct house later that night."

"Ha!" Mario exclaimed.

"But I'll tell y'all, I still never went over to that woman's place again. I may be crazy, but I ain't stupid," the Captain concluded.

"Oh, man!" Joette breathed. Ketch noticed she'd pulled her chair right up next to the Captain's, and her free hand was resting on his knee.

"Looks like he might've hooked one," Kari remarked quietly to Ketch in amusement. Ketch had to smile as well. How did he manage it, and at his age? It must be the tall tales. Some women were fascinated by the seafaring type, and some by men in uniform, and there were women who were selectively attracted to pirates and rogues, and there were those as well who were attracted to older men; and the Captain had been all of the above at one time or another.

"So is all that really true? Did he really get that scar in a bar fight?" Kari asked.

"Well," Ketch softly replied, "don't tell anyone, but I happen to know he accidentally hooked himself under that ear one time when he was fishing." Kari threw her head back and laughed. "But I imagine there was probably some kind of a fight. I think he was kind of wild in his younger days."

"And he never got married?"

"Divorced, just like me. A long time ago, in a galaxy far far away," he added, thinking of her Han Solo remark earlier.

"Just like peas and carrots!" she said, and laughed again. "Okay now, no more movie references for today!" Then she turned serious. "Never been, myself. Things just never worked out for me that way. I can't have kids anyway, but I got a niece and nephew up in Manteo. Not exactly the same thing, I know, but I guess it'll have to do." She sat up a little straighter and rubbed at her eyes. "Whoa! Where's my glass? I better finish my dinner, I'm babblin', sorry 'bout that! Oh, here it is." She drained it in one gulp. Ketch picked up her plate and handed it to her.

"So," she added, glancing around the deck. "It looks like Len and Diana, and Mario and Barb, and maybe Don and Joette." She held her empty glass out again. "So there's just me and you left."

"Yes, I guess so." He refilled her glass and stood. "Well, excuse me for a moment please, I'll be right back." It was time for a pit stop, and another bottle as well; good thing he'd bought a half-dozen of them.

"Hey Ketch," Len called. "How about fetchin' that git-tar a yours while you're in there?"

Ketch considered attempting to demur again, as he was in fact nervous about playing in front of people and always had been – but he guessed he'd probably had enough to drink, anyway more than the couple he'd anticipated this afternoon. His fingers still seemed to be working well enough, so what the heck. It certainly wouldn't be the first time he'd embarrassed himself if he botched it – nor was it likely to be the last, he thought, with the foam block floats stacked outside his kitchen window in mind.

~ S i x ~

He'd sung at night when he steered alone back in the old days.

When Ketch returned with the guitar, Len switched the radio off and gave everyone a brief introduction. Ketch made himself comfortable, and the dog came over and settled beside his chair. He liked it when Ketch played music.

"It's just a silly little song," Ketch explained further as he adjusted the tuning, "that grew in my mind out of an old joke you might have heard, about a first mate who wasn't the brightest bulb in the shed, or whatever. It's called 'Port Starbird', like it says on yonder ring. Here we go:"

"Well I mate for a charter boat captain,
He's a heck of a mighty sailin' man,
With just a compass and a twelve-pack,
He will take you anywhere he can.

Every day just before we set sail,
He reads the same piece of paper again,
He says it's a private inspiration,
That's worth more than most of his friends.

He says he's been around the world,
He can't remember all of the girls,
But if he can just remember Port Starbird,
He can die a happy man.

Port left, starboard right,
Ships that pass in the night,
When you don't know where you're going,
Any course will take you there,
Port left, starboard right.

Somehow, we always seem to get somewhere,
Though I've never seen him use a chart,
He must be a great navigator,
An expert at some old lost art.

But every time we pull up the anchor,
He reads that same piece of paper again,
He says it's a private philosophy,
That helps the means justify the ends.

He says he's been around the world,
With lots of true-hearted girls,
And if he can just remember Port Starbird,
He will die a happy man.

I want to go to Port Starbird,
I want to blow this particular harbor,
I want to sail around the world like my captain did,
I want to go to Port Starbird.

Well he passed on just the other day,
We buried him at sea,
The way that he would have wanted,
That was where he always wanted to be.

But I felt like there was something missing,
That prayer for safety that he never read to me,
Or maybe it was an old love letter,

That belonged with him down in the sea.

So I retrieved the paper from his locker,
And finally saw what the old man had read,
Every day for all our years on the sea,
And here's what the paper said:

Port left, starboard right,
Red left, green right,
When boats pass in the daytime,
Or in the night,
Go port-to-port and you'll be all right.

Port left, starboard right,
Ships that pass in the night,
When you don't know where you're going,
Any course will take you there,
Port left, starboard right.

Port left, starboard right,
Port left, starboard right."

He finished with a flourish. "Well, that's it," he said. He set the guitar aside and reached for his beer. His hand was shaking just a bit, but he felt good – he'd gotten through it without making any major mistakes. The laughter and applause started as he tipped the bottle up.

"I get it!" Len exclaimed. "You sly son of a gun!" the Captain laughed. "Hey, that was excellent, man, really!" Mario declared, and the beach bunnies concurred. "Do another one! Do you have more originals?"

Kari gave Ketch's arm a pinch. "I had no idea you were so dang clever!" she said. "Did you really make all that up by yourself?"

"I did," Ketch answered. He saw that her glass was empty again. "Here, let me top that off for you."

Len said, "Ketch, you mind if I play a little somethin'?"

Thank you again, Len, Ketch thought with relief. He'd had enough of public performing for tonight. "Not at all, please do, be my guest," he replied, passing Len the guitar.

Len wasn't much of a singer, but he was a good chicken-picker. "So, me and you," Kari mused while Len played, finding her way back to her earlier train of thought. "Kari and Storm, Storm and Kari. Sounds weird. Ha – Ketch and Kari! We could open a live bait shop!" She laughed and took another drink. "Where'd you get that name, 'Storm'? I know you don't like it, but I don't know why."

"Like Bruce Willis said in *Pulp Fiction*, this is America, names don't mean anything." Ketch chuckled. "Sorry, you said no more movie references."

"Come on, I'm serious."

"Okay. Well, my parents were a little odd. Not in a bad way, but they were definitely on a tributary off the main stream. They were big fans of pulp fiction and those old noir mysteries when I was a kid. I think they hoped I'd become either a movie actor or a famous detective, so they gave me something they thought I'd need, what they thought was a glamorous name at the time. And no middle name either, just 'Storm

Ketchum'. But I became a scientist."

"Are they disappointed?"

"Not anymore. They're both gone now."

"Oh, I'm sorry," she said. "Huh... Well now, don't we make a pair? A failed noir detective, and a jug of syrup." At Ketch's puzzled look she explained, "You know, for hotcakes, like Karo syrup, you ever had that? Your folks were just ahead of their time. I was born when a *lot* of folks were startin' to screw around with spellin' and makin' up new names to try to be different. I guess I'm lucky, though, it could've been worse. I could've been named Moon Unit or Dandelion or Lafawnduh or somethin' like that, I guess."

After Len, Barb took over – and surprisingly, she turned out to be a something of a virtuoso, obviously classically trained. You never can tell about people, Ketch thought. He hoped his own performance hadn't been too offensively amateurish for her.

"Hey, you got any of that wacky terbacky stashed around here?" Kari abruptly inquired.

"What?" Ketch chuckled. "No, I don't keep any here. You'll have to ask, uh, someone else about that." He'd almost said 'Mario', but loose lips can sink ships. Not that he didn't trust her, but who knew who she might mention it to sometime, and so on down the line. "Besides, I think you're doing fine without it."

"Oh yeah? Well, mister smart guy, you don't know everything."

"Everythin' 'bout what?" the Captain's voice suddenly projected from right behind them. Kari almost dropped her glass. Ketch hadn't noticed him returning up the steps from his cooler. "Never mind, none a my beeswax. You dawg!" the Captain leered at Ketch. "Hey, we're talkin' 'bout truckin' this party on down to the boatyard, where they got some, shall we say, additional resources, you know? We're gonna clean up here first, though. Y'all want to join us?"

"Thanks, but not me," Ketch said. "It's been a long day for me."

"Me neither, but thank you kindly," Kari immediately added, to Ketch's surprise given her recent query. "I've got to get goin' soon."

The others were starting to collect plates and bottles. "You guys don't have to do anything, don't worry about it," Ketch said.

"Hey, it's the least we can do for a great musician like you. In fact, it's a dang honor!" the Captain pronounced. "Don't worry, won't take long with us all doin' it. By the way, okay if I leave my truck here? Ain't in your way, I don't think. I'll walk down with the others and pick 'er up tomorrow, and just crash on board tonight."

"Of course, that's fine. And thank you. Just do what you feel like doing, I'll take care of the rest later."

The Captain went off to help in the kitchen. "I should help out too, I guess, but I don't know if I can stand up," Kari giggled. "So, what are you gonna do with me? I guess I shouldn't be drivin' right about now, and neither should you. Should I go on down there with the rest of them? Maybe I could crash on board somewhere too," she teased.

"Well," Ketch said. He hadn't thought about this, but in his defense he hadn't known she'd go through two bottles of wine either. He wondered what was behind that; she hadn't behaved like this when she'd been here in the past. "I have that second bedroom. It isn't very fancy, but there's a bed and it's made up. I have a new toothbrush I haven't opened yet."

"Yeah? No, wait, I'm sorry, I shouldn't put you on the spot like that," she apologized. "I might could ask the girls if I could stay with one of them. If they aren't gonna be busy later, that is, I don't know about that."

"No, you don't have to do that. You're welcome to stay here tonight. I honestly don't mind." Ketch got up from his chair and bowed. "In fact, Jack and I would love to have you, really, and we insist." He smiled down at her, sincerely enough to reassure her, he hoped. The dog joined him and wagged in agreement, with a doggy grin on his face as well. He loved company.

"Well, okay then!" she said, smiling back at both of them. "Thanks!"

The others shortly began exiting the house and reassembling on the front porch, having finished the cleanup. "Hey man," Mario said, "what's with all that stuff you got piled up out back there?"

"Yeah," Len said, "we couldn't help but spot 'em out the window when we were loadin' the dishwasher. What are they, floatation blocks? You fixin' to put up a floatin' dock or somethin' like that?"

Ketch had hoped no one would notice the blocks; he should have covered the kitchen window. He'd gotten lucky when the truck had delivered them – no one he knew had been around at the time, and as his neighbors were largely vacation renters he hadn't worried about any of them. But he supposed they'd had to have found out eventually anyway. Still, it was getting late and he didn't want to go into all the details tonight. He didn't think he had the energy to both explain everything and defend himself against accusations that he was losing his mind; which maybe he was.

"They're for the house," he said. "I want to attach them underneath it so the house will be able to float, just in case."

"Really? Wow. I've heard of people doin' that," Mario said, "but not anywhere around here."

"How come I didn't know about this?" the Captain asked. "When did you get the dang things? And what about Ingram and that lot, I thought you were gonna have to sell the place? You got a engineer?" He stopped talking and raised his arms. "Okay, sorry, too many questions." He pulled a chair up by Ketch and cast a glance around the group. "Do you know somethin' 'bout the weather we don't? Should we be thinkin' about movin' our boats?"

"No!" Ketch hastily replied. "I don't know anything, there's nothing for you to worry about." The rest of the group started settling back into their chairs, and he carefully continued. "It turns out I won't be selling the house," he began. Though this was technically true, it was of course not the whole truth. And technically speaking, were these white lies he was engaging in, or lies of omission, or just plain lies? Maybe he was just building up to the whole truth gradually, the way Emily Dickinson had advised in a poem of hers he happened to recall some of: *Tell all the truth but tell it slant, success in circuit lies, too bright for our infirm delight, the truth's superb surprise.* Yes, that worked for him, for now.

"I guess you must a just found that out, since you didn't tell me about it this mornin'," the Captain said. "But you had to've ordered them blocks some time ago, right?" He crossed his arms and put a look on his face that made it clear he was waiting for an explanation.

"They were delivered on Saturday. I ordered them when you were out of town. I'm sorry, I just didn't feel like going into it this morning," Ketch said. "We didn't have much time to talk anyway." That didn't fully explain Ketch's outburst regarding Ingram and his grandiose plans on this morning's charter, among other inconsistencies, and the Captain didn't appear satisfied – but then Kari cut in.

"Why were you gonna sell the house?" she asked. "I know Bob Ingram's gonna take the boatyard and some other nearby properties, but was he after yours too?"

"Yes," Ketch answered, and then Len rescued him once again. "How are they supposed to be attached? How much do they weigh? How do you know you got enough of 'em?" he asked.

"Well, they weigh ninety-one pounds each, and I got twenty-five of them," Ketch started to explain, grateful for the reprieve. "They're top-mount, and they attach with lag screws. Put together they're supposed to provide enough buoyancy to support a sixty thousand-pound house, which is the high end of the estimated weight of this house at sixty pounds per square foot of living space. And I did verify my figures with an engineer at the company." And the solid EPS foam blocks were polyethylene-encapsulated, making them highly UV-resistant and impact-resistant and impermeable to water as well as to marine organisms, solvents, and fuels; he hoped the others wouldn't realize tonight that this was overkill for their stated purpose. He hadn't yet worked out the logistics of getting the house into the water when the time came, but when that happened these blocks would be able to hold up under permanent immersion.

"I still don't see why you're feelin' the need to do any a this," the Captain muttered. "Seems to me you're spendin' a bunch a money for nothin'."

"You sure all that extry weight won't just pull the bottom right off the house?" Len persisted. "Maybe you'll have to jack it up here and there. And you'll have to anchor it somehow in case it ever does get to floatin'."

"It looks like you got plenty of freeboard under the house, but it's still gonna be tough workin' under there," Mario observed. "Probably have to get at least a couple jacks too to hold up the blocks while you're screwin' 'em in. Who's gonna do that? You got somebody lined up? You sure can't do it yourself, right?"

"You're right," Ketch agreed, "it's too much for me to do alone – and no, I haven't hired anyone yet."

"Well heck," Len said, "I'd be willin' to help out. I'm gettin' tired of that shit job I been workin' anyway."

"Hey, we could both do it!" Mario said, getting enthused. "I got nothin' goin' on right now. We could work out a cut rate, cash under the table. We'd get us some income, and we'd be helpin' our good friend here at the same time!"

"Sounds good to me," Len said, and the girls murmured their approval as well. "Ketch, what do you think?"

He couldn't answer immediately; there was something caught in his throat. He took a sip of his beer. "Ahem! Well – yes, I think that's a fine idea, and I think it's really great of you guys to offer to do that for me. Thank you." Thinking of his possibly severely limited timetable, he tried to sound casual as he asked, "When do you think you could start?"

"Well, maybe in a couple days or so if you want?" Mario said. "Okay by me," Len said.

"What about your job, Len?" Kari asked, from the perspective of a potential employer. "Don't you have to give notice? Would you be putting them in a bind? What if you need a reference?"

"I ain't worried 'bout all that," Len said. "I'm a good worker, but there's lots of folks needin' a job, and a monkey could do mine. I'll tell 'em I have to go back home to Tar Heel for some family thing or other."

The Captain, who'd remained atypically silent through the remainder of the exchange, stood up. "Well, now that's been settled, I guess we best be moseyin' along," he said. The others agreed, got up, and started down the steps, and Ketch stood to see them off.

"Ketch, you want these torches out?" Mario called.

"No thanks, they'll burn down on their own soon."

"Take 'er easy, you ole dawg," the Captain said, clapping Ketch on the back. In a lower voice he added, "I know you don't want to talk right now, and that's okay. But next time we meet, Lucy, you got some splainin' to do." Raising his voice again as he walked away, he called to the others, "Hey you guys, do me a favor and stick that cooler in the back a my truck!"

Trailing a profusion of thank-you's and various permutations of farewell, the group finally trundled off through the yard and down the road.

"Well, what now?" Kari asked as they disappeared from view. "Hey, there's still a little of that wine left. How about we just set out here for a spell longer? It's nice and quiet now, and it's a beautiful night."

What now, indeed? Would there be no end to this long and winding day, this confoundingly good and bad day? Should he confide in Kari now- or in anyone, ever? He knew the Captain would pry it out of him; he realized he no longer had a choice there, and really the Captain deserved to know the whole story if anyone did, no matter what he ended up thinking about it. But as for the others – it was his problem, not theirs, and he didn't see how anyone could do anything to help, certainly not in a legal sense at any rate. He didn't need their advice, either; advice was just something people asked for when they already knew the answer but wished they didn't, and adding everyone's well-meaning but impotent outrage to his own wouldn't accomplish anything. But he supposed he was only delaying the inevitable; they'd all end up knowing eventually.

"So," Kari said, "you want to talk about it?"

"About what?"

"Whatever it is you're really up to here." Smiling, she added, "Seemed like Don wasn't buyin' what you were sellin', and I don't think I do either."

"You guys are too astute for me," he said with a weak smile of his own. "You're right, there's more to it than meets the eye, but it's a long story and I'd rather tell you another time."

"Promise?" she asked. Ketch nodded assent. "Okay then, I'll wait. But not forever," she mockingly warned. "And hey – I can keep my trap shut if I have to, just so's you know."

So, he'd have to tell her, too, and soon. But not tonight. It was apparent to him that she had her own problems and something was bothering her; so for what remained of the evening, as long as his eyes could stay open, instead of talking he'd listen – a highly underrated skill, and one he fortunately happened to possess.

~ Seven ~

*There's seldom a happy ending when people
fall in love.*

*K*ari emptied the remaining wine into her glass
and put her feet up. Ketch went into the house.
The dog, bleary-eyed now, followed him in and
stretched out on the rug in front of the wood-burning
stove – which was of course not in use at the moment,
but this had become his favorite spot during their first
winter here, and he was always comfortable there. As
smart as he was (for a dog), when he was hot he'd also
lie under a ceiling fan whether or not it was on, which
Ketch found amusing; but perhaps the dog was
engaging in wishful thinking or thinking ahead, or
indirectly making a request that Ketch was too dumb
to recognize.

He came back out with two bottles of water and
some headache medicine and sat down across from
Kari. "Where's Jack, gone in to bed?" she asked. "It's
been, what, a little more than three years now, but I
still miss my dog."

"I know how that feels," Ketch said. "Have you
ever thought of getting another one? I always think I
never will again, but then somehow I always do."

"I don't know, I probably don't really have time for
one anymore. What's that you've got there?"

"Medicine. After you finish that wine, you'd better
drink all of this, and take at least a couple of these as

well," he said, cracking open one of the water bottles for himself. "Otherwise you might be sorry in the morning."

"Yes, doctor," she said, rolling her eyes. "You *are* a doctor, right? I seem to recall you mentionin' that one time. Doctor Ketchum..."

"I am, but not the kind you'll wish you had in the morning if you don't listen to me."

"Okay, okay." She rolled her eyes again. "So what's on your mind? Besides your little project, I mean. You were actin' funny today, when you came to the shop."

"Really?" What had he done differently? And how did they always know? "Oh, nothing for you to worry about. What's up with you? You're the one who's cleaning out my wine cellar," he joked.

"You have a wine cellar? Where? Oh, you're kiddin' with me, okay." She took another gulp of wine. "Well, what's *not* up with me? I'm almost forty years old and I have no family because I spend all my time on my business, which is on the ropes most of the time, and I'm almost forty and still livin' month-to-month... I can't afford to hire anybody to help at the shop – and by the way I appreciate it when *you* help me out more'n you know, so thank you for that." Another quick gulp. "So I have to be at the shop all the time, and I got some folks signed up for classes, so I'll be able to pay my rent and probably fix my car again, it's makin' a funny noise, and hopefully I'll sell some gear so I can eat and keep the lights on at night. I don't know what'll happen next month – or next winter when it gets slow again if things don't pick up soon.

Maybe I'll have to get another job." She paused again and this time emptied the glass.

"Plus I'm not seein' Mick anymore, which I know is no big loss, you don't have to tell me though I know you'd like to. He just quit callin' me, and I'm pretty sure he was cheatin' on me anyway." She reached for the water bottle. "Followin' orders, see?" she said with a thin smile, then sighed. "I'm sorry, I'm babblin' again. I shouldn't be dumpin' on you, it's bad enough I conned you into a free bunk for the night – and I drank up all your wine too, which you mightn't have realized but I know it was expensive, and that was real nice of you and thank you *again* for that. God, that was good at least." She took a deep breath and loudly exhaled. "So that's the story of me."

Cheating? On this one, this intelligent, vivacious, giving, hard-working woman, and the way she looked in the glow of the fading torchlight? Ketch stole a look into her bright green eyes. How could anyone be cruel to those eyes?

"Are you done?" he rhetorically inquired. "Well then," he counted on his fingers, "first of all, I'm your friend, and you don't have to apologize for anything. Second, you're welcome to stay here anytime you need to." Well, at least for a little while. "And third, Mick isn't worth your time and you deserve better. And fourth – well, never mind that. And fifth, I can cover for you at the shop sometimes when you need a break – all you have to do is ask." He stopped counting. "Does he even have a job now?"

"Mick? Who knows?" She sipped some water and

popped a couple of the tablets. "But who cares? You're right about him. He was mean sometimes too, especially when he'd been drinkin'. I'm done with him." After a short silence she asked, "So what was the fourth thing? See, I'm not as wasted as you thought I was," she said with a wan smile.

"Oh, I forget. Nothing."

"Oh no, you can't do that! I'm already bein' patient on the one thing, so come on now, out with it!"

"Okay, okay," Ketch smiled. "Well, I was just going to say that wasn't all of the wine, I have more. But not tonight!" he added, putting his hands up in a stop sign. She laughed. "It's getting late, and you have things to do tomorrow, as I recall," he continued. "Allow me to show you to your quarters, mademoiselle." He rose and crooked an elbow for her. She laughed again and took it and they went inside.

She sat down hard on the guest bed. "You'd get tired of me if I stayed here too often," she said. "Yeah, I heard that part too." She hiccupped. "They all do, you know, sooner or later."

"Now, that's enough of that," Ketch said as he went off to get her a tailed dress shirt in lieu of a nightgown, which he had none of on hand. Go figure... The dog came in to check on her, then trotted back out and into Ketch's bedroom.

After he'd gotten her straightened away, Ketch retreated to his bedroom as well and prepared to retire for the night. The dog was already slumbering blissfully on his own overstuffed bed on the floor beside Ketch's bed.

As tired as he now was, he found he couldn't sleep. He rolled over and reached for his e-reader on the nightstand, hoping that might make him sleepy – but it didn't work, so after a while he put it away and sat up and thought. If he remembered correctly, he'd left his laptop on the table by the recliner in the living room, rather than on his desk in that extra bedroom as he usually did. He slipped his robe on and padded out there as quietly as he could, and found he was right.

He sat in the recliner in the dark and booted the laptop, and when it was ready he brought up a browser window and returned to a page he'd earlier bookmarked about eminent domain.

There were apparently lawyers who specialized in eminent domain cases. He supposed some might think him foolish for not retaining one, but he strongly suspected doing so would just be a waste of time and money. When people like Bob Ingram set their minds on something, especially in the 'good-old-boy' type of political climate he currently resided in, it was probably pretty much a done deal.

What if he tried to stall Ingram by contesting the proposed compensation? Ketch read that this tactic wouldn't delay the seizure, because North Carolina law allows a 'quick-take' procedure in which the recipient gets the title to the property as soon as all the papers are filed, even if there's a compensation issue to be resolved in court. So, he thought, when Ingram pushes the button, the title would probably transfer immediately. He could possibly stall by instead contesting the legality of the seizure – but if Ingram had friends in high places, as he surely must given what Ketch already knew, that wouldn't help either.

Ketch hadn't heard of anyone else trying to use these tactics around here – but as he'd noted earlier, he didn't know if any of them had had to go through the eminent domain process; in fact, based on what he'd heard from the Captain, it sounded like they'd all evidently caved and sold, and probably after consulting with their expensive and useless attorneys. He thought about asking around the neighborhood to see how others had fared, but he didn't know his neighbors very well – not because he was reclusive, but again, rather because most of them were absentee owners and the people in the houses at this time of year were vacationers who came and went a week or two at a time. He didn't know who owned the boatyard, just that it was some out-of-town outfit. There was one person he could maybe talk to, the old guy with the grandfathered mini-horse farm around the bend that the Captain had mentioned; he couldn't recall the man's name, but they'd spoken before in passing. But the Captain said that fellow had agreed to sell.

Ah, here was a link to North Carolina General Statutes 40A. Interesting – there were separate articles in the statute for public and private condemnors; now why would that be, if the Assembly supposedly didn't generally allow seizures for private development, as he'd earlier read? He sighed aloud –

goddamn lawyers... But here was a glimmer of light in the darkness. It appeared that if Ingram operated as a private condemnor, there'd be meetings (plural) of county commissioners to be scheduled, where Ketch could appeal and air his grievances. Not that it would probably help in the final analysis, since said commissioners would undoubtedly have Ingram's tentacles pulling at them, but it could eat up some time. And if Ingram somehow went the public condemnor route, Ketch would have a hundred and twenty days to answer the declaration, after which it looked like maybe he could do something, but he couldn't discern what exactly. Shouldn't he also have a hundred and twenty days the other way as well? It didn't say so here. Maybe he should pay for an hour or two with a lawyer after all? He at least needed to know how long he'd have to finish the work on the house, beyond the week Ingram had given him today – if that even still held, after he'd antagonized the man. It was good that Mario and Len could start helping with the foam blocks sooner rather than later.

Now he was getting sleepy. This was just the tip of an iceberg, there were truckloads of material here he could read, but that was enough for tonight. But wait, what if he agreed to sell after all? Closings certainly seemed to take more time than people generally desired, and could be made to take even more time than strictly necessary. In either case, sale or seizure, Ingram didn't really want the house, since he'd just be demolishing it, so Ketch's plan for floating away in it shouldn't present any more legal difficulties either way. In fact, it would probably save Ingram some money, damn it. Which reminded him, he should start doing some research on squatting rights, as well as marine codes – which shouldn't apply to him, though, since his house wouldn't be motorized and should thus not be considered a houseboat...

But damn it all, he didn't need any of this. Why couldn't people just live their own lives and let other people be? It's too bad he wasn't living on a houseboat, he thought, then he could just drive the damned thing somewhere else, maybe park it right down at the boatyard – but no, not the Kinnakeet Boatyard, that was on the chopping block as well. And no, not 'the damned thing' – his house, *his* house, a place he loved and that was the epicenter of his and Jack's formerly idyllic existence.

He also needed to think more about how to get the house into the water. Add a steel frame to protect the blocks and roll it into the water on a flatbed, or maybe on some logs? Push it with a truck, or pull it with a tugboat? Were there tugs with a shallow enough draft for this sound? He'd have to get all of the existing utilities disconnected, and if he wanted to actually live in the house, learn how to rig it with standalone utilities. He'd have to use solar panels and/or wind power or a generator for electricity, probably propane for cooking and heating, make sure the wiring was waterproof, install chemical or composting or incinerating toilets, collect rainwater...

Yes, he had a lot of work to do – but he could certainly 'camp out' in the house for a while if necessary, and he knew there were resources he could tap for help and advice. Beyond the small floating cabins he'd seen, like the ones on Powell Lake in British Columbia, and the floating house everyone had seen in *Sleepless in Seattle*, these days there was literally a whole world of floating houses out there, both single- and multiple-story, and many that were bigger and fancier than most folks knew. There were hundreds of them in Seattle now, hundreds more in San Francisco and on the Mississippi River in Minnesota, thousands in Portland, Oregon, a luxury floating home community that formed a suburb of Amsterdam, near-shore communities where the docks served as roads and the floating houses had driveways with cars parked in them elsewhere in Europe, a floating city that was being planned in the Maldives... The houses could be prefabricated or stick-built, and they floated courtesy of log floats, solid styrofoam encased in rubber, foam-filled pontoons, positive concrete, concrete pontoons, concrete and foam, wood and foam, polyethylene shells with solid core polystyrene block molded inside (like the ones he'd bought), fiberglass and envirofloat, whatever that was...

Not for the first time, he hoped he'd made the right decision with the option he'd chosen. The foam blocks weren't as expensive as many of the other options, and he'd thought they were the most expedient and easiest way for him to go, i.e., the most DIY-friendly, given his locale and situation, and most importantly he'd thought they would work; and the engineer at the company (who had assured Ketch he was ethical and had encouraged Ketch to get a second opinion if he didn't believe him, which Ketch had not done) had agreed. But he still wondered if he should have gone with pontoons, so he clicked on another of his bookmarks, a company that sold individual pontoons as well as pontoon boats, and reviewed the data he found there on buoyancy, sizes, and cost. He discovered that he'd need too many of them, they wouldn't provide as much buoyancy, and they'd be more expensive and harder to install – just as he had the last time he'd checked.

Okay, enough already, time to shut down. One more thought occurred to him – would he have to make an effort to contact the media to cover the event? Probably not – he imagined they'd be coming to him, once they found out what he was up to. Either way, he'd make sure he got some attention somehow if he had to. Though he really did love the house, his main goal after all was not to save it, but rather to make a point. If all went well, floating his house and squatting in the sound would constitute a statement and hopefully a high-profile protest or demonstration against eminent domain abuse in North Carolina, resulting in publicity that Ingram and others like him would hopefully find unwelcome.

With a feeling of contumacious self-satisfaction, Ketch was starting to close windows when he heard the padding of more feet on the floor. "Hey, you," a soft voice floated across the room to him, and an apparition with a white shirt, a familiar face, and bed hair started to materialize in the dark behind the glow of the screen. "Couldn't sleep? I'm kinda restless myself." She parked herself on an arm of the recliner and squinted down at the laptop. "Whatcha lookin' at there, porn?" she innocently asked.

"No! Pontoon boats," Ketch dissembled, acutely aware of her proximity. He scootched away from her a bit to give her a little more space.

"Pontoon boats?" She laughed. "Are you serious? I never would've guessed that in a million years! I swear, you've got to be the only man I've ever known that'd be sittin' in the dark alone half-naked in the middle of the night lookin' at *pontoon boats* online! I swear..." She giggled some more, then calmed down. "What do you need one of them for?" she asked.

"I don't," Ketch said, and closed the lid of the laptop and yawned. "What time is it?"

"I don't know," she answered. "And we probably don't want to know. Hey, you want a drink?"

"Yes, thanks, why not? There's some juice in the fridge."

"You know, a pontoon boat might be handy in the sound for trainin' dives," she called from the kitchen. The dog wandered out to see what was going on, sniffed the air, and took a look around. No food. He turned and wearily shuffled back to his bed.

"Maybe. Most of the sound would be too shallow, so they'd have buoyancy problems, but I know a couple of twenty-five-foot holes. The visibility might still be too poor, though." Ketch started recalling his own certification dive, back when he'd first learned.

That was over thirty years ago now, when he'd been on vacation one time down at Wrightsville Beach, several hours south of here...

They'd gone out to a sunken tugboat in fifty feet of water about three miles offshore. It was a brutally hot day and he'd overheated while donning his gear. Sitting on the gunwale with his back to the water and sweating inside his old-fashioned rubber wet suit, he'd started to wonder what on earth had possessed him to do this crazy thing. There was no land in sight, and when he looked down behind him all he could see was murky green water. The others were waiting for him at the anchor line and he was starting to hyperventilate.

He'd practiced the prescribed rear entry from the side of the pool, but the height was greater here and the thought of letting himself fall backward into that unknown environment suddenly held little appeal. That was when the boat captain, a kindly soul, had approached him and solved the problem.

"Are you all right?" he'd asked. A silent nod. "You don't feel sick?" A shake of the head. "Let's check your gear one more time." After a moment, "Everything looks good. Put the regulator in your mouth. Good. Now put your hand over your mask." Nervous compliance. "You'll feel better when you get in the water." And then he'd given Ketch a good hard shove and sent him on his way.

Those were the days, Ketch thought; you couldn't get away with something like that now, you'd probably get sued. But that captain had been right. He'd quickly overcome his initial fear, thoroughly and competently enjoyed the dive, and returned to the boat with more air left in his tank than anyone else.

"What are you smilin' about?" Kari asked, returning to her perch on the recliner arm and handing Ketch a glass.

An arm draped across his shoulders as Ketch started to drink, and he had to manage a discreet cough before replying. "I was thinking of my Open Water certification dive a long time ago. It's a funny story. I'll tell it to you sometime."

"Well, I'd like to hear that," she said. "But some other time, it's too late tonight for more tall tales." She finished her juice and said, "Drink up, and let's get back to bed." He obeyed, and they both rose from the chair. He started to head off to his room, but she grabbed his arm and turned him around. "Nuh-uh, this way," she said, steering him toward the guest bedroom.

"Why?" he asked, startled, and then he understood. Could this really be happening? "Oh, I see. Kari, I'm flattered, really, but I don't even remember the last time I was with a woman, and I'm dead tired – and besides, just because I'm letting you stay here, you don't have to -"

She laid a finger on his lips and interrupted, "You just hush now." He stopped trying to talk and allowed her to lead him into her bedroom. "I know you've been wantin' to. And don't you worry one little bit 'bout bein' too tired," she said, and mischievously added, "I like bein' on top."

~ E i g h t ~

*It's good to be lucky, but better to be
prepared and ready when the luck comes.*

Ketch was alone when he finally woke, to a beam of bright mid-morning sunlight shining directly in his face. He rolled over and groggily scanned the room. He couldn't see the dog anywhere from where he was – which was where? Ah yes, the second bedroom. So it hadn't been a dream; or rather it had, but it was one of those rare ones that come true.

He found he was a bit sore here and there when he got up out of the bed and tried to stretch, but then he realized that despite this he hadn't felt anywhere near this good in years. He went to his own bedroom and pulled on some shorts and a tee shirt. The dog was lying on the dog bed.

"Good morning, Jack," he said to the dog, "want to go out?" The dog didn't move, except to thump his tail a couple of times. She must have already taken him out. "Okay then, how about some breakfast?" Just another half-hearted thump. She must have fed him, too.

"Hello?" he called out. No answer. He splashed some water on his face in the bathroom and then went to the kitchen, where the wall clock read 10:38. What the hell? He never slept this late. There were a couple of pellets on the floor next to the dog's food dish, so it looked like he had in fact been fed. Then he saw a small white card propped up against the plant in the middle of the kitchen table.

All it had on it was a shakily drawn generic smiley face. He picked it up and turned it over. 'Sea Dog Scuba Center, Kari Gellhorn', and so on was professionally printed on that side. A business card. No thank-you, no sappy words, no apologies, no 'call me', no schedule, no promises, no nothing. It might be possible for him to grow to like this one even more than he already did. He chose to interpret the card as an indication that she meant to keep things simple, which he didn't at all mind. Alfred Hitchcock once said a good story was like life without the dull parts. Ketch liked a good story, and it was okay with him if she wanted to leave out some of the dull parts.

He poured himself some more juice and carried it, a banana, and a buttered but untoasted jumbo bagel out to the front deck. He noticed the tank they'd forgotten about last night standing just inside the front door. She was nothing if not thorough, he thought with a flush. It was already late and he didn't feel ambitious enough to clean the boat today, so he'd just keep the tank cool and safe in the house for now. She wouldn't mind if he didn't return it right away.

He also noticed that her car was gone, and so was the Captain's truck. He wondered which had happened first. He'd hear about it later if her car had still been here when the Captain had come for his truck – which it probably had, or the Captain would probably have awakened him earlier. It wasn't like that salty dog to operate in silence, unless he'd thought he might be interrupting something important.

Oh well. He thought about giving her a call, then remembered she'd said she'd be visiting her mother today. In Manteo up on Roanoke Island, where the niece and nephew were? He'd forgotten to ask. Maybe he'd try later.

The dog moseyed out to the deck to see if there'd be any leftover breakfast food. There was, almost half of the bagel Ketch had tired of chewing. Ketch leaned forward in his chair and scanned the sky while the dog licked the butter from the bagel. Mackerel sky with mare's tails, makes tall ships carry low sails... Red sky at night, sailor's delight, red sky at morning, sailor's warning... These heuristics and others that were favored by the old-timers here may seem silly to some, he thought, but he'd fared better with them over the years than he had with the forecasts generated by the meteorologists with their fancy equipment. Not that any of that mattered at the moment, though, as he hadn't been paying attention last night and he'd missed the morning harbingers by snoozing half the day away. Whatever happened with the weather was irrelevant today anyway – it was going to be one fine day regardless.

"Well, boy, we'd better get going," he said to the dog. There were a few chores that needed doing, mostly related to the previous night's soiree, and he needed a shower – and a shave, he reminded himself. Since he'd done away with the beard he'd have to do that every day from now on, if he didn't want to look even older than he already did. And try to call a lawyer? No, not today; maybe tomorrow. Sometimes it seemed like life consisted mostly of a series of menial duties, many of them not all that pleasant – but it certainly beat the alternative and he was certainly nowhere near ready to give it up.

But maybe he should do something with the dog first. It was too hot already for the furry fellow to truly enjoy a trip to the beach, but maybe a bit of playing and a swim out back? Then they could get on with their menial duties.

"Hey Jack," he said to the dog, "let's get ready for a playtime!" The dog perked up at these words, followed Ketch back into the house, and waited fairly patiently (with just a single anticipatory bark) while Ketch exchanged his shorts for a bathing suit.

They went out to the back yard and he kicked a football for the dog a few times. His dogs had always preferred footballs over other balls, probably because their unpredictable bounces made them more exciting. Then he threw the frisbee, and he was pleased to see the dog was still adept at chasing it down and catching it in the air. The yard wasn't big enough to seriously chuck the thing, but it was still good exercise and the dog enjoyed the game. When he thought the dog was starting to overheat, he finished by sailing the frisbee into the water. When the dog belly-flopped in off the dock to retrieve it, Ketch eased into the warm water behind him. After they'd splashed around some, he took the dog back up to the house, rubbed him down with an old towel, and thoroughly brushed him. He didn't always rinse the dog with fresh water, as an occasional salt water dip was an effective flea and tick preventative.

After he'd finished his chores and made himself decent, he decided to drive the pickup down to the Food Lion at the south end of town. He hadn't done that in a while, and it was time to stock up on some things he couldn't get at Village Grocery or the Barefoot Station. It was too hot to leave the dog in the truck, so he gave him a new bone, made sure his water dish was full, and headed out.

Ketch didn't begrudge the presence of the Food Lion in Avon. It was the only major supermarket on the whole island and served everyone from Rodanthe on down to Hatteras, and he appreciated not having to drive twenty or thirty miles to get there like some folks did. Still, he lingered there only long enough to get the staples he needed, which today also included a few extra items he'd decided he should keep around the house – another toothbrush, a feminine stick deodorant and shampoo/conditioner combo, a small package of sanitary products that might or might not be appropriate and would hopefully never be needed, a box of some kind of little fruity soaps... just in case. The Food Lion didn't carry clothing, but he wouldn't know what sizes to get anyway.

When it was time to leave, he decided to turn right on 12 instead of left and continue south to Buxton, a pleasant little town that was the home of the iconic Cape Hatteras Lighthouse. Though he'd bought some perishables, it was only about five miles and they were iced down in a cooler in the back and should be okay for a while. It was a pleasant sunny drive with the windows down, and with the sound on his right and the beach dunes on his left, both mostly unspoiled along this stretch of road.

The lighthouse, the tallest one in the United States, had stood fifteen hundred feet from the water when it was built in 1870; but by 1970 steady and relentless shoreline erosion had placed it in serious jeopardy, and it ended up being only about a hundred feet from the water. In 1999 a long-planned and truly stupendous engineering project to preserve the lighthouse was finally completed, when the entire light station, including the lighthouse and all of its associated outbuildings, cisterns, and sidewalks, were lifted from their foundations and painstakingly moved twenty-nine hundred feet southwest, to a secure new location sixteen hundred feet from the water.

He could see it now coming up on his left, but though he always enjoyed visiting the site, he wouldn't tarry there today. When he shortly crossed into Buxton, it took him a few minutes to find her apartment again, since he'd only been there once and that was quite some time ago; and when he found it he discovered she wasn't there. This didn't surprise him and he knew he'd been foolish to try, so he wasn't really disappointed.

He briefly considered dropping in at Buxton Village Books, as a sort of consolation prize. It was the best little bookshop he'd ever known, but he decided he shouldn't stop there today – if he lost track of time, as he invariably did whenever he went in there, that might not be good for the groceries. Too bad... This was the bookstore where he'd found a reprint of *The Hatterasman*, the regional classic penned by Ben Dixon MacNeill in the late Fifties and which was his second-favorite book after *The Old Man and the Sea*. The store itself was actually a smallish house, old but quaint and appealing, and was distinguished by its relaxed atmosphere and an excellent selection of books about North Carolina and the Outer Banks, in addition to the standard bookstore fare; and to top it all off, the seasoned proprietress was knowledgeable and outgoing, and was herself a local treasure in Ketch's opinion.

He returned home and unloaded his supplies and took the dog out again. He might have napped if he hadn't slept in this morning. Instead, he went online, checked his e-mail, and read the day's newspaper, something he'd lately fallen out of the habit of doing and should get back to. Then, deciding he was too restless to hang around the house, he called the dog over.

"Let's go for a ride, Jack. Are you up for that, boy?" The dog indicated he was. Ketch thought he'd drive down to the boatyard, even though it wasn't that far. If the Captain was there, maybe they could get takeout from somewhere and shoot the breeze (and do his splainin', he supposed); if the Captain wasn't there, he could check to see if Kari was back and maybe take the dog and do something with her; and if neither was available, he and the dog could stop at the Subway out on 12 and take something home.

When they arrived he didn't see the Captain's truck anywhere, but he parked and walked out to the boat with the dog in tow anyway, just in case. It turned out there was no one on board, so he extracted his cell phone from its faux-leather carrying case on his belt and dialed Kari's cell number. There was no answer, and he didn't leave a message. As he was pocketing the phone, he happened to see Mick climbing into a beat-up old pickup toward the far end of the boatyard. He watched Mick start the truck, back out of his parking space, and slowly drive out of the boatyard.

It didn't appear Mick had noticed him when he'd driven by. Though Ketch knew who Mick was, Mick didn't really know Ketch and hadn't seen him in quite a while, so that wasn't too surprising. Ketch suddenly broke into a brisk walk, calling to the dog to follow. He hurriedly loaded the dog back into his truck and cranked it up. The rear wheels spit gravel as they exited the boatyard.

If Mick was headed back out to 12, he'd have to take North End Road and then Harbor Road, so that's the way Ketch went. He drove a little faster than he usually did, but despite his haste he drove prudently. It wouldn't do to be too reckless on these back roads, where children walked and ran pretty much wherever they wanted because it was usually safe to do so.

He still hadn't caught up with Mick when he reached the Route 12 intersection. If Mick hadn't turned off somewhere and had in fact taken 12, he could have gone north or south. Ketch guessed north. When he'd left the town and its 30 mph speed limit behind, he accelerated to 60, which was about as fast as he dared to drive on this road. Hopefully it would be enough for him to catch up – if Mick was indeed ahead of him. He decided he'd give up and turn around if he got as far as Salvo and still hadn't seen any sign of Mick.

He finally remembered to lower the window on the passenger side for the dog. But not all the way, as it wasn't good for him to ride with his head out the window at higher speeds, just enough to let him stick his snout out and experience the olfactory feast Ketch knew he enjoyed when they went for a ride.

Now that he had some time to think, he started to feel foolish. He asked himself why he was doing this – it was none of his business what Mick was up to, and Kari had said she was through with him anyway. But she'd also said she thought he'd been cheating on her, and though it no longer mattered, Ketch was curious – though there was no good reason for his curiosity, logically speaking. Even if Mick wasn't just running some innocent errand this evening, Ketch doubted he'd ever tell her. Doing so wouldn't accomplish anything other than make her feel bad, and he had no desire to do that. But he had nothing else to do at the moment; and he wanted to know.

When they reached Salvo, Ketch decided he'd probably guessed wrong and started looking for a place to turn around – but just then he saw Mick's truck pull out of a service station up ahead. Finally, a piece of luck. Ketch slowed and glanced at his fuel gauge, and was relieved to see he shouldn't have to make a similar stop himself anytime soon.

He followed Mick at a discreet distance, just closely enough to keep him in sight most of the time. Just like a real detective, he thought. He didn't have to use his headlights since it wasn't dark yet, so that should also help him escape Mick's notice. They continued on up through Waves, through Rodanthe, and beyond toward Oregon Inlet. The next major settlement on 12 after the inlet would be Nags Head. If it was a girl, he hoped she was worth the ride and the gas; if a job, ditto, but Mick might not have a choice in that case. The Nags Head area was more populous than where they'd come from, so naturally there'd be more work available there; and everyone has to eat.

As they began crossing the elongated, elevated Oregon Inlet bridge, which was officially named the Bonner Bridge if Ketch recalled correctly, the sun was dropping lower in the sky and he was struck as always by the glorious, panoramic views of the inlet, the ocean, the sound, and the adjacent marshlands afforded by the bridge. This was a beautiful place, and it remained virtually pristine even in these modern times. The Pea Island marsh refuge precluded development on the sound side of the Hatteras Island terminus of the bridge, but there was also no development here on the ocean side because inlets were geologically an even more unstable environment than the barrier islands they separated.

The inlets of the Outer Banks of necessity had to be considered transitory formations. The beach erosion and migration that constantly occurred on barrier islands was exacerbated near inlets, since they provided a direct pathway for beach sand to travel from the ocean side to the estuarine side of the island, helping to more or less maintain the width of the island but significantly contributing to the island's inexorable creep toward the mainland; so shorelines and depths could fluctuate. A Banks inlet itself also gradually migrated south over time, this particular one on the order of about two feet a year.

On top of all that, one good storm and everything could change quickly and sometimes drastically. New inlets could be created, and old ones could disappear. Oregon Inlet, for example, hadn't existed until 1846, when a powerful hurricane separated Bodie Island from Pea Island; and those 'islands' were no longer true islands, because other inlets had closed since then. The original Hatteras Inlet, south of the current one, had closed in the mid-seventeen hundreds, and the modern inlet had been formed by the same storm that formed Oregon Inlet.

But the north side of the inlet was a different story, and all that hadn't stopped someone from building the Oregon Inlet Fishing Center, the marina he could now see from the north end of the bridge. Well, good luck to you folks, Ketch thought.

So, it looked like maybe the Nags Head area. But then he saw Mick turn left onto 64 West at Whalebone

Junction. So it might be Roanoke Island – he hoped anyway, rather than continuing on to the mainland. Roanoke was where Kari might be today, if her mother lived in Manteo or Wanchese. He considered trying to call her again, but he didn't have a dashboard cradle for his phone and he refused to use it otherwise while driving, and he couldn't afford to pull over right now – and besides, how would he explain where he was and what he was doing?

The road, and soon the bridge, they were on now was part of the Virginia Dare Trail. This route and the county as well were named after the first child born in America to English parents, in 1587 in the old Roanoke Colony, now popularly known as the Lost Colony. The disappearance of everyone in that colony between then and 1590 is still a mystery, and is the subject of a popular play perennially performed at an outdoor theater here for the tourists. Ketch hadn't so far managed to catch a performance himself, but he'd read about it.

Once on the island they soon turned left on 345 and started doubling back to the south. A little while longer and they'd be in Wanchese, a town whose main businesses were fishing, seafood, boat building, and related maritime pursuits. Ketch didn't know his way around this town or this island very well, but his phone had a GPS app if he needed directions on the way back. It was getting later now and he was getting hungry – and so must the dog be, he realized. He hoped they'd reach their destination soon.

When they arrived in Wanchese they turned onto a

street he didn't catch the name of, and Mick shortly pulled into the parking lot of a company called Tibbleson Construction. Ketch turned onto a nearby side street and parked his truck there.

"Jack, I'll be right back. You stay here," he told the dog as he rubbed its head. "I know you're hungry, me too. Be a good boy, and I'll get you something to eat soon."

He rolled the windows down halfway for the dog. Though he'd parked in the shade, he had to – it was later in the day, but it was still hot enough that it would be inhumane to lock the dog in the truck with no airflow. Hopefully he wouldn't start to bark; if he did, they might have to leave in a hurry – which put him in mind of his cell phone, which he took the time to silence before he got out of the truck.

He made his way back around the corner of the block on foot. He wasn't used to sneaking around like this, and he was nervous. Why hadn't he brought his binoculars with him? Then he wouldn't have to get as close to see what was going on. He decided he probably wouldn't make much of a detective after all.

Mick was pulling his truck around to the back of the building now. Ketch took a chance and followed on foot, his heart beating faster. He saw there was a dumpster back there not too far from the building, which could provide cover if he could reach it undetected. He took another chance and peeked around the corner of the building. There was Mick's truck, backed up to a loading dock, but no Mick; he must have gone inside. 'Tibbleson Construction' was again lettered on the wall above the open bay.

Okay, he thought, this obviously wasn't some girl's place – so he could leave now, right? He wasn't going to see what he'd perversely hoped to see here and his mission was a bust, so he should just stop being silly and go on back home. That would be the logical thing for him to do, wouldn't it? He chanced another quick peek and then sprinted for the dumpster. His heart pounding now, he steadied himself behind it and forced himself to breathe deeply.

There was some concrete rubble behind the dumpster, and Ketch discovered that he could see over the top if he stood on a piece of it. When he did, he saw Mick come out and jump down from the loading dock, still in apparent conversation with a good-looking blond woman who remained on the dock. Ketch could hear their voices, but he couldn't make out what they were saying.

Well, maybe there was something going on here after all. No, wait... Now another man was driving a forklift whose purpose appeared to be to transport large metal drums, probably 55-gallon drums from the looks of them. Ketch could see some writing on some of the drums and some official-looking stickers, and a skull-and-crossbones symbol on one of them. What was in the drums? Fuel? Some kind of solvent? Did Mick have a job that required something like that?

Ketch didn't know why, but his instincts told him he should take a picture. Isn't that what real detectives did, when they had to document the activities of some allegedly cheating spouse in a divorce case or whatever? Now that was truly silly, he told himself. This was not a game, and he was not a detective. A real detective probably wouldn't have brought his dog with him, he wryly reflected. He'd do well to just extricate himself from this potentially embarrassing situation and get the hell out of here.

Of course, just as with the binoculars, he hadn't brought his camera either – however, his phone could take pictures, and it even had a zoom feature. The quality wouldn't be great in the diminishing light, and he certainly couldn't use the flash nor get close enough for it to help anyway, but he could give it a try. He activated the phone's camera mode, remembered to make sure it wouldn't flash, positioned himself as best he could under the circumstances, and managed to get a shot of the loading dock and all three people over the top of the dumpster as the forklift was loading some of the drums onto the truck.

Okay, now that's it, he told himself. He looked around and saw that he could circle behind a neighboring building without being seen. He could then make his way back to his own truck from farther down the street.

He succeeded in doing this. The dog finally did bark at his approach, but Ketch quickly opened the passenger side door and shushed him. He let out a long breath, hugged the dog, and tried to calm both of them down. "It's okay boy, you're a good boy," he murmured into the dog's furry neck. He probably had to go by now, he thought. "Want to go out?" Ketch stood back and let the dog hop out of the truck. After the dog had relieved himself, Ketch helped him back in. "Okay, all done now," he said. "Let's go find something to eat."

He started the truck, turned it around, and began to proceed back the way he'd come – but at the intersection where he'd turned, he had to stop and wait as Mick's truck, the bed now weighed down by several steel drums, pulled out of the construction company's driveway ahead of him. It looked like Mick was alone. Ketch slumped in his seat so his face wouldn't be easily visible, then waited a bit before continuing on.

When he reached the 345 intersection he looked left before making his intended right turn, and happened to catch a glimpse of what looked like the back end of Mick's truck. Why would he be going that way, Ketch wondered? He'd assumed everyone would be heading home now, wherever home was. He debated internally for a moment, then turned left. What the hell, he'd come this far, might as well satisfy his curiosity one more time before calling it quits. Again, some instinct was telling him that he wouldn't be sorry; though the thinking part of his brain was trying to tell him otherwise.

And so they continued south on 345, Ketch again hanging back behind Mick as far as possible and refraining from using his headlights despite the gradually failing daylight. The road was now also called Mill Landing Road. Wanchese Harbor, a working commercial waterfront, was coming up on his left. They passed by the Fisherman's Wharf restaurant and soon thereafter the entrance to a fish processing plant, and then just kept on going, onto a section of the road that was now called Thicket Lump Drive. It seemed like this road might continue forever, or at least until it ran out of island.

When it was about to do just that, Ketch saw Mick's brake lights come on, and Mick's truck turned left at a fork. Ketch stopped and idled, wondering what he should do next. He could backtrack to a small marina they'd passed not too far back, park the truck there, and retrace this route on foot – but he'd have to leave the dog behind, and if he started barking that could again become a problem. He decided to chance taking the right fork and parking a little way down there. He probably wouldn't be noticed if he kept his lights off, and if Mick came back this way he'd be unlikely to take the same fork.

He reassured the dog again, again left the windows half-open, then started walking cautiously down the jog Mick had turned onto. He saw there was a narrow channel ahead on the right with a small wooden building and parking lot nearby. There was also a patch of maritime forest by the road; Ketch stepped into it and crept closer, moving from one salt-stunted live oak to another for cover and wishing he'd worn trousers instead of shorts. He at least had his ball cap on, but his exposed legs and forearms might get scratched up if he wasn't careful. He'd have to remember to inspect them later for ticks, which unfortunately were fairly common in this part of the country.

He could see now that there was a boat dock on the channel, behind the building. The building appeared to have been some kind of sightseeing cruise business at one time, but looked defunct now. Soon he could see a fishing boat tied up to the dock, and Mick's truck parked nearby. There were no more trees to hide behind, so he crept a little closer and crouched behind a dense clump of scrub where he could see the dock. He didn't dare proceed to the building; it was too close to the dock. It was officially dusk now, so if he didn't move much he shouldn't be spotted – he hoped.

Though he knew he was taking chances, he didn't feel quite as foolish now as he had earlier; maybe his instincts had been right after all. It looked like Mick and another man, whose voices he could again hear but not always clearly, were preparing to transfer the drums from the truck to the boat. It didn't look like the boat had a winch or hoist, but it appeared they had wood planks and a drum caddy. They could tilt and roll the drums if they had to. It looked like they weren't open-top, but rather welded-top drums with bungholes.

Still, it looked like it would be a project. Ketch knew that a gallon of water weighed over eight pounds, so if those drums were full of water they'd weigh over four hundred pounds each. Maybe they weren't full, or maybe they contained a lighter liquid, or perhaps a powder of some kind. But they couldn't be light no matter what, and it would certainly be easier to do this at a commercial dock where they'd have better equipment to help them – but he doubted a legitimate harbormaster would approve of this particular activity. He'd initially wondered what these guys were doing here, but it hadn't taken him long to arrive at the obvious and odious conclusion.

Why would people transport drums containing apparently toxic materials by boat, when they could more easily be transported by truck? Because they were being shipped overseas, obviously inapplicable here given this kind of boat, or maybe for a project on an island that was only accessible by boat – but why do it at night, and at an out-of-the-way location like this, and with less than optimal gear? And as for this old fishing boat, there were regulations to be observed regarding the type of vessel to be used for transporting such materials.

This old fishing boat... Ketch squinted in the fading light and realized this boat looked familiar. And then one of the men's words floated up to him like a feather on the wind – "amigo". Yes, that was Mario down there with Mick; and that was Mario's boat; and they were going to illegally dump toxic waste at sea.

Indiscriminate ocean dumping of drums like these containing hazardous waste had been allowed at one time, but when it was learned the drums could corrode and disintegrate faster than had been thought, the practice was halted, at least in civilized parts of the world. Especially when dumped on the continental shelf or in shallow seas, it was understood that this kind of pollution could easily contaminate fish and shellfish harvested for human consumption.

But money talks, as they say, and Ketch supposed this was one way to make some when you were down and out; and though it was utterly abhorrent to him, they probably had few if any qualms about doing it, other than worrying about getting caught. And with all the environmental regulations in place today, doing it this way was undoubtedly less expensive for the company than doing it the right way would be.

Unbelievable... Mick's involvement didn't surprise him, but he'd thought Mario was more ethical than this. Granted that might seem incongruous to some, given Mario's lifestyle; but though it might not appear to make sense, to Ketch there was a distinction between being an outlaw and being a criminal – especially an environmental criminal, which to him was one of the worst kinds of all.

The oceans were not limitless, as many people seemed to believe, and there would eventually be far-reaching consequences if people didn't stop polluting them – and soon. In addition to contamination of seafood, there was the seawater itself to consider. Ketch had read that this state was one of those that didn't regularly monitor water quality at its beaches; well, they'd have to when people started getting sick, as he knew had happened from time to time at some of the beaches in New York and New Jersey.

And what about the myriad other creatures that didn't have the option of leaving the water? There was legislation nowadays, to be sure, but it never seemed to be enough, as evidenced here tonight. There were sea turtles now with fibropapilloma tumors; fish with ulcers; coral reefs dying from bleaching and black band disease; and shellfish, numerous bottom dwelling organisms, and seabirds poisoned by algal blooms. A huge garbage patch had been discovered floating in the middle of the Pacific, consisting of particles of pelagic plastics, chemical sludge, and other debris trapped by the currents of the North Pacific Gyre; estimates of its size ranged from a quarter million square miles to over five million.

Marine mammals were also being impacted, including dolphins, which Ketch personally admired more than the vast majority of people he'd ever known. Chemicals, sewage, nuclear waste, lack of food due to overfishing, all were starting to take their toll. Several massive die-offs, each numbering in the thousands, had occurred in recent years. The populations of harbor seals in Europe, bottlenose dolphins in the Gulf of Mexico, and striped dolphins in the Mediterranean had been dramatically reduced. And some years ago over half of the bottlenoses on the East Coast had been killed by some kind of bacterial infection. Where would it all end?

Extinction, that was where. And when the seas and the rain forests are dead, mankind will soon follow. We may be among the last to go, Ketch thought, but go we surely will. Mother Earth will inevitably assert her regulatory powers and right the wrongs just as she always has, and she'll expunge us without a second thought.

Red-faced now and dangerously stimulated,

Ketch's first instinct was to jump up, run down there, and stop them – but fortunately his thinking brain overruled the instinct this time. Mario might possibly listen to reason and Ketch believed he wasn't a violent man, but who knew what Mick might do? Maybe he was being overly dramatic, but he decided it would be wise to not risk ending up in the hospital, or worse yet wherever those drums were going. Maybe he could call the Coast Guard later, after he'd gotten safely away from here.

So he maintained his position and fished his phone out again. Despite the poor lighting, he got a zoomed shot that would be unacceptable to a serious photographer but did clearly show what was happening. Then he quietly retreated back up the road and returned to his truck.

A couple of short barks ensued at his arrival, but that was probably okay since those two down the road would be occupied for a while and there'd be no lollygagging on his part this time. He started the truck and turned it around as quietly as possible and drove, again with the lights off for now.

He wished he knew where that boat would be going. Maybe if he'd gotten closer and stayed longer and listened harder... But Mick and Mario might not have a firm destination in mind anyway. They might just motor out a ways and do the deed wherever it felt 'right'. He thought again about alerting the Coast Guard, but he couldn't provide a course or destination. They wouldn't be foolish enough to jettison the drums in the shallow sound, right?

Probably not; Mario at least should know better than that – unless he knew of a deeper hole. But they'd most likely head out to the Atlantic through Oregon Inlet, and with their running lights off – another reason it would be difficult for anyone to find them. And if he could convince the Coast Guard to mobilize, it would take time (it wouldn't take them *that* long to load those drums), and by then it would be too late to intercept them in the inlet, and maybe too late as well to catch them before they dumped, which would be a waste of everyone's time. If only he knew for sure where they were going...

Well, he couldn't know where they were going right now – but he thought of a way he might be able to later find out where they'd been. He couldn't try that until tomorrow, though; but with any luck he'd then have all the information he and the Coast Guard would need.

Assuming of course that he was right about what they were doing. Though Ketch considered it highly unlikely, it was possible that there was a perfectly innocent explanation for what he was seeing, one that wasn't occurring to him for some reason; in which case he'd only embarrass himself at best, and unnecessarily kill a friendship and make an enemy at worst, by reporting them without cause. Another good reason to wait until he'd gathered more evidence.

Okay then – he had a plan. Meanwhile, his stomach was rumbling, which was not surprising since he'd eaten nothing since his meager brunch earlier in the day. It would soon be full dark and he was famished – and the dog as well, he imagined. He needed to find them both something to eat.

~ N i n e ~

Each time was new, and he didn't think about the past.

*K*etch pulled into the parking lot at Fisherman's Wharf and parked as far from both the road and the building as possible. Granted it was a weeknight, but during the season places like this usually stayed open later to cater to the tourist trade, and the lights were still on here. He figured that although this was a full-service restaurant and not a fast-food joint, he should still be able to get some kind of quick takeout. If they kept driving there'd be some other options in Wanchese proper, around the Junction, and then in Rodanthe, but he didn't know their hours; and they were here now and they were hungry.

He let the dog out for a couple of minutes to give him a chance to stretch and relieve himself, then helped him clamber reluctantly back up into the truck. "This is a restaurant. I'll get us some supper. Be good, and I'll be right back," he said. "And be quiet." He left the dog behind once more and headed across the parking lot.

He reasoned it should be safe to take a short dinner break here. Mick and Mario should be occupied for some time with loading the drums, and then with driving the boat to wherever they were going and back again. In the unlikely event only one of them took the boat out, it would be Mario, and in that case even if Mick stopped here Ketch doubted he'd be recognized, especially without his beard. So there was no need for undue haste now – except that he did sincerely want to get home.

Home... Wonder where that'll end up being when all's said and done, he thought. He turned to look back at the dog, who was tracking Ketch's progress with sad eyes. Dogs were indeed the most loyal of friends. Though he wasn't in a joking mood, an old one popped into his head – if you don't believe a dog is man's best friend, lock your dog and your wife in the trunk of your car for an hour, and then observe which one's glad to see you when you let them out. And here he was dragging the poor creature with him all over the Banks.

Ketch entered the restaurant and ordered a dozen hush puppies and a serving of chicken tenders. After a short visit to the rest room, he also selected two large bottles of water from a cooler, and a Diet Pepsi to provide some caffeine on the drive back, and set them on the counter. It wasn't much, but it would be relatively quick and enough to tide them over. Someday when he had more time maybe he'd return here and leisurely enjoy some of the fresh and supposedly delectable seafood he'd heard this place was noted for.

And so, he thought while he waited – there was the business with the house, and now this business with toxic waste dumping... It seemed to him that his once pleasantly laid-back life was getting more complicated by the minute. And speaking of complicated, now there was also Kari – who'd flown completely out of his mind with everything else that had been transpiring. He remembered his cell phone was still silenced. He activated it and saw an incoming voice message flagged on the screen. She called, he thought; that's a good sign. He listened to the message.

"Hey there hotshot, where are you? Tried to return your call, couldn't get you so I dropped by your place and the boatyard when I got back, but you were nowhere in sight! Guess you're busy – anyway, catch you later!"

Well, at least she sounded cheerful and not upset that he'd been incommunicado this evening. And she'd tried to find him. He should call her back. But when he did, what was he going to tell her about where he'd been tonight? He could just say he'd been running errands, but that wouldn't fly this late in the day. Would she, and others as well, find out if he turned Mick and Mario in to the authorities?

He'd intended to not tell her whatever he learned about Mick, but how could he avoid it now, given the circumstances? Would his name get into the newspapers? And whether it did or not, would Mick and Mario find out it was he who'd reported them? Ketch thought he'd heard that anyone against whom a complaint had been filed had a legal right to know the identity of the complainer. Did he care? Not so much about Mick; but he was sorry Mario would know he'd betrayed him, since he considered Mario a friend.

But wait, maybe he should care about Mick – he

could be the type that might seek some kind of retribution or revenge. Could he report them anonymously? Would he be taken seriously if he did that? But he couldn't just call, he'd have to show them the pictures. Could he send them a letter? This was starting to give him a headache.

"Sir? Sir?" Ketch realized he was being addressed. "Sir, your order's ready." He paid, thanked the girl, and carried the food back out to the truck.

The dog appeared happy to see him but too tired to bark; and he was panting, so he was probably thirsty. Ketch glanced around the interior of the cab, which was unfortunately shipshape as always, and saw nothing he could use as a water dish for the dog. He could go back into the restaurant and ask for the cup he should have thought to request before, but he didn't want to leave the dog again. He decided his ball cap might hold long enough for the dog to get a drink, so he removed it from his head and poured half a bottle of water into it.

The dog drank fast enough to lap up almost all the water before it had time to soak through the material, and then started sniffing at the bags. Ketch hand-fed him half of the tenders and some of the hush puppies one at a time while he himself devoured the rest, almost keeping pace with the dog. Then he filled the hat again.

He'd been exceptionally lucky tonight, he thought as he finished off the other water bottle. There were so many things that could have gone wrong – he could have been seen, he could have forgotten to silence his phone, he could have left the flash on, the dog could have barked, he could have guessed wrong and never found Mick in the first place – and his impulsiveness could possibly have gotten him injured or maybe even killed. And then what would have become of the dog, who he shouldn't have brought with him in the first place? And no binoculars, no camera, no food, no water... Not even a pot to piss in, as they say (as some mysteries he'd read had also suggested carrying). Not a well-planned or executed surveillance or stakeout or whatever, that's for sure. Some detective he'd make.

He disposed of their debris in a nearby trash can and wrung out his hat, and they finally hit the road to head for home – definitely this time, no more detours. He decided to put off calling Kari until they got there. He was tired, and for now he still had his self-imposed ban on using a cell phone while driving to fall back on. The ban was self-imposed here because unlike some other states, North Carolina only disallowed it for school bus drivers and novice drivers instead of for everyone, which he didn't agree with.

Or should he wait until the morning to call her? He didn't want to wake her if she was asleep. He knew the Sea Dog didn't generally open until noon, but she usually did her instructing in the mornings when she had a class. He remembered she'd said she had one coming up soon, but he didn't know when; though probably not tomorrow since she hadn't asked him to help. But then again, she didn't always ask. He sighed and rubbed at his tired eyes one at a time. More complications... At least Mick hadn't shown up at the restaurant. He decided he was overthinking this; he'd call when he got back, regardless. If it was too late and she didn't want to answer, she wouldn't have to.

He tried to relax and just enjoy the ride. There'd be nothing else to do for a while anyway, and the scenery was still inspiring to him even at night. He succeeded for a time, but then a nebulous thought started to nag at the back of his mind... Yes, Tibbleson Construction, that was it – something he'd earlier filed away for later reference, the place where the drums had originated. Where had he heard that name before? He couldn't place it at the moment, but he was sure he knew it. Or maybe he just thought he did because it sounded a little like 'Tillet', one of the names he knew of the historically prominent families of Hatteras Island, like the Midgetts, the Etheridges, the Jennettes, the Grays, and so on.

He was especially familiar with the Midgett name because a remarkable number of Midgetts had served as surfmen at the old lifesaving stations and several of them had won Lifesaving Medals; and because nowadays the name was advertised everywhere in the form of Midgett Realty, a major one that also managed over five hundred vacation rental houses on Hatteras Island alone.

Midgett Realty... HatterasMann Realty... Ingram... Tibbleson... Now he had it – Tibbleson was the maiden name of Bob Ingram's second wife, the one who'd disappeared. Could there be a relationship of some kind between Ingram and Tibbleson Construction? He'd have to remember to see what he could dig up on that. He could do it right now with his phone provided it had network connectivity here, but he certainly wouldn't try that while driving and he didn't want to stop. He'd just have to be patient.

Okay, so there were four things he had to remember to do – call Kari, check out where the boat had gone, do a web search on Tibbleson Construction, and print his pictures. 'Four' was the operative word – rather than try to remember each individual item, he'd remember the number four and then trust his brain to supply the remaining details when he needed them. This was also how he did his grocery shopping. Though he always returned with the number of items he'd set out to buy, he occasionally mistakenly ended up buying the wrong thing. But the system worked pretty well as a rule, so he filed the number away and tried to focus on the remainder of the drive.

The number resurfaced in Ketch's weary mind as they finally approached the outskirts of Avon. He doubted he'd get to any of the items tonight except for calling Kari, though he might have some more energy if he showered again. "We'll see, Jack," he told the dog, who yawned back at him. Maybe both of them would simply crash tonight instead.

He turned onto Harbor Road at the Barefoot Station intersection, then onto North End Road – again. How many times had he traversed this route in the last three years, counting both directions? Still, it hadn't gotten old yet – and if it ever did, there'd be nothing to be done about it anyway since it was the only way out to the main drag from where he lived.

When their house came into view, he didn't immediately notice the car in the driveway, and in fact came close to sideswiping it in the dark. Good thing he hadn't looked away for a second, he thought, a bit shaken. Whose car was it? The dog knew, and was already up and wagging. Ketch shut everything down, opened his door, and stood aside as the dog bounded past him and up the front steps.

"Jack! Hey there, big fella!" Ketch heard from the shadows on the deck. It was Kari's car. What was she doing here at this hour? He hadn't checked lately, but it had to be after ten, at least. He hiked his shorts up, straightened his shirt, grabbed the empty Pepsi bottle from the drink holder, locked the truck, and started up the steps.

"Kari," he said, with a mixture of perplexion and pleasure – which however quickly changed to apprehension. What was he going to say to her? Before he could say anything, she disengaged from the dog, got up from her chair, and wrapped him in a bear hug. The dog went back down to the yard to water some of the foliage.

"I'm glad you're back," she breathed against his neck, then pulled away to arm's length. "I hope you don't mind. I didn't feel like goin' home, so I got somethin' to eat and then just came on over here and hung out. I figured you'd be back sooner or later. I didn't try to go in, but it's probably locked anyway, right? I don't know if you have a hide-a-key somewhere." She sat back down and repeated, "I hope you don't mind." She distractedly ran a hand through her hair and then looked wide-eyed up at Ketch.

"Of course I don't mind," he said. "You're always welcome here, you should know that now." Though he'd noted she hadn't yet asked him where he'd been, he was still a little anxious – and grubby, and still exhausted – but his concern for her outweighed everything else. She must be here for a reason.

"Let's go inside, you must be getting bitten up out here," he said. He unlocked the door and Kari and the dog obediently followed him in. "Turn that lamp on and sit down and relax, and I'll go get us something to drink."

"Okay, thanks, thank you," she said. "But no wine tonight, I had enough of that last night to last me a little while." Noticing the scuba cylinder standing in a corner, she asked, "Are you finished with that tank?"

"No, sorry, I didn't get around to that today," Ketch called from the kitchen. Figuring a little more caffeine wouldn't hurt either of them, he brought two tall frosted beer mugs of ice-cold soda – or rather, 'pop' as they called it hereabouts, he remembered – back to the living room. He handed one to Kari, who was on the undoggy end of the couch, then settled into his recliner. The dog stretched out on the blanket covering its end of the couch, happy to have someone close enough by to scratch his butt if he should require that service.

"So what really brings you here tonight?" he inquired, in an attempt to draw her out. "Not that it matters, and you don't have to have a reason." Though he imagined she probably did. "Like I said, you're always welcome here. How was your visit with your mother?"

"Well... She's okay, thanks for askin'." She took a drink. "Shoot, I guess I'm too tired to think right now, it's been a long day." It certainly has, Ketch thought. "I guess I was mostly just lonely, and I missed you. You know, since we found out last night what good friends we are." She paused again, then tentatively asked, "Listen, would you mind if I stayed over again? It's late and I have to get an early start tomorrow, and I don't feel like drivin' home and back."

She still wasn't asking him where he'd been – so were they still keeping things simple then? He hoped so. But then again, it occurred him to wonder, how 'simple' was going to someone's house unannounced and uninvited and waiting out on the deck for who knows how long? But he still didn't mind.

"Not at all," he replied. "And you can sleep wherever you want, in case you're wondering about that. I'm not expecting anything. I'm tired too." He stood up, stretched, and yawned. "I need a shower, though, before I do anything else. So if you'll excuse me for a few minutes?"

"Sure, no problem. A shower? I could use one myself." Brightening a bit, she added, "Hey, mind if I join you?" Before the slightly flustered Ketch could answer, she got up and said, "Oh, don't be shy now, come on!" and headed off to the master bedroom, beckoning him to follow.

When they came out of the shower, the dog shuffled into the bedroom and curled up on his bed, and Kari got into Ketch's bed. With a little continued encouragement that had begun in the shower, he was pleased to discover he wasn't quite as exhausted as he'd thought – though he did basically pass out almost immediately afterward. But this time he woke in the morning before she did.

And considerably earlier than the last time as well, which was good since he had a lot to do today. Although the number he'd stored the night before was already flashing in his mind, she was curled up at his side and still breathing evenly, with an arm and a leg draped across him and her face resting on his outstretched arm, so he didn't try to get up right away. Instead, he tried to relax and enjoy the moment.

But even with her rhythmic exhalations tickling his skin, and the light of the barely risen sun just beginning to poke through the blinds to illuminate the dust motes circulating beneath the slowly rotating blades of the ceiling fan, he couldn't help recalling the last time he'd truly savored an interlude like this one. Although there'd been a couple of casual flings in between over the years, it had been a very long time.

His wife had been younger and tantalizingly delightful for a while, just like this one, but the honeymoon had ended even before the birth of his son. The eventual split hadn't been amicable and she'd somehow managed to gain full custody. After his career had taken him to another state, he hadn't had as much opportunity to spend time with the boy as he would have liked, and after a while the boy hadn't wanted him to anyway. Ketch knew he'd gone to college and he should have been out a year ago, or maybe two; but he hadn't been invited to any celebrations. He wondered if the boy had actually graduated, and if so whether he'd decided to go on to a postgraduate school of some kind.

And then he decided to stop wondering. What will be will be, and the past will never change and it's pointlessly crippling to try to live in it. There are at least three things in life you can't ever get back, he reflected – words you've said, time you've wasted, and ephemeral moments like this. And maybe fine wine if you leave it where this one can find it.

He let his appreciative eyes wander down the length of the naked and now softly ochre body lying next to him in apparent blissful oblivion – and saw that an ugly-looking bruise had formed on the upper arm lying on his chest. Why hadn't he noticed that earlier? They'd only used a night light when they'd showered and then it had been completely dark after that, and granted his mind had been on other things – but still... Had he somehow done that to her?

She stirred next to him, and he saw her face contort into a frown. Her eyes remained closed, but her lips started moving. He leaned his head down a little closer to hear what she was saying. It sounded like, "I'll get it, I'll get it..." Her eyes suddenly flew open and scanned their surroundings in a momentary panic.

"Oh, hey..." she said, then smiled up at him. "Good mornin'!" She gave him a hug and sat up and stretched. Ketch thought he detected a wince as she extended the bruised arm. "I'll be right back, hear? Nature calls," she said, padding off to the bathroom. Ketch didn't know if he was supposed to stay put, but said Nature then answered that question for him and he got up as well, gave the dog a pat, and hurried out to the other bath. Fortunately there was a bottle of mouthwash in there, which he also took advantage of.

By the time he returned she was already back in bed and under the covers. "Hey, get back in here," she directed, "I'm cold!"

He was not, but he did as he was told. The blood runs thinner when you live down South, he knew. He'd seen the natives dress in layers when the temperature dropped to a point where he only considered maybe not wearing shorts. He'd thought the scuba diving season would be longer here, too, but most of them wouldn't even go in with a wetsuit until the water temperature got up into the eighties, whereas sixty-five was tolerable to him, and even less with the right gear. He guessed he just hadn't lived here long enough yet.

"That's better," she said, wrapping herself around him to utilize his body heat. He responded quickly – and so did she, he noticed. "Hey, I forgot to thank you for buyin' that soap and shampoo and all. You're gettin' to be quite the ladies' man now, huh?" she teased. "Okay, so how about I cook us up some eggs? You got eggs?"

"Yes. How'd you get that bruise?" he responded.

"Oh, this here, on my arm? Don't worry, you didn't do it," she said. "I just bumped into somethin' is all."

He didn't believe her, but then she threw back the covers and began to straddle him. "Life's short, dessert first," she said. "Let's just take care of this real quick, and then I'll get to those eggs. It won't take long."

She was right, it didn't take very long at all, and he could tell she wasn't faking. He was amazed – this just kept getting better and better. When they were both done she got up and pulled on another shirt from his closet.

"Okay, I'll get to work in the kitchen," she said. "Hey, you want coffee?"

"No thanks," Ketch replied. "I don't drink it. I've found I have expensive tastes. I can tolerate it if it's outrageously expensive, but even then I don't like it enough to bother with it. But you go ahead. There's a coffeemaker on the counter."

"Gotcha. Say, you probably want to let Jack out, right? When you do, could you please bring in that bag I left on the back seat in my car?"

Ketch dressed quickly and again did as instructed. When he opened the back door of her car he saw what appeared to be an overnight bag – no, more than just an overnight bag. It wasn't completely zipped, and he could see it contained multiple changes of clothing and various other sundries.

"Jacky, there's somethin' good in your dish! Come on boy!" Kari called when Ketch and the dog reentered the house. The dog trotted into the kitchen to find a bowl of the usual dog food, but this time with a fried egg on top. He stretched out on the floor with his back feet extended and his snout over the dish and began to leisurely feast on this unexpected bounty. He liked having this female here.

Ketch set the bag down just outside the kitchen, then added the newspaper he'd found on the deck to the ever-growing pile in the basket by the recliner. He was still behind on that, and he realized he also hadn't turned on the flat-screen TV he'd thought he needed even once in the last few days. He wondered if there'd be a Yankee game on this weekend; he'd have to check later.

He went to the kitchen and took over at the toaster. "Looks like you're planning on staying a while," he commented, nodding toward the bag.

"Oh, I just needed somethin' clean for today, and maybe tomorrow," she said. "I'm havin' a little problem at my apartment. The landlord said he'd try to get the exterminator to come out today. If he does, I thought I'd bunk at the shop for a night or two. I can't abide that smell."

A little too pat? Maybe, maybe not – but Ketch was sensing something off-kilter here, even through the fog of his infatuation. This exterminator story didn't jive with her reaction at first seeing him last night, nor with her remark about simply not feeling like going home; and both that remark and the exterminator bit were inconsistent with the duffel bag, which contained more than a day or two's worth of clothing and was clear evidence of premeditation. The questionable instincts of his fledgling detective alter ego again, like last night?

It was probably callous of him to be suspicious, and ungrateful as well considering the circumstances. He should just drop it. But he still couldn't help wondering – why didn't she want to go back to her apartment, really? Why did she really come here last night? Where did she get that bruise? What was she mumbling about in her sleep? She still hadn't asked him where he'd been yesterday – and not only did he appreciate that, he also correspondingly respected her own right to privacy. He decided he wouldn't push; if there was something she wanted to talk with him about, she'd bring it up when she was ready. But he thought of an experiment he might try, just to see what happened.

"Nonsense, you don't have to stay at the shop. I told you, you can stay here whenever you need to." That number four started flashing in his mind again, and it occurred to him that her staying here might crimp his style, so to speak – but he meant what he said. He couldn't let her sleep alone on some old cot in the back of a store.

"I know you did. It was the second thing you said the other night. See, I told you I wasn't that wasted," she reminded him with a quick smile. "But I didn't want to wear out my welcome, so I wasn't gonna ask."

Right, he thought – she was instead going to plant a seed and let him work his way around to it on his own, as he'd just done. He was finally starting to learn now how this worked. Or was he just being paranoid? But it was all right with him either way- and he'd be an ingrate to complain, with everything he was getting in return. He made a mental note that they'd have to at some point start working on communicating better with each other, and more honestly, assuming of course his feelings for her were reciprocated. He figured that might come naturally with time, though, and meanwhile putting up with a little subterfuge, if that's what it was, now and then wasn't all that much trouble.

"Well, consider it done," he said. "You'll stay here, for as long as you need to."

"Thank you so much!" she said. "I mean it, I gotta admit I wasn't lookin' forward to stayin' somewhere else. I mean, at the shop, I spend so much time there already as it is." She stopped what she was doing and gave him another hug. This is ridiculous, he thought – he was already ready again. But refusing to let himself be distracted this time, he performed his experiment instead.

"It's nothing, say no more about it," he said. "And by the way, don't let me forget, before you leave this morning I want to give you a check for that class I signed up for. I'd like to get that out of the way. And I want to pay your individual instructional rate. Your time is valuable, and I don't want to take advantage."

The effect was almost magical. She went completely limp in his arms, like a helpless rag doll – muscles of hers that he hadn't even known were tensed, and that she might not have known of herself, were no more, and she hugged him even tighter. "Thank you," she said, "God knows, I could use it." She backed away a little and looked up at him. "You've got really good timin', you know that? And I don't just mean with this." Then she looked away and said, "Come on, let's eat."

Small talk occupied the rest of their short time together this morning. Again Ketch didn't press, as he'd earlier resolved not to – but it was apparent to him that her coming into a little money had made a noticeable difference in her demeanor. She was even more effervescent than usual, and she looked like a weight had been lifted from her.

So was it just a temporary financial reprieve for the shop that was responsible for this, or did she need the money for something else? 'I'll get it,' he remembered she'd said in her sleep. Get what, money? And for whom? Was this connected with however she'd really gotten that bruise? Was someone 'shaking her down'? Was that the appropriate noir mystery term? And if so, why? Or did her mother need money, maybe for a medical expense or some other kind of emergency? Did Kari herself have a medical problem of some sort? It was all just conjecture at this point. He was sure he'd find out eventually. Meanwhile, it would be interesting to see if she still felt the need to stay at *Port Starbird* with him after she cashed that check. He hoped she would.

While he was trying to prevent his imagination from running away with him, she finished eating and said, "I better get goin'. You could stop by the shop later if you want. If you've got nothin' else to do, I mean." But he did indeed have things to do – three more, in fact. "Or are you gonna clean your boat today?"

"I should," he said, though he knew he wouldn't. "I'll tell you what, I may not be able to get there earlier, but I'll be there by closing time, and I'll bring the tank. Then I'll take you to the Froggy Dog for dinner, how about that?"

"Oh, I'd love that, I haven't been there in ages! I don't get there much. It's kind of on the expensive side, you know."

Before she left the table he wrote out the check and gave her an extra house key. Then, after she'd gotten herself together and departed for wherever it was she really had to go this morning, Ketch shaved, took the dog out again, and prepared to head down to the boatyard. It was time to check a second item off his virtual to-do list.

~ Ten ~

Now it was time to think of the one thing for which he was born.

*K*etch had seriously considered tailing Kari, the way he'd done with Mick, but he'd decided against investigating further at this time. First, he thought it would be wrong to invade her privacy; second, he didn't know if he could pull it off in broad daylight and he'd be mortified if she caught him at it; and third, he had an important task to cross off his list right now, one that might be time-sensitive and that should thus be completed as soon as possible.

Listen to me, he thought as he drove down to the boatyard – 'tailing' her, not just 'following'; and 'investigating', and 'premeditation', and 'shakedown'. And he was driving the pickup rather than walking or biking, with his backpack within easy reach on the seat beside him; he'd left the dog at home; and the backpack contained a set of binoculars, his camera, three water bottles, three granola bars, and a large empty wide-mouth jar. His cell phone was clipped to his belt, and he had a small notebook and pen in his shirt pocket. Finally, his camera and cell phone batteries were fully charged, and the truck had a full tank of gas after a quick stop at the Barefoot Station.

His parents might be pleased if they could see him now – even if he was still missing many of the classical noir trappings, like the fedora, the cheap suit, the drinking problem, and the long-legged dame with a hidden agenda. Though on second thought, maybe he'd come close enough this week on that last item. Oh, and a gun, he supposed.

Where indeed are his folks now, he wondered, and not for the first time. He had no idea, and he didn't think anyone else really did either. He sometimes wished he could blindly believe in something, the way most people did – heaven, hell, nirvana, reincarnation, astrology, voodoo, witchcraft, black cats, *something* – but he couldn't stomach any of the organized superstitions, as he liked to term the world's prevailing religions. While there might well be some sort of greater power or powers at play in the universe, he was certain it would be nothing like any of the anthropomorphic and dogmatic representations that had been variously foisted on the gullible masses throughout history.

He wished he could at least know that sentience doesn't simply cease to exist at death – but he did recognize the falsity of human conceit, and that could be something. Despite the expansive breadth and depth of all our accumulated knowledge, we really know next to nothing about the incomprehensibly profound and innumerable intricacies of the infinite wilderness of space and time we exist in – and because of this, perhaps all things were possible, and maybe that was enough to allow the faithless like himself to hope.

And that's enough deep thinking for one day, he decided as he pulled into the boatyard. Back to business.

It looked like things were pretty quiet here this morning. Those who had somewhere to go had apparently already gone, and those who didn't might still be asleep. He saw that Mario's boat was tied up at the dock, and he wasn't detecting any overt activity there either.

Okay, mister smart detective, he suddenly thought – ever picked a lock? It had just occurred to him that if Mario wasn't on board his boat, as he'd initially hoped, then the cabin door would probably be locked. What would he do then? Well, as Senator Ted might say, he'd drive off that bridge when he came to it.

He left the truck and strode purposefully out to Mario's boat, just as if he had a good reason to be there. He boarded the boat and found the door was unlocked. He took a quick, light-footed stroll around the perimeter of the cabin and glanced in through the windows. He couldn't see any movement, but he did see the GPS unit he was after. Congratulating himself on his luck, he thought about just opening the door and going in. But then he decided to try knocking first.

It was a good thing he did. Mario came to the door almost immediately and squinted at Ketch through the glass. Maybe he'd been in the head. He swung the door open and spread his arms.

"Hey Ketch, what's up amigo?" Mario said. "Come on in!"

"Thanks, Mario. I hope I didn't wake you."

"Nope, I just got up, so your timing is perfect." It

must be, Ketch thought – this was the second time he'd heard that this morning. "Hey, you want some coffee?" And that, too. "I just made some."

"No thanks," Ketch said. Mario motioned for him to sit at the table and then joined him with a steaming cup.

"So what can I do for you, my man? By the way, thanks again for havin' us over the other night, that was a nice little party."

"You're quite welcome," Ketch said, "and thanks for coming." Now what? He had to come up with some reason for being here. He tried to concentrate. "Well," he started, "I was just wondering about something..." Wondering about what? Ah yes – the obvious finally jumped up and smacked him in the face. He should have thought of this right off.

"I don't usually do this, but I was wondering if you might be able to spare a little weed? If you have enough, of course. Not a lot, just a little for some company I might have coming into town soon. You know me, I like to be a good host, keep the customers happy, and these people..." he said, and then forced himself to stop talking.

"Sure thing, amigo! Not a problem! What are we talkin' here, enough for a couple joints? Three, four, half-ounce, ounce?"

"Oh, probably three would be good," Ketch said, and then added in another moment of inspiration, "and would you mind rolling them for me? I've tried it before, and I'm no good at it."

"No problem! I'll just go on down right now and

get that taken care of. Hey, you want me to teach you how to do it right?"

"Actually, thanks anyway, but would you mind if I took a look at your GPS while you're doing that? I'm thinking about buying a new one, and I noticed you have a Garmin, which is what I'm considering."

"Sure, go right ahead, man." Mario rose from the table and headed off, cup in hand. "Back in a flash if not sooner!"

Could it really be this easy? Could Mario really be that guileless? It would seem so. Still, he wasn't completely out of the woods yet. He'd have to work fast – but that shouldn't be a problem, as he was in fact already familiar enough with this GPS, since luckily he already owned almost the exact same model – and both of these models had memory.

What could be a problem would be if Mario hadn't set a waypoint at the dump site – which he may well not have if they were just dumping the drums at random. But even then, Ketch knew there would be a track log, which Mario was likely to have used, and from which the tracks had to be manually cleared. So if he hadn't deliberately cleared the track from last night, Ketch could still find out where he'd dumped those drums.

As it turned out, there was a waypoint in the Atlantic east of Oregon Inlet that looked promising – and only one, not several, which could be a good thing as it implied there might be only one dump site. He extracted the notebook from his shirt pocket and jotted down the numbers. Again, could it really be this easy? He wondered how long this lucky streak he'd been on lately would hold out.

Mario hadn't returned yet, so Ketch glanced at the track log – which hadn't been cleared. He found the track from last night and saw that it matched up with the waypoint; and a quick scan through the log showed no other tracks that seemed relevant. He switched off the GPS just as Mario came back with his contraband.

"Here you go, my man!" he said, holding up a plastic baggy with three exceptionally fat joints in it.

"Thanks, they look great, really," Ketch said. Thinking fast, he added, "I made a note of this model number, so I wouldn't forget it." He quickly pocketed the notebook and took the baggy. "So, how much do I owe you?" he asked, carefully stashing the baggy in a pocket of his cargo shorts and zipping it shut. "For parts and labor," he lightly added.

"Hey, for you? Nothin' this time, amigo – on the house!" Mario replied. Through a brief storm of protests, Mario continued to insist and Ketch had to finally acquiesce. Despite what Ketch now knew, he still felt a stab of affection for this generous outlaw – or rather, criminal now, he supposed. He'd be genuinely sorry when he finally did what he knew he had to do.

"So, you want to talk about the job?" Mario asked, referring to Ketch's floatation blocks. "Or should we wait 'til Len's around?"

With everything else that had been happening, Ketch had almost forgotten about that. Another complication... How could he make this man work for him and then turn him in? But he guessed he didn't have much choice at this late stage of the game. And anyway, who said he had to name names, after all? While he wouldn't at all mind punishing Mick, whom Ketch had never liked and who probably amply deserved some kind of punishment, Ketch didn't feel the same compulsion where Mario was concerned. Maybe he'd just let the authorities figure it out for themselves, if they could – and if they couldn't, then so be it.

"Um, yes, that's probably a good idea," he stammered. "We'll get together then. I'll give you my cell number, and you can give me a call sometime when you're both available."

He extricated himself as graciously as possible. As he disembarked, he noticed the Captain was puttering around now on the *Minnow*. He didn't really want to take the time right now to go into the explanation he knew the Captain was waiting for, but how could he avoid it? He tarried on the dock where a houseboat shielded him from the Captain's view, then started to thread his way back to his truck as unobtrusively as possible.

But not unobtrusively enough, as evidenced by the familiar booming voice that now shattered the early morning quiet of the boatyard. "Ahoy there, Mister Ketchum! Top a the mornin' to ya!" Ketch heard several kerplunks from the neighboring marsh; probably bullfrogs. He turned and backtracked a bit in the direction of the Captain's boat, just so they wouldn't have to yell to each other.

"Good morning," Ketch said. Before he could continue, the Captain spoke again.

"Hey, I been meanin' to ask, how come you-know-who's car was still parked at your place yesterday mornin'? Is that why y'all didn't want to come down here with the rest of us? You dawg! Come aboard and tell me all about it! And while you're at it, I still wanna know what the Christ you're really up to with them blocks!"

Since the Captain was grinning at him, Ketch briefly grinned back, but then he said, "I'm sorry, but I can't talk right now. I have to get going."

"Oh." The Captain's grin faded. "Hey, sorry if I offended you."

"No, not at all, I'm not offended," Ketch hastened to reply. Though he hated doing it, he could see it was time for another lie. He wondered how a habitual liar could keep up the charade for very long; he was already starting to lose track. "I have an appointment."

"Oh yeah? What kind? You finally decide to sell?" the Captain asked – testing, apparently.

"No, it's something else. It's nothing to worry about. I'll explain later, maybe tomorrow, okay?"

"Tomorrow? Must be some appointment," the Captain said. "Did you have another one down here at the yard this mornin'?" Ketch shook his head and turned to go. "Okay, never mind, I'll mind my own bidness. Hey, before you run off, I got a dive charter on Saturday. You interested?"

"Yes, and thanks!" Ketch called. He waved once and kept walking. He needed to get out of here.

And he was greatly relieved when he finally did, though he knew the reprieve would be short-lived; the Captain wouldn't let him slide for too much longer. But he'd gotten by for now, and he had the coordinates he needed; plus a little of Kari's 'wacky terbacky' to boot, which his new paramour might appreciate. He wondered what it would be like with her after a taste of that; he'd never tried that before.

He suddenly became cognizant of the fact that, since his confrontation with Ingram earlier this week, he hadn't been having any more panic attacks – and in fact, today he hadn't even broken a sweat so far, not with Kari or Mario or the Captain anyway. It seemed he might be getting a little better at handling stressful situations and thinking on his feet, and better as well at sneaking around and being duplicitous. But while that latter might have impressed his parents, he wasn't entirely sure it was a good thing.

It also belatedly occurred to him that maybe he could have investigated the dump site on Saturday, when the Captain took his dive charter out. Mario's boat hadn't gone too far out last night, only a few miles east out of Oregon Inlet from what he'd seen on the GPS, so there was an excellent chance of the site being well within the depth limit for recreational diving. He knew from the Captain's charts that one would have to sail farther out than that to get to a canyon, and farther still to finally leave the relatively shallow continental shelf behind and enter the realm of the true abyss.

In either of those cases those drums would have been virtually unreachable, and would almost certainly never be seen again by human eyes. He wondered whether Mick and Mario were ignorant of these facts, or if they couldn't go out that far for some reason, or if they were just plain lazy. Maybe Mario's boat, old as it was and not very well maintained, no longer had the range, or maybe it wasn't reliable enough to trust it going out that far; or maybe Mario simply wasn't a great navigator.

But the feasibility of the Saturday plan would depend on the dump site's proximity to the planned dive site or sites, which he'd neglected to ask about, and on cooperation from both the Captain and the divers. And most of the divers who came here wanted to dive on the historic shipwrecks of the Graveyard, not on a heap of barrels – not to mention they might be concerned about their safety, and rightfully so. Maybe as the second dive of the day? But even if they agreed to do it and they found the drums, one or more of them would probably be as outraged as he himself was, and they'd want to report the crime immediately – whereas an alternative idea was now beginning to take shape in the back of his mind, something he hadn't considered earlier and which might accomplish more than one objective. And if it could, it would require continued secrecy on his part, at least for now. He'd have to look into that further when he got home.

Although he was anxious to get all of the items checked off his list, he experienced a pang of guilt when the dog greeted him at the door. The dog was more energetic and impish than usual, sticking his head into Ketch's backpack and coming out with one of the granola bars, which Ketch had to chase him around the room to retrieve. After Ketch had let him out and back in again, the dog went immediately to where his leash and Ketch's walking stick hung on a peg in the kitchen, and sat there wagging and intently staring at Ketch.

"I'm sorry, boy," he said, squatting and giving the dog a hug. "I've been neglecting you, haven't I?" He didn't want to take the time to drive the dog to the beach, which was probably what he was angling for, but he decided he should at least take him out back and play with him again, as he'd done the day before. It wouldn't take long, and he'd have to change into a swimsuit anyway before he took the *TBD* out. "I'll make it up to you later, I promise," he said, then stood and proclaimed, "Let's get ready for a playtime!"

If the dog was disappointed, he didn't show it. He paced excitedly and panted while Ketch changed, then eagerly followed Ketch down to the back yard. They went through the same basic drill as they had the previous day, with the football and the frisbee and the water-play, and the dog behaved as though it were the first time for any of it, as he always did. Ketch knew he wasn't just meeting the dog's needs for attention, stimulation, and exercise, but also satisfying a characteristic craving for routine, and his guilt abated as he saw he was succeeding on all counts.

When they went back in and he'd gotten the dog

settled with another bone, he draped a beach towel over a chair at the kitchen table, sat down, and booted his laptop. The first order of business was to verify the depth of the ocean at the dump site. Since he still didn't have his own set of coastal navigational charts, he'd have to find an appropriate chart on the web. The NOAA had an online chart viewer that should do the trick.

Yes, here was a good one... He consulted his notebook for the coordinates and zoomed in on the section of the chart he needed. As nearly as he could tell, the depth should be no more than sixty feet, tops, and likely less. That was certainly doable, as the maximum recommended recreational depth was a hundred and thirty. Beyond that was tec diving territory, and he was not a trained technical diver.

And now, while he was at it, what about Tibbleson Construction? He unfortunately had less luck this time. All he could find through Google were phone directory-type pages, and while some of the companies listed there had their own websites, they didn't often name names; and Tibbleson was no exception.

He needed to know who ran the show there. How could he find out? He heard his cell phone ring from the other room; he'd put it in his backpack so he wouldn't forget it later, and when he got to it he saw it was Kari. He considered answering the call, then decided against it. Let her think he was out cleaning his boat or whatever for now – he didn't want to be interrupted, or worse yet talked into doing something that might force him to scuttle his plans for the day. After all, there are schedules to be maintained, even in Colombia, he thought in a Hollywood Spanish accent. Since the Sea Dog wouldn't be open yet, he hoped she wouldn't just show up here unannounced again.

He could see she was leaving him a voice message. He'd check it later. Meanwhile, he went to his desk and found the most recent letter he'd received from Ingram. The phone was free by the time he returned to the kitchen, so he tapped in one of the numbers he found on the letter.

As he'd anticipated, he got some kind of receptionist or secretary on the line. Implying he was a client, he inquired how he might get hold of the owner of Tibbleson Construction, which had been recommended to him for renovation work at the implicitly expensive beach house he implied he'd recently bought through HatterasMann Realty, and did they ever use this company themselves? The girl replied yes and that would be Bob Ingram, who also ran the realty, and who was not in the office at this time and would he like to leave a message? Ketch thanked her, politely declined to identify himself, and said he'd call back another time.

So, he'd covered three of the four items on his list now – and *now* he was a private eye, wasn't he? Right, he thought, sure. He wondered if one needed a license to hang a PI shingle in North Carolina. Anyway, the pieces were starting to fall into place. Next on the agenda was verifying the dump site and getting some more photos, which would enable him to check the last item off his list. He moved to the guest bedroom and started assembling the gear he'd need to accomplish that.

~ Eleven ~

*He sailed on, with hope and confidence
freshening like a rising breeze.*

There were a few scattered light clouds as Ketch motored up the sound toward Oregon Inlet, but none of the long white plumes the old mariners had called mare's tails, and none that looked like fish scales. The sky had been a gorgeous panoply of reds and oranges at sunset the night before and hadn't been earlier this morning, and the moon hadn't been ringed last night. His wind sock indicated a light westerly, which he estimated at about five knots. Finally, the birds he was seeing weren't perched or flying low, which could indicate decreasing barometric pressure and changing weather.

And just to be sure, he'd also checked the weather report on his marine radio. So he'd probably be okay out there today weather-wise at least, which was good because taking anything smaller than a twenty-footer out to sea around here could be iffy. But his seventeen-footer was adequately powered and stable enough for nearshore sailing under reasonable conditions and mild current. It should also have range enough, and he'd brought a container of extra fuel for backup.

As for the rest of this little outing, he didn't need a specialty diving class to know he'd be violating some cardinal rules today. For starters he'd be diving solo, without a buddy who'd at least theoretically be able to rescue him if he had any trouble. He also didn't have a redundant air supply other than the half-dozen breaths he might get from his Spare Air, and he'd be leaving his boat unattended in open water when he descended to survey the dump site.

But he had after a modicum of internal conflict decided to follow one rule, that being to file a 'flight plan' with someone back on shore just in case. Though he had a radio, that wouldn't help if he couldn't use it for some reason. So he'd sent the Captain a message on his phone asking him to come get him if he hadn't called in by a certain time, and he'd given the Captain the coordinates – but still no explanation. Poor old salt... The Captain had always been a good friend, he deserved to be treated better than Ketch had treated him this morning, and he was after all a bit of an outlaw himself. Ketch was fairly certain he could and would keep his mouth shut, his public persona notwithstanding – he just needed to find the time to fill him in. And Kari as well, he remembered.

Speaking of that particular devil, he'd forgotten to listen to her phone message. He'd meant to check it right after she'd left it, but he'd gotten caught up in his snooping and then in packing his gear; and he'd again meant to do it when he'd sent the Captain's message, but he'd put that off until departure time and then set out immediately after. He felt bad now about forgetting, and he hoped it hadn't been something urgent.

In his defense, since he was a competent and

(usually) conscientious diver, packing for a dive trip was a highly organized affair; one didn't just jam whatever was handy into a bag and hope for the best. In his case the dive bag was also a backpack; though oversized, he found it easier to handle than a duffel-type bag. Working from both a written checklist and a detailed step-by-step mental visualization of the planned dive from start to finish, he'd ensured that he packed every essential item, big and small, bar none. It was always important to do all that, but obviously even more so when there'd be no one else around to borrow anything from. And he'd wanted to leave as little time as possible between the Captain receiving his message and himself getting underway. But he knew those still weren't great excuses; he'd have to do better.

There might be no cell reception at the dive site later, so he decided to start doing better right now. He idled the outboard to cut down on the noise and, still keeping an eye on the GPS, extracted his phone from the dry bag that also held his wallet and various other landlubber flotsam. He relaxed as he listened to the message – she was thinking of closing at six instead of seven, that was all, nothing to worry about except that he hoped he'd make it there on time. He stowed the phone and throttled back up.

He'd deal with that, and all the rest of it, later. Right now he needed to focus on his GPS, his compass, and the water ahead of the boat. He shouldn't have a problem navigating the shallow sound with the *TBD* unless he got truly unlucky, since it had only a nine-inch draft, but he thought he should still keep a close watch.

The *TBD*... He silently apologized to her once again. When he'd gotten the boat he'd had to register and name it, and he'd been in some kind of creative trough at the time and hadn't been able to dredge up anything that really resonated with him. He'd figured he could just rename her later, but then he'd learned it was considered bad luck to change the name of a boat. That was of course just more superstitious nonsense, so he'd still change it when he got around to it. Probably.

With the inlet coming up soon, his thoughts turned to the single waypoint he'd found on Mario's GPS. If Mario had participated in more than one dumping operation, could that mean they'd always deposited their nefarious cargo in the same general area? If so, that would be both better for the environment and convenient for those who'd be involved with the cleanup Ketch assumed would eventually happen. But it could also mean other boats had been used in the past and Mario had only done it once, or that Mario had done it more than once but not very often.

Well, he'd find out soon enough, some of it anyway. It wouldn't take too long to get through the inlet, and then he could go almost full throttle. Once he did that, reaching the waypoint would be a matter of minutes.

He made it through the inlet without mishap and wound her up. When the GPS told him he was at the waypoint, he throttled down and slowly circled the area, trying to see if he could eyeball anything below. But the visibility wasn't good enough here for that, so he picked a spot, cut the engine, and dropped anchor.

He counted the intervals on the braided anchor rode as he fed it into the water. When the anchor hit bottom and the line went slack, he was able to estimate a depth of about forty feet, give or take. He wouldn't need to consult a dive table or his dive computer for forty feet; he'd empty his tank before he reached the no-decompression time limit for that depth.

But even though the dive tables already incorporated safety margins, each person's physiology was a little different, and the risk of decompression sickness, or 'the bends' as it was commonly known, increased with age, among other factors. So for a safer dive profile he'd round up to fifty feet, which he knew carried an eighty-minute limit on bottom time; he wouldn't remain at depth more than seventy minutes; and he'd make a five-minute safety stop at fifteen feet on his ascent. And of course he'd use his dive computer to track depth and time.

He hoped that would be enough time to find the drums, if he hadn't landed right on top of them. He had only the one tank, so there'd likely be no trying again at another spot. He paused a moment to reevaluate the dive conditions. The surface was fairly calm, it looked like the weather was holding, and things were generally pretty quiet out here today. So, this was it.

The first thing he did was set out the ladder. He could manage to get back aboard this kind of boat later without it, but ever since he'd seen the film *Open Water 2* he'd made it a habit to take care of the ladder before he did anything else. It would be profoundly embarrassing to him if he ever ended up stranded like those dumb-asses had, when they'd all gone snorkeling off their yacht at the same time and no one had thought to set out the ladder.

Then he began to don his gear, starting with the uppermost items in the bag and working his way down to the bottom, having methodically packed the bag earlier in the reverse of the donning order.

For a wetsuit, he'd brought his 2mm jumpsuit. He probably could have gotten by with his shorty today, since he didn't chill as easily as the locals did – but even though the water temp was in the eighties at the surface, that was still lower than body temperature, and it would be cooler at depth. Though it was a hot day up top and he was sweating now, he knew enough of his body heat would dissipate during the dive that he'd be glad to get back up into the warm sun by the end of it. Plus the long sleeves and legs, and the light gloves he'd also wear, would protect him from abrasions and jellyfish stings, if he should happen to encounter any of those.

While he was suiting up he decided to violate another safety rule – he wouldn't fly his 'diver down' flag today. There were no other boats anywhere in sight at the moment, but in case that changed while he was underwater, he thought it might be wise to avoid advertising the fact that someone was diving here. He'd be careful on his ascent as always; he wouldn't get run over.

When he was otherwise ready, he carried his fins over to where he'd left the tank racked despite having attached the regulators and buoyancy compensator to it earlier. Although it was essentially weightless in the water, as Kari had pointed out this kind of tank weighed about forty pounds on the surface when filled with air, and you didn't want that rolling or sliding around loose on deck. The BC's integrated weights were already in place, and the accessories Ketch would need were already clipped to the BC as well. He slipped it and the fins on, inflated the BC halfway, double-checked his gear again, glanced one more time at the ladder, and did a back roll off the port gunwale.

He swam to the anchor line, deflated the BC, and began descending down the line, clearing his ears every few feet along the way as the ambient pressure steadily increased. As he neared the sandy bottom he made himself neutrally buoyant to avoid stirring up sediment and reducing visibility. He noted his depth was forty-two feet at the moment; it could vary throughout the dive, but the computer would keep track of it.

First he checked on the anchor. The Danforth fluke was the best kind for this type of bottom and it looked as secure as could be expected, but he clipped the end of the line from the wreck reel he was carrying to the anchor line so he'd always be connected to it. He didn't see any drums so far, so he'd have to do a search; and if the anchor dragged, there was no one up top to chase him down if he got separated from the boat. The viz looked to be about twenty feet, so he wasn't shocked that he hadn't seen anything yet. This wasn't the kind of visibility featured on postcards and in travel brochures; that was rare this close to shore. But it would do.

He started executing a circular search pattern centered on the anchor, and switched on his dive light. It wouldn't penetrate much farther, if at all, than his eye could see, but it would provide more color contrast and make it easier to discern objects such as the drums, which could be half-buried in the sand or silted over. And if there were some that had been there a while, they could be encrusted with marine growths.

Sunlight in seawater was progressively weakened by absorption and scattering as the depth increased, and colors were steadily lost to view as a result. Red, orange, and yellow were the first to go, being completely absorbed by thirty feet; after that everything was shades of green, blue, and violet. The sea usually appears blue-green to our eyes because those wavelengths penetrate the deepest and are the ones that are scattered back to us. Shining a white light on an object at depth restores its true colors.

He'd reeled out about forty feet of line when he found the first clutch. That's apropos, he thought – a clutch of toxic eggs. There were a half-dozen of them clustered fairly tightly. He could tell these were not the ones from last night, because coral had started to accrete on them, and that took some time.

He hovered and began to frame a shot. His camera was just an entry-level digital model with a built-in flash, no fancy strobes and such, but it would do the job, and he also had the dive light to help illuminate the subjects if needed. He wasn't interested enough in underwater photography to spend the time and money it would take to obtain magazine-quality photos, and he didn't need that kind of quality today anyway – he just had to show what these were and how many of them there were. He gently finned as close as he could get while still including all of the drums in the shot.

Continuing his search pattern, over the next thirty-five minutes he found three more similar groupings, ranging from six to eight drums each. One group looked fairly clean, and they were blue and orange like the ones he'd seen last night. He took pictures of all of them – and since they were digital, he could already see he had enough that were acceptable for his purposes. No more waiting, these days, with fingers crossed for film to be developed to see if he'd been successful; that was why he'd sprung for this camera.

He wondered if there were more drums down here. There might well be, but he decided he'd obtained enough evidence to meet his needs. His air supply was fine, but he'd soon need to start his ascent and it would take some time to reel in his line on his way back to the anchor.

When he reached the anchor, he saw it was still dug in where he'd left it, but it shouldn't be too difficult to dislodge and haul up later. He began a leisurely ascent toward the surface and stopped at a depth of fifteen feet. This was always the part of the dive he had the least patience with. He'd dived safely today, decompression-wise anyway, well within the limits; and he was sorely tempted to skip this safety stop. But he had plenty of air left, so he decided to wait it out. No sense taking any more chances, he thought – he'd already taken enough of them today.

So, he thought while he hung on the anchor line and fiddled with his buoyancy, which was always tricky business for him at shallow depths – twenty-eight drums. And counting perhaps, if he'd continued searching. They'd been doing this for some time then, and fortunately for everyone else it appeared they'd been consistent. They were almost all the 55-gallon kind from the looks of them, but he'd noticed several drums that were bigger; they were probably 85-gallon salvage drums, which were used for transporting leaking, damaged, or otherwise non-compliant smaller drums.

He hoped none of these particular drums were leaking yet, for his own sake as well as that of the environment. He hadn't observed any severe corrosion on what he could see of the ones he'd found. The conventional drums looked like they'd all had welded tops with bungholes, and the bigger ones were open-tops sealed with ring clamps.

The five minutes passed more quickly than he'd expected. See, that wasn't so bad, he told himself. He ascended to the ladder, removed his fins, climbed aboard, and geared down. He didn't take anywhere near as much care repacking his bag as he had with the packing earlier; his main concern now was just to make sure nothing would get damaged. He didn't have that big a buffer between now and Kari's new closing time, and the dog had been alone long enough and he wanted to get going. There were still no other boats in the immediate vicinity, which he was grateful for. He took in the ladder, hoisted the anchor, and got underway.

Though anxious to get back, and now hungry as well, he made himself take the same care in the sound as he had going out. He hadn't had lunch nor brought one with him, and as usual post-dive he was ravenous. He ate all three of the granola bars he'd been carrying around with him all day, but still found himself wishing he'd taken time to pack something more substantial. Well, he guessed he'd get his money's worth at the restaurant later, that's all.

He thought back to the phone call he'd made this morning to HatterasMann Realty. So Tibbleson Construction must have been the second wife's company, and it was being run by Ingram now. He found that fact extremely interesting, as it meshed perfectly with the embryonic plan that had started forming in the back of his mind last night, and which had now moved to the forefront.

Had she been declared dead, or was she still officially missing? He didn't know, but he suspected the former since Ingram was now at the helm. Though it might not matter if it was a family-owned business, as was likely. There must not have been a pre-nup, he thought, or if there had it had been engineered in Ingram's favor. Ditto for the first wife and the realty, he imagined, since Ingram had gotten his talons into that one, too. He wondered if Ingram knew much about construction; or much about anything else, for that matter. But the question was probably irrelevant – you didn't have to be an expert to be an owner, as you'd have your 'people' to take care of the details. And you'd have your money, of course, which may not always buy happiness but can make otherwise impossible things possible.

But regardless of whatever you did or didn't do yourself, as the owner you could be held responsible for everything that happened under your purview. Legally speaking, he knew an absence of hands-on involvement was not always a protection against prosecution. He looked forward to checking online later to see if that applied in the case of illegal ocean dumping.

When Ketch pulled up to his dock, he finally realized how tired he was. Diving burned a lot of calories, usually more from heat loss than exertion, and he might also be a little dehydrated from saltwater immersion. He needed more food and more water and a little rest. But he couldn't slack off yet – though he still had some time to spare before he needed to be at the Sea Dog, he had to take care of the dog, tend to his gear, and get himself cleaned up. Oh, and call Kari.

And call the Captain, which he'd better do

immediately so he wouldn't forget. It was bad enough he'd put the man off this morning – to then send him on a wild goose chase with his boat would be unconscionable. Ketch had no doubt his good friend would be steaming up the sound five minutes past the deadline otherwise. He dashed off another short and otherwise uninformative message as soon as he'd tied up.

He lugged his gear back to the house and dropped it in the driveway, then picked up the mail and trudged up the front steps. He needed a shower, though it should be a lukewarm one at best. His tissues had today absorbed more nitrogen, an inert and ordinarily harmless gas, than normal from the air in his scuba tank due to the increased pressure at depth. The pressure started at one atmosphere at the surface, and then increased by another ATM for every thirty-three feet of depth. He thus had to breathe the air from his tank at a higher pressure in order to fill his lungs. The regulator's function was to deliver air to him at the necessary pressure.

Since the body doesn't metabolize nitrogen the way it does the oxygen in the air, his body was working to get rid of that excess nitrogen, now that he was back at normal air pressure – a process that had begun as soon as he'd earlier started to ascend from depth. If the nitrogen remains dissolved in the blood on its way out through the lungs, no problem – but if there's too much nitrogen and the pressure decreases too rapidly, nitrogen bubbles can form in the blood and end up lodging somewhere undesirable, resulting in symptoms that can range from fatigue, skin rash, and numbness to severe joint pain, paralysis, and death. This is the bends.

Hot water can stimulate off-gassing of residual nitrogen from the body's tissues, and getting bent after a hot shower was not unheard of. Though unlikely given the kind of diving he'd done today, Ketch again figured why take chances, especially at his age. So no hot shower, not until tomorrow.

The dog was barking inside the house, knowing Ketch was back. He greeted Ketch with something akin to ecstasy as soon as the door opened, almost bowling him over in the process.

"Whoa boy, settle down!" Ketch admonished. "What's the matter, were you worried about me? I'm okay, it's okay now." He knelt on the deck so the dog could hug him, and he hugged the dog back. "You're my good boy. Come on, let's go do our chores," he said, and the dog followed him down the steps.

Ketch hosed the salt water from his gear while the dog took care of his own set of chores, which consisted of patrolling the perimeter of the yard, tracking recent interlopers, and re-marking the territory. When he was finished with the hose, Ketch hauled the gear up to the deck and spread it all out to dry, out of the direct sun. He'd bring it inside before he left for the shop, though, dry or not; he was willing to trust those few of his neighbors who were permanent residents, but not the vacationers. He stowed the tank in the capped bed of his pickup so he wouldn't forget that later, and carried his dry bag into the house.

The dog followed him in and Ketch gave him a biscuit. He refilled the dog's water dish, then decided it was close enough to his dinnertime and filled the food dish as well. Wouldn't want to forget that either – it was bad enough he'd soon have to leave him alone again for a while. Ketch decided he was just too busy for the both of them lately. How had that happened? Well, he guessed he knew. He resolved to take the dog for a serious hike on the beach, the kind he liked, first thing tomorrow no matter what.

What next? He could call Kari, but that might take too much of his remaining time, so he decided to just send a message saying he'd gotten hers and would be there soon. Then it was off to the shower.

He ended up making it to the shop a few minutes before the amended closing time. Not too shabby, he thought – and he was both clean and clean-shaven, and restored and chipper after the shower, such as it had been. And hungry, and dressed for dinner in khakis and a tasteful Hawaiian shirt – if there is such a thing, some might say, but Ketch believed there was. When he carried the tank in he saw that he was again the only customer. He hoped it hadn't been that way all day, but he suspected it might have since she'd wanted to move up the closing time; though that had been this morning.

"Hey, you!" He barely had time to set the tank down before getting caught up in a quick but warm embrace. "Done with this, huh? I tried to call you after I got your message," she said as she carried the tank into the back. "I can't wait to get out of here. Let's make like a tree and lock up!" she laughed.

"Whatever you say. I was probably in the shower," he called. "Say, do you happen to have two filled ones back there? The Captain has a charter on Saturday."

"No," she said. "Believe it or not, I actually had a little run on rentals on Monday and I was off yesterday, and I only have a few filled now and they're accounted for. We can do a couple more before we go if you want."

"No, let's take off before someone else comes in," he replied, knowing it was the right thing to say. "I can get them anytime."

"Right, you know where I live," she laughed again. She seemed to be relaxed and in fine spirits; the money he'd given her this morning must indeed have helped with something important. She tossed him a set of keys. "Lock the front door, set the alarm, and hit the lights. I'll get my stuff and we'll go out the back. I'll chauffeur you tonight, you're probably tired from cleanin' your boat."

"Okay, but I'll need to get my truck later," he said. It sounded like she was still planning on staying with him; that was good. As for the boat, he wasn't ready yet to tell her that if there'd been any hull cleaning done, it had been accomplished by putting the pedal to the metal in the open ocean.

"I'm jealous of you," she said on the way to the restaurant. "Do you know how long it's been since I went divin' anywhere just for fun, without students?"

"Well, you could take my place on Saturday if you like, and I could cover the shop. The Captain wouldn't mind," he offered.

"Thanks, but I'd rather do it with you," she demurred. "I'd rather go divin' with you too," she added with an evil grin.

"Bada boom," he said. "You should try stand-up sometime. They'd probably let you do it at the Barefoot Station."

"Yeah right, I don't think so. We're here!" Since the Froggy Dog was again on the north end of town, it wasn't far from the dive shop. They probably could have walked – but hey, this is America, he thought, and this is how we Americans roll.

They parked and went in. "Can we get a drink first, before we get a table?" she asked. "I love this bar, it's gorgeous!"

"Lead the way," he answered. Though he was starving, a beer would help. Alcohol in excess was another decompression sickness trigger to avoid immediately after diving, but one beer now and a glass of wine at dinner and water otherwise shouldn't hurt.

As it turned out, they never left the pub area. They claimed two semi-facing seats at an end corner of the bar, ordered drinks and appetizers, and then migrated to a small table nearby when the entrees arrived. She drank most of the bottle of wine Ketch had ordered, while he himself adhered to his two-drink limit.

"Do you mind if we stop at the gift shop on the way out?" she asked toward the end of the meal.

"Not at all, whatever you want to do," he said with a satisfied smile. Sated at last and slightly buzzed, he might agree to just about anything right now, he thought.

"Hey, you know what? This was our first date!" she returned with another smile. "But it's not quite over yet." She leaned forward across the table on her elbows and feigned solemnity. "Your place or yours?" she whispered with a straight face.

Ketch laughed. This had indeed been like a date. They'd had a fine dinner, enjoyed each other's company, and talked about practically everything under the sun – except anything important, of course.

He found a tee shirt he liked at the gift shop, and bought her one as well. As they drove back to the Sea Dog to get his truck, he decided that when it was time to come clean with both Kari and the Captain, he'd do it when they were all together. Weren't they after all his two best friends in the world? And it would be easier to tell both of them at the same time. Unlike the Captain, Ketch didn't enjoy repeating his stories.

Tomorrow night; that's when he'd do it. Meanwhile, he still had a couple of things to get out of the way between now and then – the final item from last night's list, and now an additional one if he could swing it.

~ Twelve ~

He was awake awhile before he recalled that his heart was broken.

*K*etch woke before dawn, completely refreshed and keen to dig in on his plans for the day. This wasn't an unusual occurrence when he had something to look forward to – he'd been this way all his life, though it had almost never happened on a workday like today until after he'd retired. And surprisingly, though he'd never really enjoyed sleeping all night with anyone as a rule, not even when he'd been married, he'd been sleeping quite well these last few nights. He wondered if that would last.

Kari had also stirred when he'd awakened, so it had been a little while longer before he'd been able to start bustling about the house, which he was now doing while she slept in – if one could call sleeping until at least daybreak 'sleeping in'. The sacrifices he had to make, he thought, though not with any degree of dissatisfaction. He knew he'd be a fool to not fully enjoy this ride while it lasted.

The dog had been taken out and fed, and there was a bagel in the toaster. He'd quickly shaved and was now multitasking during the toasting cycle, restocking his backpack and filling his canteen. Before he did anything else today, he intended to keep his promise to the dog – and a promise he'd made to himself as well when they'd first moved here, that being to spend more time watching the sun rise and set over the sea. There were fewer excuses now not to, or should be, since he was no longer a serf to the corporate warlords; and since he lived by the ocean, failing to occasionally avail himself of the restoration and rejuvenation he derived from especially a good sunrise on the beach seemed a crime.

When they were ready to leave, Ketch went into the bedroom, sat on the edge of the bed, and lightly stroked her hair one time. A sleepy smile grew on her face and her eyes half-opened. "Are you sure you don't want to go with us?" he asked.

"No thanks," she mumbled. Drifting back to sleep, she breathed something else that Ketch didn't quite catch, '(something) you'.

He quietly led the dog out the front door, down the steps, and into the truck. He stowed his backpack and walking stick behind the seat, then tossed his tarp hat back there as well, since it was hard to drive while wearing it.

They made their way out to Route 12 and headed south toward Canadian Hole, Ketch sharing his bagel with the dog along the way. It took only a few minutes to get to the day-use parking area on the sound, where they left the truck. He kept the dog leashed until they'd crossed the road and reached the top of the primary dune line. He paused there to release the dog onto the beach, then stretched contentedly and surveyed his surroundings as the dog began his own explorations. There were already a couple of people out fishing the surf, but the dog knew to stay away from them.

There were no beach houses here, nor much of anything else that was artificial in origin. Many would consider Ketch's view from atop the dunes a barren one, but the island was far from barren to an educated observer. What you can perceive and appreciate often depends on how much you know, he might say to the uninitiated.

The sun was beginning to rise now. Diurnal and tidal activities were cycling, and patterns seen and unseen were subtly shifting. The parts of the island in his field of vision were taking on a mottled glow, sharp patches of light alternating with deep shadows in the hint of maritime forest he knew lay a couple of miles or so to the south toward Buxton on Cape Hatteras.

The birds were becoming more active, and nocturnal animals would be leaving the dunes and marshes to seek shelter for the day among the stunted shrubs and trees in the thickets and forest, except for some raccoons that would stay out a while longer to gather shellfish at low tide in the marsh. Also in the marsh, periwinkles that had climbed stalks of spartina to avoid drowning at high tide would be inching their way down again. The vegetation gently bending in the light wind was adapting to the new day, greedily absorbing the sun's rays as it reverted from nighttime respiration back to photosynthesis.

The sea was not yet completely illuminated, and the light from the nascent sun made the foam on the breakers appear to stand out from the surface as if the scene had been sculpted in bas-relief. Strange creatures from depths where no sunlight penetrated that had ventured closer to the surface to feed during the night would be descending again. The screeching of the gulls and terns, mostly territorial and antagonistic in origin but musical to Ketch's ear, was building as they came out to forage along the shoreline in the ebbing tide. He watched the dog playfully chase a straggling ghost crab back into its daytime refuge at the base of the dune.

Throughout this pristine part of the island, a diversity of indigenous life forms existed that was remarkable in its adaptations to the extremes of temperature, salinity and moisture it had to endure. The primary dune was stabilized by a variety of pioneer plants, the slender sea oat with its long and narrow leaves curled to prevent water loss being the most common. There were also stately clumps of tall panic grass, low sea elder shrubs with their bright green succulent leaves, clumped stalks of sea rocket, so named because its flowers resembled little rockets, spreading mats of seaside evening primrose with its fuzzy leaves and yellow cuplike flowers, the fragrant croton, and the flat, radiating doily-like branches of the dune spurge.

The secondary dune they'd earlier passed, a back dune partially protected from the ravages of the sea and its salt, was able to support the beach morning glory with its pink trumpet-like flowers, the prickly sandspur, catbriar, and taller species such as the broom-like broomstraw rush, salt meadow hay, and the sword-like yucca, or Spanish bayonet, which could grow as tall as nine feet.

Between the primary and secondary dunes, in the low area called the swale, the temperature was significantly higher during the day than on the dunes themselves because the sloping sides of the dunes reflected the heat inward. The only plants that could survive there were the beach pea and the prickly pear cactus. The cactus was low-lying and could be quite painful when stepped on or nosed at, so Ketch and the dog both avoided walking in the swale whenever possible – as they largely had today, having opted to cross the dunes at the old haulover site.

Back across the road on the sound side he could see some of the salt marsh that defined much of the western shore of the island. Despite the wide variations in salinity that occurred there, even the marshes contained a variety of plants. Shimmering waves of cordgrass or spartina predominated, but there'd also be the sea oxeye with its yellow sunflower-like flowers, the marsh rosemary whose tiny lavender flowers would bloom later in the summer, black needle rush, cotton bush, marsh elder, salt meadow hay, wax myrtle with its distinctive bayberry aroma, and the yellow flowers of the seaside goldenrod, among others.

The island harbored a surprising abundance of animal life as well, aside from the many cetaceans, fish, turtles, crustaceans, mollusks and so on that could be found in the waters of the ocean and the sound that together surrounded the island. Several common species of insects existed across the island, dragonflies being prevalent in the marshes. Small translucent ghost crabs, seen mostly at night, frequented the front dunes and strand line, as did the sand hopper or beach flea, a tiny shrimp-like amphipod. Some of the forest animals, such as the meadow mouse and cottontail rabbit, foraged on the dunes at night. The forest also sheltered raccoons, and the yellow rat snake and an entertaining lizard called the six-lined racerunner.

The watery marshes, aside from their important role as a nursery for juveniles of many species of shrimp and fish, supported blue crabs, fiddler crabs, marsh crabs, the diamondback terrapin, clams, oysters, mussels, and several types of snails. On the tidal flats, anaerobically pungent and sometimes broad expanses of detritus-blackened muddy sand that were exposed at the marsh's edge at low tide, could be found a variety of mollusks including scallops, clams and oysters, several kinds of shrimp, hermit crabs and blue crabs, corals, sponges, and bryozoans, and the occasional squid and horseshoe crab.

The beach itself had its clams, ghost crabs, mole crabs in the surf zone, and other bottom dwellers such as starfish, sand dollars, and urchins, washed in from deeper water, and seasonal visitors like the endangered loggerhead turtle, which laid its eggs above the high tide line.

And of course there were the birds. Common terns, herring gulls, willets and sandpipers frequently scavenged along the shoreline, and Ketch had seen laughing gulls, oystercatchers, skimmers, an occasional cormorant, and several other types of tern there and toward the sound. There were sometimes brown pelicans, ibises, egrets and herons in the marshes, including the great blue heron which stood over four feet tall, and once he'd seen a seahawk dive to the sound for a fish from what must have been a height of a hundred feet.

Ketch contentedly took it all in as he descended to the beach and started hiking south along the high tide line, envisioning the island and its myriad natural inhabitants as the synchronized entity it truly was, the whole dependent on all of its parts and each part ultimately dependent on every other. If he had to believe in something, he thought, he could believe in being a part of this. As he strode on, alone in this better world except for the dog, it pleased him to imagine that it all belonged to him.

But of course, it didn't. And soon neither would even his humble abode back in town. He walked for a while longer, loath to exit his lucid dream, then reluctantly called to the dog. They'd gone more than halfway toward Buxton Woods, the largest remaining stand of maritime forest on the Carolina coast, and he wanted to hike its trails again sometime – but not today.

He removed his canteen and the collapsible dog dish from his backpack and gave the dog a drink, and then started retracing his steps. It was time now to begin the unavoidable devolution back to reality.

It was still early when they arrived back at the house, early enough to catch the paperboy delivering the morning newspaper. The boy stopped and dismounted his bike when he saw the dog get out of the truck, and the dog's tail started wagging furiously.

"Jack? Hey Jack!" the boy called. The dog glanced at Ketch for permission, then assumed he had it when he didn't hear otherwise and ran to the boy. "Hey, Mister Ketchum!"

The sun was in Ketch's eyes. He shaded them with a hand, then said, "Henry?" What was he doing delivering newspapers? Wasn't he on vacation?

"Yes sir," Henry replied. Before Ketch could inquire, he said, "We're here for the summer, me and Mama and my sister. My dad still has to work some, so he comes when he can."

"So you decided to get a summer job? Where are you staying?" Ketch asked.

"In a house down by the canal." Still petting the dog, Henry said, "Yeah, I want to make some extra money this summer. My allowance isn't that great. I'm savin' up for somethin'."

"Are you? Well, good for you, Henry."

Ketch already admired this boy for the way he'd handled himself on the Captain's boat earlier this week, and now he was even more impressed. Unlike many nowadays, this one wasn't wasting his time playing video games, he was respectful, and it looked like he had a good work ethic. His parents must be teaching him well.

"How old are you, Henry?" he asked.

"I just turned twelve, sir. Say, do you need your grass cut or anythin'? It's okay if you don't," the boy quickly added.

"Well, now that you mention it, it could use a trim." Another thing he was falling behind on, and he doubted he'd have time to do it himself today or tomorrow. "Do you know how to run a power mower? Is it okay with your mother?"

"Oh sure! I've done it at home, and for a couple neighbors. She doesn't mind."

"You're sure?" Ketch pressed. "Should I talk with her about it first?"

"You can, but she'll be okay with it. Want to use my cell?"

Ketch shook his head. "No, that's all right. How much would you charge?"

The boy named a figure and Ketch said, "That's way too low. If you charged twice that, you'd still be cheaper than the pros. So that's what I'll pay you." He saw the boy's face light up. "I have to go out later, but I'm not sure when. I'll leave the mower out behind the house, and I'll pay you now. You come back later and do the job, and if I'm not here leave the mower in the shade when you're done. How does that sound?"

"That sounds great! Thanks, Mister Ketchum!"

Ketch gave the boy his money and sent him on his way. Before he went inside, he got the mower out and filled its gas tank, then wheeled it around to the back of the house and parked it where it would remain shaded. Then he and the dog went into the house.

"Hey, you!" Kari called from the kitchen, where the

dog immediately headed. Not only did he need another drink, the woman was cooking as well. "How was your walk? I waited breakfast for you. Go on and wash up, and then get back in here. Everythin's just about done except the eggs, and they won't take long."

Ketch returned to find a plate of scrambled cheese eggs, bacon, orange slices, and biscuits waiting for him. "You're going to spoil me," he said, "and probably make me fat, too."

"Nah, I'll make sure you work it off," she said. "Who were you talkin' to out there?" He told her about meeting Henry on the fishing charter, and what the boy was up to now.

"Huh, sounds like a good kid. It's nice of you to help him out," she said. "So what are you doin' today?"

"Oh, you don't want to know. Chores and errands. I have some things to do on the computer."

"That reminds me!" she exclaimed with a mouthful. She swallowed and said, "I wasn't snoopin', honest, but I saw some papers on your desk and I couldn't help but notice. Are you writin' a book or somethin'?"

"Well," he said, looking away in embarrassment. "It's just some short stories I started fiddling with when I moved here, and now maybe it's turning into a novel, I don't know."

"A novel? No kiddin'! What's it about?" Before he could answer, she continued, "And you've been workin' on it for what, three years? It must be good!"

"It's a piece of crap," he said. "But it might be good

someday, and meanwhile it's something I can relax with. I don't watch a lot of TV, as you might have noticed. I'll let you read it sometime, if you'd really like to."

"I would! But no pressure, I'll wait 'til you're ready," she said.

They ate in comfortable silence for a while. Even the dog, who sat on the floor between them, was silent as he patiently waited for the occasional scrap. That was when it occurred to Ketch that he might be in deep. He'd known this woman on a casual basis since shortly after he'd moved here, and now... As the Captain might put it, when two people were comfortable enough with each other to just shut the hell up, that was serious. To sit in silence once in a while without one or the other feeling the need to manufacture conversation, that meant something.

Toward the end of the meal she announced, "Well, I've got some paperwork at the shop this mornin'. It's almost dang tax time again! Every three months, I swear... But I'll clean up here before I go." He started to protest, but she cut him off. "I have time, and besides you have a dishwasher, silly! Anyway, if you can stop by the shop later, I'll have your tanks ready for you. Or I can just bring 'em with me tonight."

Ketch considered for a moment. "Thanks, but I should be able to drop by later this afternoon."

It sounded like she might be hoping to stay here again tonight, which would make the fourth night in a row. He wondered what she'd say if he inquired about that likely mythical exterminator, then thought better of it for the time being. Whether it was a deliberate strategy or just her nature, she wasn't demanding a lot or interfering much with his activities, and he didn't want her to go home yet.

In fact, he was tempted to ask her right now if he could help her move in here for good, or at least for the foreseeable future. No longer having to pay rent for an apartment would be a financial boon for her, and she didn't seem to mind cooking – not to mention the other fringe benefits. But then he thought of what could still be lying in wait in his and this house's future, thanks to that damned Ingram; he shouldn't be counting his chickens just yet. And who knew, maybe he'd change his mind after a while and regret what he'd set in motion. Remember what B.B. King advised, he told himself, and don't make your move too soon.

So for now he just bided his time and helped her with the dishes instead – and after he'd walked her out to her car, he went straight for his laptop.

He settled in at his desk in the extra bedroom, where the printer was, and transferred the pictures from his phone and his underwater camera to the computer. Genuine photographs might arguably make more of an impression, but he didn't have a photo printer and he didn't want to waste time taking the files somewhere to have prints made or ordering prints online – and in any case he didn't want anyone else to see them just yet anyway. Color printouts should serve the purpose for now.

It would take a while for them all to print. While

he waited, he backed up the files to his external drive and to disk, then attached them to e-mails and sent them to himself. If something happened to his printouts or his equipment, the photos would still at least be floating out in the ether somewhere where he could retrieve them. The ones on the phone were automatically backed up to a phone company server as well.

Then he visited the home page of the New York Yankees. Yes, Saturday's game would indeed be televised. Since he'd be diving that day, he went to the living room and set up the DVR to record the game.

What next? The printer was still chugging away, so he considered trying to make a dent in his accumulating stack of newspapers – but no, another time for that. He decided to instead return to the laptop and his good friend Google. He started with ILLEGAL OCEAN DUMPING. It wouldn't hurt if he was a little better informed later.

Well, this was interesting... It looked like the kind of dumping he'd witnessed could be considered a felony under the Clean Water Act or the Ocean Dumping Act; he wasn't sure which. A federal crime, and perhaps with multiple counts, each carrying a fair-sized fine and possible imprisonment. And his criminals were U.S. citizens and hadn't dumped in international waters, which made things simpler.

It looked like they'd finally started getting serious about this issue back in the Seventies, and had ramped up the enforcement and the penalties beginning in the Nineties. It appeared the EPA was responsible for regulating ocean disposal of everything other than dredged spoils, which were handled by the Corps of Engineers; and the Coast Guard was responsible for surveillance of ocean dumping.

So he guessed he could report his crime to either the EPA or the Coast Guard – or easier yet, here was a link to something called the National Response Center where he could file a report online, or he could call their 800 number. The state also had similar laws and programs, but whether his concerns were founded or unfounded he was too paranoid now about Ingram's political reach to go to the state; and for a similar reason, the Dare County Sheriff's office, which covered all of the unincorporated settlements on Roanoke and Hatteras Islands, was also out of the question.

He read that during the past ten years, a federal initiative called the Vessel Pollution Program had generated over $200,000,000 in fines and a total of seventeen years in prison for ship officers and executives. Executives? Good, but had they themselves been imprisoned? That wasn't clear in most cases, and they definitely hadn't been in some. Also, that had mostly to do with ships discharging used oil and oily bilge water, and disposing of such wastes in violation of or without permits; but still, it was encouraging.

Permits – now that was disturbing. Apparently it was still possible to obtain permits for a limited range of ocean disposal activities. Could Tibbleson

Construction have a permit allowing Mick and Mario to do what they'd done? Ketch decided that was unlikely, since they'd loaded the boat at an isolated location away from any working waterfront, and at night; or if they did have one, their methods would again indicate that they were probably violating its terms. Plus he remembered reading that dumping hazardous waste in shallow waters was no longer allowed.

He glanced at the printer's output tray and checked the time. The pictures would be done soon, and if he took a quick shower right now, he could easily make it to the offices of HatterasMann Realty before lunch hour. Not that Ingram would necessarily be there, or would be available if he was since Ketch didn't have an appointment. But he figured Ingram would agree to see him if he thought Ketch had decided to sell; and if it turned out Ingram wasn't there, maybe he'd find out where he was and track him down.

He thought he might have a shot now, and he wanted to take it without further delay, partly because of the suspense and partly because his conscience was bothering him. He should have immediately reported the illegal act he'd witnessed, and under ordinary circumstances he thought he would have done just that, the potential reactions of those involved be damned. But those drums weren't going anywhere, and he didn't think they were leaking, so they could wait a bit longer. The main reason he felt guilty about putting off reporting them was that he was about to try to leverage the sordid situation for personal gain. However, he didn't feel at all guilty about how he intended to do that, nor about whom he intended to do it to.

And why should he? He was certain things like this happened all the time in Ingram's world, and probably usually to Ingram's personal advantage. So Ketch figured there was no harm in his dabbling in that game as well. It was just business, right? That was undoubtedly Ingram's take on what he was trying to do to Ketch. Maybe he wouldn't be needing those foam blocks after all; could he sell them on eBay? He'd seen pontoons for sale there.

When he got out of the shower, he quickly dressed and gathered his printouts into a manila envelope. He let the dog out, apologized to him yet again, gave him another bone, and hit the road.

HatterasMann Realty was at the south end of town, so he was parking the truck there in just a few minutes. Another reason the north end was better, he thought, though he hadn't known of this particular reason when he'd bought the house. It was an attractive building in its way, he noted, a tastefully sided and appointed example of modern sterile beach architecture; and it had a club associated with it for the vacation rentals the realty managed, with tennis courts, a playground, and an outdoor swimming pool for the rentals that didn't have private pools. But he wasn't impressed by any of this today, and he marched into the reception area without giving the club a second look.

He stopped at the long bar-like reception counter and waited for someone to become available to help him. To his surprise, it turned out to be one of his dinner guests from Monday night. He tried to remember their names – Barb, Diana, Joette... Yes, this one was Joette, the one who'd been hanging on the Captain.

"Well hey there Ketch, what can I do for you?" she inquired with a genuine smile.

"Hello, Joette," Ketch said. Dispensing with further pleasantries, he pressed on. "If Mister Ingram is in, would you please tell him Mister Ketchum would like to see him?"

"I could," she said, lowering her voice. "But I gotta tell ya, he's in some kinda mood this mornin'. He's been yellin' on the phone, and he told us no interruptions."

"Really? Well, I'd appreciate it if you'd try. Or just point me in the right direction, if you'd rather, and I'll go knock on his door. I really need to see him, and I think he needs to see me." Having been lucky enough to find the man in, and feeling the adrenalin now, he was anxious to complete his business.

"Well, I don't know..." she said.

"I'm afraid I must insist," he said, determined now to not leave here empty-handed, not when he was this close. He clutched his envelope more tightly and waved it at her. "He has to see this today."

Joette shrugged. "Okay, it's your funeral." She leaned across the counter and jerked her head toward the back hallway. "Take a right, last door on the left.

Don't say I sent you."

Ketch thanked her and hurried off in the indicated direction. It was time to get this over with.

~ Thirteen ~

He wished he could see him once more, to know what he had against him.

He drew his weapon, held it straight out in front of him, and zigzagged toward the office in a semi-crouch, quickly verifying that each intervening room was clear along the way and taking care to avoid tripping on his trench coat. Procedure be damned – there'd once been a time for talk, but it had expired. When he reached the closed office door, he lowered his shoulder and rammed it without preamble, executed a forward roll through the splintered doorway while simultaneously sweeping the room with staccato bursts from his semi-automatic, and came to rest on one knee with the barrel of the gun pointing straight at the chest of the lone man left standing behind the desk. He still had his hat on, and he was in charge now.

Ketch briefly wondered if he could use this daydream somewhere in his gestating (or would 'festering' be a better word choice?) novel. His parents might have enjoyed reading a hunk of cheese like that, he supposed, but he doubted anyone else would nowadays. He refocused and knocked politely but firmly on the door.

"I said no interruptions!" came an angry voice from within. Then shortly, "Oh, never mind, come on in." Ketch turned the knob and opened the door.

"Sorry, didn't mean to bite your head off, it's been a hell of a mornin'..." Ingram started to explain, then stopped when he looked up and saw who his visitor was.

"You!" he exclaimed. "What are *you* doin' here?" He exhaled loudly and sat back in his oversized leather desk chair. "Who let you in here? You don't have an appointment, that I can recall." His eyes bored straight into Ketch's and the impatience in them was obvious. "Well?"

Ketch's mouth suddenly went dry again, and he was afraid he wouldn't be able to speak. But wait – wasn't it just yesterday he'd been congratulating himself on his newfound composure under duress? He could do this, he told himself; he *had* to do this.

He looked away from Ingram's stare and tried to generate some saliva by thinking of something appetizing – the crab puffs at the Froggy Dog, the gourmet pizza at Gidget's, a sundae at the DQ, Kari earlier this morning... Whatever it was that finally did the trick, it worked. He swallowed once, resumed eye contact, and started talking.

"No, I don't have an appointment, and I apologize for that," he enunciated clearly, managing to keep his voice even in the bargain. "But we have some urgent business to attend to."

"Do we now? Well, I guess I might could humor you, since you're here anyway." Ketch silently closed the door and took a seat in front of the desk. "So, what's so damn urgent? I'm busy here. Did you finally decide to sell? Is that your big news?"

Ketch skidded his manila envelope across the desk. "Please take a look at these pictures."

"Pictures? Of what?" Ingram snatched the envelope, dumped its contents onto the desk, and quickly fanned through the printed photographs. "What the hell is all this?" he demanded.

"I'll summarize for you," Ketch said. Now that he'd gotten some traction, it seemed to be getting easier. "Those are pictures of hazardous waste from Tibbleson Construction being illegally dumped at sea. The ones on your left were taken on Roanoke on Tuesday night. The ones on your right were taken at the bottom of the ocean yesterday afternoon."

Ingram stared at Ketch, then looked more closely at the pictures. "What the hell..." he mumbled. "Where'd you get these? What's this got to do with me? These don't even look real. What are you tryin' to pull here?" he asked, his voice rising again.

Ketch remained calm, outwardly at least; so far so good. "I took them, and they're real. These are just computer printouts, but I have the originals. I can have a nice set of glossies made up for you if you like, I'll be making a set for the Coast Guard and the EPA anyway. And what they have to do with you is this – since you're running Tibbleson Construction now, you're liable for numerous felony violations of the federal Clean Water Act and Ocean Dumping Act, and some state laws as well. From what I've heard, the fines could be hefty, and someone might go to jail."

"You don't say? Well, they might have to stand in line if they want it to be me." Ingram ran a hand through his hair and rubbed at his eyes. Ketch wanted to ask what he meant by that, but he didn't get the chance. "Assumin' you're tellin' the truth, what do you want me to do about it? Why are you here?"

"I'll tell you -" Ketch began.

"Forget it, this is bullshit," Ingram suddenly interrupted, waving Ketch off. "I need this right about now like a hole in the head. I know nothin' about any of this, it isn't my concern. I'm too busy for this."

Ketch cleared his throat and leaned forward in his chair. "It will be your concern, if I report this."

Ingram's eyes narrowed. "What do you mean, 'if'?"

"Well," Ketch began again. Here goes nothing, he thought. This is it, the big kahuna. Though his heart rate was elevated now and he had to work at it, he continued to keep his cool. Just a few more minutes, that was all it would take – and then everything would be right with his world again. "Here's the deal. I won't report this if you do two things. First, you see to it these drums get salvaged and disposed of properly, according to the law. Second, you promise to stop trying to take my house. In writing."

Ingram's eyes widened and then he let out a great bark of a laugh, startling Ketch back into his seat. "Are you kiddin' me? You tryin' to blackmail me? *Me*? Jesus H. Christ!" He stopped laughing and swept the pictures from his desk onto the floor. "Who the hell do you think you are?" He rose from his chair and pointed a finger at Ketch. "Blackmail is illegal, sir! Get out of my office before I call the sheriff!"

Ketch felt his face redden. This wasn't turning out

to be quite as easy as he'd hoped. "It isn't blackmail, it's a business deal. You do something for me, I do something for you. Weasels like you must make backroom deals like this all the time."

"What? You're callin' me names now?" Ingram exploded. "Damn you! I should call the sheriff on you right now!"

"Go ahead," Ketch said. "It'll be your word against mine. And I'll call the Coast Guard, and then maybe you'll get fined and run out of money and I won't have to worry about my house anyway." He stood and pointed a finger of his own, surprising himself again with his audacity. "You have one hour to decide, and then I'm calling the Coast Guard." He started to turn toward the door.

"God damn it!" Ingram was shouting now. "I will *not* be ordered around by the likes of *you*! Get out!"

Ingram was bluffing; he'd see reason, he'd call. He had to – didn't he? "You can keep the pictures for your scrapbook, along with the ones of your murdered wives," Ketch tossed back over his shoulder, in what he thought was a nice noir touch.

A second later something whizzed past said shoulder, ricocheted loudly off the far wall, and bounced across a table. It looked like a paperweight. Ketch spun around in surprise. "You son of a bitch, I said *get the hell out*!" Ingram bellowed, groping this time for a rather large stapler.

Ketch fumbled with the knob for a moment that seemed to last forever, then got the door open and himself out of the room before anything else could come flying at him. He took a few shaky steps down the hall toward a rest room he'd noticed earlier. He went in, locked himself in a stall, and leaned against the wall. He was dizzy and having trouble catching his breath.

When he felt he could walk again, he cautiously exited the rest room into the fortunately empty hallway, then stood as straight as he could and marched back outside to his truck, ignoring the curious stares of the employees in the reception area. Joette started to follow him out and tried to say something to him, but he didn't know nor care what and didn't acknowledge her. He climbed into his truck, quickly put it in gear, and spun out of the parking lot.

He made it back to the house safely, though he'd driven on autopilot and wouldn't remember anything about the drive later. He stormed in and went immediately to his bathroom, paying no attention to the dog's initially excited attempts to greet him. Seeing that his face in the mirror was alarmingly red, he ran the water as cold as possible and splashed copious amounts of it over his head, then held both of his wrists under the faucet for a while. Though it was but a dim and vague memory now, the dog had seen behavior like this before and quietly held back, watching Ketch closely.

When Ketch abruptly stomped out to the kitchen without bothering to towel off, the dog followed but kept his distance. Ketch grabbed a couple of bottles of beer from the refrigerator and went out to the front porch. The dog made it through behind him before the screen door slammed shut. While Ketch ensconced himself in a chair and worked at twisting open one of the bottles, the dog discreetly went down to the yard, did what he had to do, and returned to the porch. He again took up a position near Ketch, but not too near, and lay down and continued to observe.

Ketch essentially chugged the first bottle, then immediately popped the second one. He was calmer now and would sip this one more slowly. He put his feet up on a table and finally noticed the freshly and neatly trimmed lawn. It looked better than when he did it himself.

"Well, that's something," he said aloud. "Might not matter much now, though." He'd have to remember to put the mower away later. The dog, encouraged, crept a little closer to test the waters. Though Ketch had never hit him, he wasn't quite sure what to expect next.

"Jack," he said. The dog's ears pricked up. "Come here, boy." The dog got up and went to Ketch and rested his head in Ketch's lap. Ketch softly stroked his head and neck, and the dog relaxed.

"I'm sorry, boy. You're a good boy," he said. He continued to pet the dog for a while and sipped at his beer. "So, what do we do now?" he unproductively inquired of the dog. Things certainly hadn't worked out the way he'd hoped. He hadn't thought much about what the ramifications would be if his little ploy tanked, as it apparently had. There was probably no way in hell Ingram would let him sell now – he'd just seize the house, to save time and maybe out of spite as well. But still, even if Ingram ignored Ketch's ultimatum and failed to call, wasn't there a chance that turning him in to the feds might have some effect on the bastard's immediate plans? Doubtful, but possible.

He found himself wondering why life had to be so hard for him, then mentally reprimanded himself. Granted some parts of his life had gotten messed up along the way – okay, some major parts – but it was generally he who'd messed them up, truth be told; and he knew life was a lot harder than this for an awful lot of other people in the world. At least he didn't have to eat bugs for lunch. Closer to home, he thought of his father, who'd grown up during the Depression and had been a fighter pilot in World War II. Everyone else from his flight class had died in that war, but he'd gotten lucky. Not so much afterward, though; there hadn't been money for college and though they hadn't technically been poor, there were not a lot of extras when Ketch was growing up. The only truly useful thing he'd inherited from his father was a stack of durable work bandanas, most of which he still used.

Ketch had never had to serve his country. Viet Nam had lurked in the background when he'd gone off to college, but he'd had a student deferment and the draft had ended before he graduated. So he didn't have any post-traumatic stress disorder to use as a crutch or an excuse for his troubles, nor substance abuse problems, physical infirmities, or unusual personal tragedies, no more so than most middle-class Americans normally had to deal with; he only had his own defective self to blame.

He started to nod off in his chair after he finished the second beer; he tried to sit up a little straighter to forestall it, but then thought, what the hell, why not? Every day was Saturday now, right, since he was retired? Though more often than not, he'd found it to be like a Saturday with all the Saturday chores. But sleeping had always been his best defense against unpleasantness, so he let it happen.

A single bark from the dog woke him some time later. He winced when he sat up; his head felt like someone had put a bucket over it and was banging on it with a wooden spoon. Squinting, he panned his eyes around the yard to see what was bothering the dog, which turned out to be Kari's car pulling into the driveway.

It looked like she was in a hurry. She barely gave the car time to come to a stop before hopping out and bounding up the front steps. "Are you okay?" she asked Ketch. She gave him a quick hug, then sat in a nearby chair and gave the dog a pat. "Hey, Jack, good boy. So?"

"I guess I'm okay," he said, a bit puzzled. Why was she here? "I fell asleep."

"Joette stopped by the shop on her lunch break. She told me what happened with you at the realtor's. I stuck a note on the door, locked up, and came right over. She was worried about you."

"Really? Well, you can tell her I have a headache, but I'm fine otherwise."

"Are you?" she frowned at him. "Look, I know I said I'd mind my own business, but maybe you should tell me what's goin' on with you, do you think? I mean, I'm worried about you too. Maybe there's some way I could help."

Ketch frowned back at her. He actually didn't feel all that great, and he wasn't ready to do this right now. Why couldn't people just leave him alone? "I could ask you the same thing, you know."

"Huh? What do you mean?"

"I mean, what's going on with *you*? For example, why do you need money, who bruised your arm, how's the fumigating going, and why are you practically living here now?" he rattled off, immediately regretting having done so.

She remained calm and regarded him evenly while he rubbed at the back of his head. "I'm goin' inside to get you a cold drink and somethin' for your headache. I'll be right back," she said.

Damn; he shouldn't have done that. While she was gone, he decided to check his phone in case he'd been sleeping too soundly. Nope, no missed calls from Ingram, just the three from the Captain that had accumulated since yesterday and which he'd been ignoring, and it had been well over an hour now. So, the game was afoot... He'd better assemble his packages for the Coast Guard and the EPA, and put Mario and Len to work on those floats. Would it take them more than a week? Maybe not, if he could get them to hustle – but then, would he even have a week before Ingram lowered the boom? And would he have a week if the Coast Guard went after Mario? Maybe they wouldn't be able to identify Mario's boat from the pictures. Oh, and he should make sure he picked up his tanks for Saturday, if he could still take the time to play divemaster then; should he, or not? And... He should stop overtaxing his brain and get rid of this headache. But first of all, he should apologize, something he knew he'd never done enough of in the past.

"I got you a pop, figured you might could use some caffeine," she said, returning with his drink and pills.

"Thank you," he began. "Now, before you say anything else, I want to apologize. I have a headache and I'm frustrated. I shouldn't take it out on you, and I'm sorry I did that." There, that wasn't so hard; in fact, just saying it was making him feel a little better already.

"Well, okay, I guess you're forgiven. Did you have any lunch at all? No? All right then, I'll go back and fix you a sandwich. You just rest here and come on in when you're ready."

He took his pills and her advice, and tried to relax. Though he'd managed to extract himself from the self-pitying mindset he'd started falling into earlier, he had to allow himself the opinion that life, his and everyone else's, was seldom simple; it's often more than just the joy and pain of the path followed, it can also encompass alternate paths, the endless permutations of branches and forks not taken, the stuff of remorse and regret, all crowded together in one finite mind struggling to understand – if you let it. No wonder we get headaches, he thought – and with that thought, he decided to think of nothing.

Which was easier said than done – but still, after a short while he felt considerably better. "Come on, Jack, let's have lunch," he said to the dog, who had stayed with him instead of following Kari despite the possibility of food. Ketch was impressed; he'd make sure he saved some of his sandwich for the dog.

When Ketch entered the kitchen, Kari said, "Before you sit down, let me hug your neck," and proceeded to give him a long warm body hug that pretty much took care of the rest of the headache. He saw she'd made up a plate for herself as well. They sat down to eat.

"I didn't get lunch either today, hope you don't mind," she said.

"Of course not. What's mine is yours."

"Yeah, well, about that... I don't have to stay here anymore, my apartment is livable. You know, if you're gettin' tired of me bein' around." When Ketch attempted to protest, she cut him off. "No, I understand, believe me, if you need some alone time. I do too, from time to time. It's not a big deal."

"I see," he said, then stopped. He knew he'd already been nosing around the hook, and for longer than just this past week; was he now on the verge of also taking the line and sinker? Well, if he was, then so be it. Realistically, at his age there might not be enough time left to permit the luxury of procrastination; he should either do it or get off the pot. What was the worst that could happen? "The truth is," he started, "I'm getting used to having you around, and I like having you around." He looked down at his plate and cleared his throat. "I've always been fond of you, and a lot more so lately. I hope you'll stay as long as you like."

"Really? You really mean that?" she said, brightening. He nodded. "Well okay then! But tell you what, let's get a couple things straight before we go any further. I told you my apartment's tolerable now, so don't be shy about kickin' me out for a while if you need to. I'm not itchin' to move in with you for good, not right now anyway. This is sorta like a little vacation for me, that's all, which is somethin' I don't often get. And I always need money, you know that. And for the record, I've mostly been hangin' around here because I think I'm fallin' for you too. So there you go!" she concluded, and rose to clear the dishes.

So, now he'd gone and done it. He felt his stomach drop, but he wasn't sure if it was from giddiness or dismay. Oddly enough, he thought it might be both, not unlike the mixed emotions he recalled experiencing while watching the terrorist attack on the World Trade Center in New York City on live TV years ago. He'd since read somewhere that this was not an atypical reaction to certain kinds of disasters. Was this then a disaster in the making? He guessed time would tell.

He noted that she hadn't said anything about her arm, which raised a small flag, but maybe that was just an overly suspicious artifact of his new detective persona. But even if she wasn't yet telling him the whole truth, he decided that if she was going to be an integral part of his life from here on, then he should proceed with his plan and be honest and come clean with her. If you want to have a good neighbor, you have to be a good neighbor, right? He probably didn't have a choice anyway, practically speaking – which went for the Captain, too, of course.

"Well, it's good you're not giving up your apartment just yet, because I may not be in this house much longer." In response to her not unexpected look of concerned surprise, he continued, "I have a story to tell you, but the Captain also needs to hear it, and it would be easier to tell it once. So I'm going to go give him a call. If he's available later, what time would be good for you?"

"Uh huh. Okay, I'll try to be patient. Any time at all is fine with me, I'm not goin' back to the shop today. I'd only be open a couple more hours or so anyway, and you and I both know I probably won't be missin' out on much."

Ketch went out onto the deck to make his call, and to pick up his beer bottles; if he forgot about them and left them there, especially overnight God forbid, his deck could turn into Roach City. He was able to placate the somewhat irate Captain by promising to explain absolutely everything to him later and offering to come to him at the boatyard; and also by promising to bring shrimp, hush puppies, and beer.

"He's out and about right now, so we'll bring supper down to the *Minnow* later," he called as he reentered the house. "Kari?"

"In here," she called back from his bedroom. When

he entered the darkened room and saw her lying naked and smiling at him on the bed, all he could do was smile back. "I should have known," he said.

"I just figured we should do somethin' useful while we're waitin'. And then you can take a nap after, I bet you could use one." She patted the mattress. "Come on now, time's a-wastin'!"

~ **F o u r t e e n** ~

Forgoing unnecessary chatter while at sea was considered a virtue.

*B*ut though they'd be on a boat, it would remain docked. The Captain started pawing through the bags as soon as Ketch and Kari arrived with the dog in tow. "Dirty Dick's hush puppies – nothin' finer!" he exclaimed, popping one into his mouth. "Srimp's good too. And crab pops? I must a died and gone to heaven!" The dog moved closer to him and sat and wagged.

"Not so loud, we didn't bring enough for everyone in the boatyard," Ketch said while Kari set places for them at the Captain's table. "And be sure to save a few of those hush puppies for Jack," Kari added, "we got more than enough."

The Captain tossed one to the dog, who caught it in the air. "And I see you brought the right beer. You, sir, are almost forgiven – almost!"

After Ketch opened the bottle of wine he'd brought, they all sat down and started to dig in. The sun hadn't quite started to drop yet, and the bugs weren't bad and it wasn't unbearably hot, and the drinks were cold. Pleasantly muted music wafted across the still water from one of the houseboats. The setting was peaceful, certainly more so than the new Dirty Dick's would have been if they'd decided to eat there; though their food was excellent as always, it was crowded and noisy and it lacked the old-timey atmosphere Ketch had appreciated at their previous location. He still liked to eat there occasionally, but he had to be in the mood for it. A fine, quiet evening like this at the old boatyard was eminently preferable to him most of the time. Too bad the place was doomed.

"God, I do love this wine!" Kari said to him. "You've got yourself into some trouble with this, mister. I don't think I can drink that old stuff anymore."

"Oh, so you're going to turn high-maintenance on me now, are you?"

"Hey, I'm not *that* high-maintenance! And even if I get to be, you know I'm worth it!" she declared with a suggestive smirk.

"So you're with this damn yankee now? I knew it," the Captain said. "Ketch, you dawg! But hey, get a room, I got bidness with ole Lucy here," he admonished. "For starters, Mister Storm Ketchum, tell me if you please what in holy hell were you doin' out in the middle a the dang ocean yesterday in that bathtub toy a yours? You like to worried me half to death!"

"What?" Kari exploded, almost choking on a hush puppy. "How do you know about that? I didn't know." She turned to look at Ketch. "I thought you were cleanin' your boat!" Her face started to color. "What exactly did you do with that tank I gave you?"

"All in good time," Ketch said, raising his hands to forestall further inquiries. "It's a long story, and it would be better if I started at the beginning."

And so he finally did, starting with the series of letters he'd received from Ingram offering to purchase *Port Starbird* for a barely acceptable price. He told how they'd progressively escalated in tone, culminating in the ultimatum that threatened imminent seizure via eminent domain at an even lower price.

"So now he's just gonna take it? How can he do that?" Kari asked in disbelief.

"I told you," the Captain said. "Did you talk to a lawyer?"

Ketch tried to give a succinct explanation (which wasn't easy) of how eminent domain worked and how it was being abused these days in North Carolina and elsewhere, and why Ingram thought he could get away with what he was doing. "And no, I haven't talked to a lawyer. I've done my homework, and I think it would be a waste of time and money to hire a lawyer to tell me what I already know. There are ways I might be able to delay him for a while, but I don't believe I can legally stop him – short of some extraordinary event like finding an ancient burial ground or some unique organism that would become extinct. Though it's a little strange," he mused, "I ran into him after our charter on Monday, and he offered me one more week to sell, even though I'd missed his deadline. I think it was because he'd save money and avoid legal hassles that way, that's all. It certainly wasn't because he's a nice guy, I can tell you that, the smug bastard."

"Well then, why don't you just sell out like everybody else?" the Captain asked. "Sounds like you'd get more money that way at least."

"Because I refuse to, that's why. You know how I feel about this island, and this town. I'm against that man and everything he stands for, and there's no way in hell I will ever cooperate with the likes of him." Ketch paused and then sheepishly added, "Besides, I doubt that offer still holds. I insulted him and made him pretty angry."

"Down at Oden's, this was? No wonder you was off your feed on the way back."

"Yes, and again just this morning – which Kari already knows something about. But I'll get to that soon."

"Why didn't you tell us about all this before?" she asked.

"Oh, he told me some of it early on," the Captain said, "but he's been holdin' out on me ever since. You, he ain't been close with that long – but when me and him's been good friends like we have, that kinda ticks me off, I have to say."

"Well, I'm sorry, I really am," Ketch apologized. "I figured it was my problem, and there was nothing anyone else could do to help. I think I was a little depressed about it too, and I didn't want to bother you with all that. But I should have told you."

"Damn right," the Captain said. "Even if we can't do squat about it, we're your friends. Now tell me 'bout them floats you got at the house. If you ain't gonna be livin' there, why in hell you wanna spend all that money'n do all that work?"

"They weren't cheap, but they're one of the

cheaper options, and it wasn't as much money as you think. Plus the company doesn't charge for delivery in North Carolina," Ketch added weakly. Well, here we go, he thought – here's where they'll probably start beating him over the head with something in earnest. "The protests and petitions of the environmentalists and preservationists didn't accomplish anything, as you know," he continued, "and the politicians in this state don't seem to be motivated to do anything about eminent domain abuses right now. I know I can't stop Ingram's project either, but I thought of a way I could help bring more attention to those issues, maybe even on a national scale, and the more people become aware of these things, the more likely it might be that something will be eventually be done about them. So..." he took a deep breath. "I'm converting *Port Starbird* into a floating house. I'm going to float it out into the sound and anchor it there, I'm going to tell the media why I did it, and I'm going to embarrass crooks like Ingram and the politicians they have in their pockets. I hope," he concluded, and then braced himself.

To his great surprise, the Captain let out a great whoop. "What the hell! Are you kiddin' me? Oh, that's rich!" he howled. "I love it!"

"Huh!" Kari said with a shell-shocked look on her face. After a bit she commented, "Well, I think it's kinda crazy – okay, maybe just extreme, not crazy – no, *way* extreme – but I guess it might could work. It sure would get you some attention anyway. But how can you do that? If you do it before you lose the house, wouldn't you get less money, and if you do it after, wouldn't you be stealin' somebody else's property?"

"I'll do it right after the eminent domain settlement is directly deposited in my bank account. I suppose it won't be legal, but Ingram might not file a complaint. It would make him look even worse in the public eye, and he's only going to demolish it anyway, so I'll actually be saving him money by moving it off my lot. That's the one part of this whole thing I don't especially like."

"The *one* part?" the Captain snorted. "That's the only part you don't like?" he got out before dissolving into a series of belly laughs. When he could breathe again, he said, "I'm sorry, I know this mess ain't really all that funny, but I couldn't help it, it just tickled me." He pulled out a handkerchief and wiped at his eyes. "Okay, so here's a thought – even if Ingram and the cops don't bother you, what are you gonna do if the Coast Guard gets after you? What if they end up makin' you pay to tow it somewhere and scrap it?"

"I don't know, I haven't thought much about that yet. But even if that happened, the publicity might be worth it. I know I'm not wealthy, but I'm getting old, and you can't take it with you."

"You're not *that* old," Kari said. "Who knows, you might live another fifty years."

"Well, I'd probably still have some savings left, plus my pension and Social Security later on. And if they wait long enough to act, maybe I can claim squatter's rights and gain adverse possession of whatever property I'm floating over. I read about that, too. Or maybe I could find a boatyard or marina somewhere that would take me."

"I guess you really did do some homework. You sound like a dang lawyer," the Captain said.

"Okay, so what about the secret mission you went on in your boat?" Kari asked. "I think it's time we heard what that was all about."

"All right, but you might not like this part very much," Ketch said, meaning specifically three parts, actually – the part about him following her old boyfriend to Roanoke, the part about Mick and Mario illegally dumping the drums, and the part about him diving alone. He managed to get through it all with minimal interruptions, mainly because he insisted on brooking none this time until he was done.

"So, there's that part of the story," he finished. "All this talking is parching my throat," he said, and took a break to pay some attention to the beer he'd been neglecting.

"I can't believe you went divin' like that all by yourself," Kari said, shaking her head. "That was really dangerous. You know that, right? You better not ever do it again, I'll tell you that, or me and you are gonna have a serious problem. I can't believe you did that," she repeated.

"I know," Ketch said, "and again, I'm sorry. I should have asked for your help. Both of you."

"Well, at least you had enough sense to give me your position just in case," the Captain said. "But still... Christ, man, you could a got seriously hurt out there all by your lonesome – and maybe if those two scallywags had caught on to you too."

"I wish I could say I also can't believe Mick did all that, but I'm not real surprised," Kari said. In an apparent attempt to make amends for her recent sternness, she added in as deep a baritone as she could manage, "He's a sneaky little shit, just like you."

"The dean in *Animal House*," Ketch said with a relieved smile. "Yes, I guess I am. And again, I apologize for that."

Kari gave him a quick smile back, then got serious again. "So what does all this have to do with your house?" she asked. "It seems like a totally separate thing."

"Well," Ketch said, "I guess that brings us to what happened at HatterasMann Realty this morning. Which is the final part of this story, I promise."

"I recall you said somethin' 'bout pissin' Ingram off this mornin'," the Captain said. "What happened, you go down to his place? How come?"

"Well, it turned out there is a connection between my house and that toxic waste business. I found out Bob Ingram now runs Tibbleson Construction, because it was his wife's business. The second one. So that makes Ingram criminally liable for what Mick and Mario did. I researched that as well. If I report the illegal dumping to the Coast Guard and the EPA, Ingram could be heavily fined, and possibly jailed, for felonies under the Clean Water Act and the Ocean Dumping Act, and maybe the Hazardous Materials Transportation Act."

"That's interestin'. And you have pictures..." the

Captain mused. "Wait, don't tell me, lemme guess –
you tried to put the squeeze on the man to save your
house, and he didn't react real well to that. Am I
right?" Ketch didn't have to verbally corroborate the
Captain's theory; that was basically it in a nutshell,
and a single rueful nod sufficed.

"He sure didn't," Kari said. "I saw Joette after, she
works there, and she said Ingram was hollerin' and
throwin' stuff at Ketch at the end of it."

"Throwin' things? No shit!" the Captain chuckled.
"I gotta tell ya, you sure know how to get on the right
side a folks. You ought to run for somethin'!", he
added before succumbing to another series of
convulsions. "Oh lordy, I'm sorry," he said, wiping his
eyes again. "I just can't help it. I wish I could a seen
that!"

Ketch stood. "I need a break," he said. On his way
back from the head, he glanced around the darkening
boatyard and noticed Mario on the deck of his trawler
a few slips over. When he returned to his seat at the
table, said scallywag was coincidentally the current
topic of conversation.

"I gotta tell ya, I don't really know Mick, can't
hardly remember what he looks like even," the
Captain was saying. "But I'm real disappointed with
Mario."

"I am, too," Ketch said. "But I still like him
anyway, odd as that may seem. I decided I'm not
going to mention either of their names when I report
the dumping to the authorities – which I'm going to
do anonymously, by the way – and not just because he

offered to help with the house. He's just trying to get by, and I only care about netting Tibbleson and Ingram. If they figure out on their own that it was Mick and Mario and they end up being prosecuted, I can't help that, but it won't be because I ratted on them. So I'd appreciate it if you'd both refrain from mentioning any of this to Mario."

Kari and the Captain promised they wouldn't. "What about the other part, though, losin' the house? It'll probably get around anyways," the Captain asked.

"I don't care anymore who knows about that," Ketch replied. "Everyone will know when it's floating out in the sound. But I'm not going through all this storytelling again. I'm not like you," he said, directing this remark to the Captain, "I find it exhausting. So if someone else wants to tell it, okay, and do it when I'm not around."

Exhausting, yes – but also cathartic, Ketch realized. Finally telling his story to Kari and the Captain hadn't changed anything, as he'd known it wouldn't; but he was gratified to know he had their empathy and their support, and he felt like a great weight had been lifted from him. The difference between these folks and a therapist was, these people cared about him, and that was a world of difference to him. Also, they were cheaper. He wished he'd done this sooner.

He wondered how things might have turned out if he'd had friends like these a few years earlier – when, he knew now, he'd been in real danger of running completely off the rails. The divorce, still a source of angst though many years had passed; the estrangement from his son; the loss of his parents and his dog, all in the same year; his career, such as it was...

He'd gotten hired as a researcher at a pharmaceutical company after the Ph.D., and had gradually moved away from the lab and into clinical data analysis as he'd developed his computer skills, initially as a hobby, along with that then-emerging technology – and despite his value to the company (though admittedly self-perceived), he along with a goodly number of the other employees had been overworked and underpaid, and basically treated like dirt in many respects by the soulless corporate machine. There'd been some casual friends, but he'd been essentially alone at that time and just watching the wheels go round and round, as John Lennon had put it; he'd felt like a powerless bystander just growing a little older every day as things around him kept changing for the worse, if they changed at all – and there came a point when he just hadn't been able to stand it all anymore.

He might have had a nervous breakdown or something enough like one, or a severely deep depression at least; but his innate obstinacy had fortunately precluded thoughts of suicide. He'd be damned if he'd ever kill himself; his attitude was, if I'm feeling bad enough to think about doing that, then I want to know who it is who's making me feel that way – and that's who I'll kill. But instead of going postal, he simply dropped out. He'd been there long enough to retire early and start collecting a pension, so that's what he did; and when he did that, he moved to Avon.

Kari's siren voice put an end to his introspection; and he decided he was glad to be here now, despite everything, and he had no desire to be anywhere else. "Do you think bein' charged with those felonies you talked about might slow Ingram down?" she asked. "Maybe he won't be able to afford to keep on with his project if he gets a big fine. Maybe he won't take your house!"

"I thought about that – and in fact, I pointed that out to him this morning, but he didn't seem impressed. Investigations and legal actions take time, and even more so once the lawyers get involved, so it probably wouldn't happen soon enough."

"Huh, that's too bad."

"You know, gettin' that house in the water is only the beginnin'," the Captain observed. "You're gonna have to do a lot more work on it to make it livable, you thought about that?"

"Yes, I know. I have a rather large to-do list already for that," Ketch said. "But I decided to be practical about it. I might not be able to go on living there, as you mentioned earlier, so before I spend a lot of time and money on it, first I'll just do some minimal things to make it 'campable', so to speak. Like maybe get a chemical toilet, a generator, a battery-powered lantern, some of those big jugs of water..."

"Hola, amigos! Permission to come aboard,

Cap'n?"

"Mario! Come on in," the Captain said. "Oh hey, you got Len there with you too? Well, you boys just grab yourselves a cool one and set on down, we'll make room."

"Sure we're not interruptin'? Okay, thanks!" Len said, "We heard y'all bustin' a gut over here, and we wondered what's so dang funny?"

"Ah, well, you had to be there," the Captain said. "Say, bring me another one a them bottles if you don't mind, I'm too fat and lazy to get up since I ate all that good stuff these other two here brung me. And speakin' of, there's some left over if you're in the mood for some munchies. Which, knowin' you two, wouldn't surprise me," he insinuatingly added.

"Thanks, man, don't mind if I do," Mario said, sampling a hush puppy.

"So Ketch, what you wanna do 'bout them floats?" Len asked. "Today was my last day on the job, I quit that ole mess."

"Well, you can get started whenever you're ready. Is tomorrow too soon?"

"Heck no, we can do that, right bro?" Len said.

"Sure, why not?" Mario agreed. "But we still need some equipment, right? So how about if we stop by in the mornin' and check things out? And then we can go get what we need and get to work in the afternoon, or Saturday, dependin'."

"That sounds great – and thank you again for doing this, I really appreciate it. I'll go to the ATM in the morning so I can give you cash for whatever you need. But Captain, that reminds me, I was thinking I should pass on Saturday's dive charter, with all this going on. Are you okay with that?"

"Oh hey, sure, no problem. Them particular boys don't really need a divemaster, and I can get by without a mate since they ain't gonna be fishin'. They're locals, so I can get one a them to handle the lines and such."

Ketch and Kari stayed through one more drink and then made their farewells. When they were about to get in her car to return to the house, Ketch said, "It's such a nice night, it's too bad we can't just walk back. I think Jack would enjoy it, too, after lying around on the boat all evening."

"Well, why can't we? It's not that far, and we can get the car tomorrow. You could walk me back, or you could drive me back, or I could walk back by myself... Anythin's possible!" she laughed.

"You're right. Okay, let's get walking then," he said, and they left the car behind. "Do you really believe that anything is possible? I think there are things that are obviously impossible – I'm not going to sprout horns before we get back to the house, for example – but I think I believe it on a grander scale. I agree with Douglas Adams."

"Huh? What do you mean? Who's that?"

"Douglas Adams wrote some very clever books. Have you heard of *The Hitchhiker's Guide to the Galaxy*? That's my favorite of his. Anyway, Conan Doyle, in his Sherlock Holmes stories, said that when you've eliminated the impossible, what remains must be true, however improbable. Well, Adams added a corollary to that. He said you should also consider that when you've eliminated the improbable, what remains might be true, even if it seems impossible."

"I see – I think. Tray deep, O Wise One. Hey, speakin' of Sherlock Holmes, you really are a sneaky little shit, you know that? I can't believe you were off doin' all those crazy things all week long, and I was stayin' at your house and I didn't have a clue!"

"I know, and again, I'm sorry about that."

"Oh please, will you stop sayin' that? I think you've said 'sorry' more'n enough times already for one night. I'm over it, mostly anyway. I won't hold it against you – not 'til we get home, anyway, if you catch my meanin'."

"Subtlety is not one of your many talents, my dear."

"Nor one of yours, sir. I know you were jealous."

"Jealous? Of what?"

"All that detective stuff you did, followin' folks around, hoodwinkin' Mario so you could get to his GPS, takin' all those pictures, gettin' that dirt on Ingram – that all happened because you followed Mick, which you did because you were jealous."

"I was curious, not jealous."

"Uh huh, you just keep tellin' yourself that. Meanwhile, mister noir detective, I was wonderin' before, how did you distract Mario so you could look at his GPS?"

After a short internal debate, Ketch decided to tell her. What the hell, he'd told her everything else. "I got him to roll some joints for me."

"Ha! Are you kiddin' me?"

"No. Why don't we try one tonight and see what happens? I mean, since we're being so adventurous already, walking home and all. But please, tell absolutely no one where I got them. I don't want to be responsible for getting Mario busted for that, either."

"Okay, you got it. Wow – you really are breakin' bad these days, huh? I like it!"

"Anything for you, milady," he said – and meant it, for now anyway.

~ Fifteen ~

*When we start living outside ourselves is
when it gets dangerous.*

They both arose at the same time the next morning, at Ketch's usual hour and more than usually a bit on the silly side, and drove the dog to a north end beach this time for a relatively short, but to Ketch still soul-soothing, sunrise hike. They parked the truck at the Avon Pier and picked up some takeout breakfast from there to bring back to the house, to avoid missing the promised arrival of Mario and Len. Ketch had made a quick stop at the ATM and then dropped Kari off at the boatyard to pick up her car on their way back, and she'd gone to the shop after breakfast. Ketch and the dog were now relaxing on the front deck, Ketch with his laptop and the dog with a new filled bone to gnaw on.

He'd originally wanted to generate glossy photos from his digital files to send to the authorities, as neither the pictures he'd taken on Roanoke nor the underwater ones had looked that great when he'd printed them out. But he'd learned he'd have to drive to another town to have that done, which he didn't want to take the time to do this morning since Len and Mario might show up at any moment. He still wanted to make his report and get his evidence into play as soon as possible, though. Who knew, maybe it might help stall Ingram — though realistically, he doubted it. But it was worth taking the shot.

The images looked fine on the computer screen, and considerably better than they had on the printouts he'd left behind in Ingram's office during his hasty retreat yesterday morning – which he could now chuckle a little about as well as the others, he discovered. He'd made the right choice last night.

He knew from his earlier research that he could submit an incident report online, which would certainly be faster than snail-mailing one anyway, and maybe he could attach the picture files to it. But he'd wanted to do it anonymously, and they'd want his e-mail address and other personal information. Well, he could easily create a new e-mail account on Google with a fake name and phone number, right? They could trace the IP address back to him if they really wanted to, though – unless he used Tor, free open source software that provided anonymity, which he also didn't have yet. He could download it sometime, but he didn't feel like doing it at the moment. They'd need to get a court order to identify him, and would they go to all that trouble? He didn't think so.

But if they tried to call and couldn't reach him, they might think it was just a hoax, some smartass kid horsing around on a computer. If he didn't name Mick and Mario, what would be the harm in letting the authorities know who he was? His friends now knew what was going on and he didn't care if Ingram found out about it, as he'd already told the man what he was going to do and it shouldn't come as a surprise to him; and if Mick ever got caught and found out who had reported the violations, he could legitimately feign innocence. Okay then, he'd play it straight.

He navigated to the NRC link he'd bookmarked. The National Response Center, he read, was now the national contact point for reporting all illegal discharges of all potential environmental pollutants anywhere in the United States and its territories. It in turn reported to numerous federal agencies including the White House and Homeland Security if necessary, and worked with the Coast Guard and the EPA. It looked like this outfit did a heck of a lot more as well, including getting involved in national disasters, transportation of munitions, and in fact just about everything under the sun that might have anything to do with the environment, national security, public health issues, or any combination thereof. The NRC had a National Response Team (NRT), Federal On-Scene Coordinators (FOSC), Regional Response Teams (RRT), an EPA Response Team (ERT), a Coast Guard National Strike Force (NSF), and a slew of other sub-entities. The superabundance of ominous-looking acronyms made him a little leery; he wondered how much of a shitstorm he might be about to unleash.

It had to be done, though. And it also said here that he should expect to be contacted with an official NRC Report Number within thirty minutes after submitting an online report, via e-mail it sounded like. He found a snail mail address as well, and a toll-free number – but online was definitely the way to go for him, he decided, so he clicked on the link to the online reporting app and got started.

It didn't take long; except for some text to describe the event, he only filled in the starred fields. He didn't know what kinds of materials were in the drums, nor the quantities, so that made things easier. He was of course able to give the coordinates for the dumping location, thanks to his stellar sleuthing, and he named Tibbleson Construction as the offender. He entered 'UNKNOWN' for the name of the vessel, and gave no names of any of the individuals involved; they could find out who ran things at Tibbleson pretty easily on their own, he figured, and as he'd decided earlier, he wasn't going to be the one to implicate Mick and Mario. He was disappointed to find no way to attach his picture files, but there was a box where he could make additional comments, so he used that to state he had pictures and could e-mail them if necessary.

So, that was that. He pushed the button and launched what he'd done out into the ether. Now all he could do was wait. He reminded himself to remember to check his e-mail later.

Before he shut the laptop down, he decided to take another look at the pictures. The faded stenciling on the stern of Mario's boat had definitely been indecipherable in the printouts, and he hoped the same would be true when the pictures were viewed on the screen. Ah, good – you couldn't make out the name of the boat that way, either.

Glancing through the rest of the gallery, he came across an anomaly in one of the photos that hadn't caught his eye in the lower-quality printouts. It looked like one of those larger 85-gallon salvage drums had something with what appeared to be orange and yellow stripes on it sticking out from under the lid. He didn't recall noticing it either when he'd been at the bottom of the ocean taking the picture, but that wasn't strange as everything had been shades of blue and green to his eyes due to the absorption of the red and yellow wavelengths of the sunlight at that depth; those colors would have only been visible to him during the momentary camera flash and if he'd shined his dive light directly on that spot, which he apparently hadn't.

Now what could that be? He zoomed in some on it and was able to determine that it wasn't a discoloration or label on the surface of the drum, nor did it appear to be any marine organism that he knew of. It was kind of wavy and floating maybe an inch or two from the side of the drum – that is, its free end was not attached to the drum, and the other end was definitely protruding from under the ring clamp that surrounded the edge of the lid. It wasn't very thick, and it looked too flexible to be plastic unless it was something like a household trash bag; but he'd never seen orange and yellow striped trash bags. Maybe a plastic shopping bag? But then it probably wouldn't be undulating in the current in that manner. Could it be part of a flag or a sign, a piece of detritus that had blown or fallen into the drum while it was being sealed? It couldn't be paper; this particular drum had been there long enough to accumulate accretions, and a loose piece of paper like that wouldn't have remained intact for very long down there. So it was probably some kind of fabric. Part of an article of clothing, perhaps, like a scarf or a shirtsleeve? Or a bathing suit? Or maybe a dress?

A thought struck him then that made him sit up straight in his chair and almost caused him to drop the laptop – which startled the dog, who he had to take a moment to reassure. "It's okay, boy, I'm okay," he said as he gave the dog a distracted rub on the head. But no, it couldn't be – could it? That was crazy. Or was it? Could Mario have been dumping these drums every now and then for about the last, say, two or three years? Had he even been in town then? Ketch tried to remember. He doubted that, in the vast expanse of the Atlantic, someone else would have chosen the exact same dumping spot. Or maybe that drum had been stored somewhere for a while and then dumped into the sea later on.

Ingram's second wife had disappeared about three years ago, around the time Ketch had moved to Avon, and no one had ever been able to find out what had happened to her. No one even knew for sure whether she was alive or dead – she'd simply vanished into thin air. Was it so crazy to think her remains might in fact be inside that drum?

Ingram certainly had a hand in whatever went on at Tibbleson, so he could have arranged it; and though it would probably be hard to stuff a body into one of the 55-gallon ones, Ketch imagined it could be managed with a salvage drum. It would be a pretty effective way to dispose of a body; who would ever find it at the bottom of the ocean? Well, Ketch had, maybe – but if whoever unloaded the drum there had had half a brain and gone farther out to deeper water, no one would have ever found it. Maybe Mario or whoever it was hadn't known what was in the drum, and had just dumped it along with the rest of one of their usual loads. He hoped Mario hadn't known, if it had been him.

He checked the time on his laptop – 10:38 again. That was when he'd awakened the morning after his little house party, at the beginning of what had turned out to be a rather wild week for him – but also a strangely satisfying one as well in certain respects, such as the one he'd gone beachcombing with early this morning. It seemed like such a long time ago... That one he'd gone to the beach with just might be almost worth all the other aggravation, he thought – and it occurred to him that this picture might be worth even more.

He thought of an observation someone had made in some book he'd read that true happiness generally seems to go hand-in-hand with pain. Maybe that was really so, and maybe it was necessary; maybe if there was no strife or struggle to stimulate awareness, you couldn't really tell whether or not you were happy. Would a victory like the one this picture potentially represented be as savory without the occasional defeats in the mix to spice it up?

Well, we'll soon see what that picture's worth, he thought. He tried to quell his mounting excitement for the time being and focus on the here and now. Len and Mario must be keeping banker's hours, he guessed, and it was getting hot out on the deck, so he started thinking about going back inside and giving the Captain a call.

Just then an old pickup truck pulled into the driveway, and the two of them stepped out and waved hello. As the dog descended the front steps to greet them, Ketch shut down his laptop. He'd have to see what Kari and the Captain thought about his theory as soon as possible, that was for sure; but for now he'd better settle himself down and deal with these guys. He tried to banish the thought of Mario as an accomplice to murder from his mind, and forced a smile onto his face.

"Hey, Ketch," Mario called. "Sorry we didn't get here sooner. Guess we're not much good at bein' early birds."

"Yeah, we don't catch too many worms down there at the boatyard," Len grinned. "But don't you worry, we'll git 'er done."

"I'm sure you will," Ketch said. "I'm not worried, and thanks again for coming. Let me show you how the blocks work, and then we can take a look under the house."

They discussed what additional materials they might need in order to attach the foam blocks to the underside of the house. Mario thought if they had three people, two could hold a block up while the third screwed it in, but Len disagreed, citing the cramped work space and the difficulty of holding a heavy weight over one's head for any length of time.

"Besides, no offense intended, but ole Ketch here

is gettin' a little gray around the gills," Len said. "He probly shouldn't be doin' this kind a work, and I don't imagine he wants to neither – that's why he hired us."

You got that right, Ketch thought; thanks for saving me yet again. "No offense taken, and you're right, I don't think I should get too physically involved with this," he said. Not to mention he was chafing at the bit and had no desire to spend any more time than strictly necessary on this at the moment. "I think you should get a couple of sawhorses and try using two hydraulic jacks with wood planks above and below, to hold up the blocks one at a time. I saw some reasonably priced jacks down at Ace Hardware a while back; it would be cheaper to just buy them instead of renting. I have enough extension cords, but I only have one power drill, so I think you should buy another one. If they don't have the lumber we need at Ace, you can get that at Dare Building Supply in Buxton."

"All right," Len said. "We might need some more lumber than that anyway. I'm thinkin' we shouldn't be screwin' these things into your floor, so I think we should put up some more crossbeams here and there. We can pick up some two-by-fours and four-by-fours and cut 'em to fit. You got a saw?"

"I have a circular saw, and hammers and nails," Ketch said.

"We might have to take the sides off your storage area under there to fit all those blocks in," Mario said, "but maybe not. Anyway, you okay with that, Ketch?"

"Yes, but save that part for last. Now let me make

you a list and give you some money. I think you should go get what you need and then try to install one block. If everything works out, you can do more after that, or you can come back tomorrow instead, whatever you want to do. Lastly, tell me what you like and I'll go pick up some subs for lunch."

"Thanks, Ketch, that's right nice of you!" Len said.

After he'd finally gotten them off on their errands, Ketch got the dog settled inside. It was too hot now to leave him in the truck. Who to talk to first? He stowed the laptop in his backpack and decided to head over to the shop. He figured he'd have time enough to quickly show Kari what he'd found in that picture and stop at Subway before Len and Mario returned.

Kari was glad to see him, but she actually had a customer for a change. She was able to wrap that up in just a few minutes. Ketch, fidgety as he was, decided to use the time to give the Captain a quick call on his cell phone. Good, now that was done.

"Well hey, this is a pleasant surprise!" she said with an easy smile when the customer was exiting. "To what do I owe the honor? How come you're not out detectin' somethin'? Gallant knight, have you come to take me away from all this?"

"Sorry, but no, not today. I can't stay long, I've got Len and Mario working at the house," he said as he booted the laptop on the counter. "I found something interesting that I wanted to show you, and I decided I couldn't wait until later. Come on, you dog," he said to the laptop. "I have a theory, and I want to know what you think about it. The Captain, too, I called him and asked him to meet us at the bar at the Froggy Dog later. Is that okay with you? Oh, good, here it comes, finally..."

"My goodness, you're just jabberin' away there, what in the world are you so hopped up about?" she asked, looking over his shoulder at the screen. "Is that the pictures you took this week?"

"Yes," he said, and then proceeded to show her what he'd found and told her what he thought it might mean. "So, what do you think?"

"Oh wow... Do you really think?" she said. "That's... I don't know..."

Ketch saw that her face had turned pale. "Are you all right?" he asked. "Are you going to be sick? Should I get you a chair?"

"I... No, thanks, I'll be okay. Maybe it was somethin' I ate, maybe there was somethin' wrong with that breakfast sandwich, I don't know, I been feelin' funny this mornin'." She took a deep breath. "Well, that's an interestin' theory. Did you send in your report on those drums yet?"

"Yes, why?"

"Well then, when the Coast Guard or whoever checks that out and salvages those drums, they'll find out the answer then, I guess, won't they?"

"Probably, assuming they'll do all that. But who knows how long that will take?" Conscious of her discomfort, he tried to rein in his enthusiasm as much as possible, but he wasn't entirely successful. "How many lift bags do you have here? I'd like to buy some."

"Lift bags? Yes, I have some, but why? Are you

thinkin' 'bout tryin' to raise that drum?"

"Yes! Don't you see? If Ingram's wife is in that drum, there could be DNA evidence. They could put him away for good with that, and then no more development! We'd be able to save not only *Port Starbird*, but also the boatyard and all the other properties that crook has tried to bully people into giving him!"

"Well," she said, still somewhat nonplussed, "that's certainly a noble thought. And if it's true? Wow. But what if it is her? Wouldn't it be a bad thing for us to tamper with the evidence? Maybe it wouldn't be admissible then."

"We wouldn't have to tamper with it. We can bring the drum to the surface, stabilize it, and crack open the lid just enough to take a peek inside. If it's what we think it is, we close the lid and radio the Coast Guard to come and get it. If it isn't, we just drop it back down to where it came from and go home."

"Huh. Well, I still don't know..." She considered for a moment. "You said Don's gonna meet us after work? How 'bout we wait and see what he thinks?"

"That's the plan," Ketch said. "Meanwhile, I've got to get going, I promised Len and Mario lunch from Subway." He drew her to him for a quick hug, and tried to inject a little levity into things. "Hey, you should be glad I'm listening to you, and not running right out there and doing it by myself again, right?"

"True," she said, extricating herself with a wan smile. "Okay then, come pick me up later when it's time."

"Right, see you then!" Ketch said as he stuffed the laptop into the backpack. "I hope you feel better soon," he called as he headed out the door.

On the way back from the Subway, he started to wonder whether he should have Len and Mario continue with their work or not. If Ingram's plans were finally scuttled, he wouldn't be needing those blocks after all. But then his new-found pragmatism asserted itself, and he decided he should proceed with his original plan. It wouldn't do to jump the gun, get disappointed somehow, and then be left in the lurch. Any number of things could go wrong – his theory might not pan out, Ingram could find some way to get himself off the hook even if it did, someone else could continue the development project... He'd certainly been burned before when he'd gotten his hopes up – most recently, just yesterday morning, for example. Had that only been yesterday? He again had the feeling he'd been caught in some kind of time warp this past week, so much had happened in such a short time...

Surprisingly, when he got back to the house Len and Mario were there and unloading their truck. There was also a bike leaning against the railing, and a boy sitting on the front steps. "Hello, Henry," Ketch called from his truck as he gathered up his backpack and the Subway bags.

"Hey, Mister Ketchum," the boy replied. "Need a hand with that stuff?"

"Yes, thank you." Ketch passed the bags to him. "What brings you around today, Henry?"

"I was just passin' by and I saw these guys cartin' stuff out of their truck. You doin' some work on the house?"

"Well, they are. I'm not doing much of it myself. Thanks for doing such a good job with the mowing, by the way."

"You're welcome. I can do it again next time too if you want. Say, do you think I could help those fellas out with whatever they're doin'?"

"I don't know. We could ask them. Would you like to have lunch with us? You could have half of my sub and some chips, I'm not all that hungry."

"Sure, that'd be great — thanks! I'll just call my mama quick, so she doesn't get to worryin'. You want these bags in the kitchen?"

Once the dog had gotten over his ecstasy at having more company, Ketch had Henry set out some plates while he himself handled the beverages. Len and Mario came in soon after and Ketch introduced Henry to them. While they ate in air-conditioned comfort, with the dog lying on the floor in a strategic position to facilitate possible handouts, it was decided that Henry could serve as gofer on the upcoming job. They didn't really need a gofer, but Len and Mario both implicitly understood that Ketch liked this boy and wanted to help him out, and they were agreeable.

It would cost him a few more bucks, but so what. Ketch figured it was a small price to pay. It seemed to him there were too few youngsters these days with Henry's mettle, and he wanted to encourage the boy. He was aware that part of his motivation was also that

Henry reminded him of his own son – or at least, of the way he chose to remember his son. He didn't have any idea what his son was like now; he supposed he should try to do something about that one of these days.

He decided he'd watch the hired help work for a while after lunch, to make sure everything went okay, and then get himself cleaned up and gather some laundry. He hadn't had time to do any all week and the immediate future didn't look promising that way either, so he'd drop a couple of bags off at the service he occasionally used. He certainly didn't have time right now to sit around the house doing laundry all day, even if he'd felt like doing that in the first place. But he guessed he should at least change the bed sheets while he was at it, so he'd do that, too. Oh, and he should check his e-mail, he remembered.

Then perhaps he'd go back to the shop a little early. Maybe he could help out some there, fill some tanks or something. He'd be needing some for himself anyway come Sunday, assuming he got his way tonight.

~ Sixteen ~

The shortest answer is simply doing the thing.

*L*en and Mario appeared to have developed a workable process for installing the foam blocks. They'd cut some wood, put up a couple of crossbeams, and managed to get one block installed. They'd decided to call it a day at that point, since it was Friday and Happy Hour was approaching, and had promised to come back 'early' (or their definition of it, anyway) Saturday morning to continue the work. Henry was also planning on returning, after he was finished with his paper route.

Having paid them all off, fed the dog an early dinner, and dropped off the laundry bags, Ketch was now on his way back to the shop. He hoped Kari was feeling better by now. Had there been something wrong with the food from the pier? He'd never had a problem himself there, including today. Maybe she'd picked up some kind of bug. She couldn't be pregnant; she'd said she couldn't have children, and neither could he anymore after a minor elective surgery years ago, so they were doubly insured that way – which was fine with him, as the dog was responsibility enough for him at this stage of his life.

Speaking of which, he should do something fun with the poor little guy tomorrow; he hadn't been spending enough time with him lately. The Captain's boat was spoken for due to his dive charter, and Kari shouldn't close the shop to accompany him to the dump site anyway; she could use the Saturday business, such as it was around here, so he knew he'd have to wait until Sunday. Despite Kari's peculiar reaction at the shop, he was sure he could convince both of them to help him do what he knew he needed to do then, and was not considering alternatives.

In spite of his impatience at the delay, he recalled thinking earlier this week that he'd like to hike the trails again in the maritime forest of Buxton Woods. He knew the dog would enjoy that, too, and would have access to the water there as well. Maybe they could do that in the morning and then spend the afternoon at the shop with Kari, while his coolies slaved away with the foam blocks. The dog liked going to the shop as well, and Ketch could line up the gear they'd need for Sunday.

He'd remembered to check his e-mail before leaving the house. He'd found one from the NRC as promised, but it was just an automated response saying they'd received his report and giving him his report number. Nothing about sending in the pictures yet. Since the weekend was coming up, he supposed he might not hear more until next week. Well, it was a start anyway. Maybe his photo would turn out to be the icing on that particular cake.

He pulled into the parking lot at the shop just as another pickup was pulling out. He didn't see who was driving, but he didn't need to – he recognized the truck.

"Well hey!" Kari said with a startled look on her face as he entered the shop. "You're early."

"Yes. Things went well at the house this afternoon and they've knocked off for the day, so I thought I'd drop by and help you out here if I could. Is there anything you'd like me to do?"

"Hmm, I don't know, let me think," she said, somewhat distractedly it seemed to him. "Oh hey, I almost forgot somethin' – come over here, you!"

When he did, she wrapped her arms around him and gave him a long hug. "Was that Mick I saw leaving when I came in?" he calmly inquired.

She disengaged and started to blush. "Yeah, 'fraid so. But don't worry, it doesn't mean anythin'."

"No? Well, what did he want?"

She hesitated for a moment, then exhaled loudly. "He wanted to borrow some money from me, can you believe that? I mean, the nerve – I hadn't seen him in forever, and like I said he never called, and now he wants money. Like I have any anyway. Can you believe it? I told him to shove off."

He'd gotten to know her considerably better over this past week, and what she was saying didn't quite ring true to him. He recalled the questions he'd been asking himself about her earlier in the week, many of which had still not been answered. Was this why she was staying at his house, to avoid Mick? But she was still going to the shop, and Mick obviously knew he could find her there, so maybe not. But was this why she'd been so relieved when Ketch had given her that money for his upcoming (someday) solo diving class?

Was Mick threatening her somehow?

He gave her a good long look. There would come a day when his patience would run out – but it didn't have to be today. She looked stressed and he didn't want to add to that, so he decided to continue to let things ride for now. There may also come a day when she'd decide on her own to be more forthcoming, he thought; and given everything that had happened this past week, he supposed he should grant her a decent grace period. He hoped he wouldn't regret this decision; but there it was.

"So anyway," she went on, "you don't have to be jealous, there's nothin' goin' on that way, I promise. Like I told you before, I'm long done with him."

"I trust you," he said, though meaning only in 'that way'. "And if you ever need my help with anything, I hope you'll trust me as well." She still looked a bit flustered, so he added with a friendly smile, "Well, at least you've got some color now. I take it you're feeling better?"

"Yes I am, and thank you for askin'," she said, looking up at him appraisingly. "You're a good man, you know that?" He didn't know for sure about that, as a matter of fact, but he didn't say so. "Hey, look," she said, "why don't we close up early and go on over to the bar? It's close enough to quittin' time, and there isn't really anythin' here that needs doin' right this minute." He allowed as how that sounded like a right fine idea, and she laughed at his clumsy attempt at Southernese. "Please don't do that again," she joked, "it makes me downright cringe, I kid you not!"

"I know, it's hopeless. And even if I took lessons, I don't think I could ever leave the 'h' out of 'shrimp' like you people do. I just can't wrap my mind around that concept."

Since it was Friday and Happy Hour to boot, the lot at the Froggy Dog was just about full. They had to scout around some for a parking spot, but they managed to luck into a table for four in the Groggy Pub. Ketch ordered a pint and a bottle of wine.

"By the way, I haven't had time to do laundry lately, as you now know," he said, and was rewarded with an eye roll. "So I turned our worn clothes in to my laundry service. I hope you don't mind. They're good, and they follow the cleaning directions on the labels. They'll probably be done on Monday."

"That's fine, and thanks for doin' that. I doubt they could do much harm to what I been wearin' this week anyway – or not wearin', half the time it seems." The drinks arrived, and Ketch poured her a glass of wine. "You know, you're spoilin' me so much I might never want to leave. Down the hatch!"

"I just love this place!" she reiterated after draining her first glass. "And this is the second time this week I've been here!"

"Well, don't get too used to it," Ketch advised her. "This has been an unusual week. I don't generally eat out as often as I have this week."

"Oh, come on! We could come here once a week anyway, couldn't we? Maybe we don't always have to eat, that'd save some money. Oh look, there's Joette. Hey Joette!" she called, waving a hand in the air.

Joette joined them at the table and occupied the fourth chair, Ketch's backpack having been placed on the third one. "Hey, Ketch!" she said, giving him a once-over. "You doin' okay?"

"Yes, thank you," he sheepishly acknowledged. "No permanent damage."

"Well, that's good. Hey, have I got some scuttlebutt for you-all! Guess what happened at work this afternoon? You know how they been talkin' on the news the last couple days 'bout a retrial for Bob, 'bout his wife that disappeared I mean, on account of there's rumors 'bout some kind of new evidence?" Ketch and Kari glanced at each other in confusion. "Hadn't y'all heard 'bout that?" Joette asked in disbelief.

"No, I haven't been reading the paper much this week, and I haven't turned on the TV all week," Ketch said. "Me neither," Kari added, "I guess we were just too busy."

"Huh, how 'bout that?" Joette said. "Well, that's why he was in such a bad mood when you came to see him yesterday, Ketch. Seems they found some more blood traces somewhere, or somethin' like that. He's been talkin' to his lawyers, and also his backers. From what I heard, it sounds like they're havin' second thoughts 'bout investin' in the marina development."

"He has backers?" Ketch asked.

"Oh yeah, I mean he's got money, everybody knows that, but not enough to do all that all by himself. So the marina might have to be put on hold. And I'll tell you what, I'm thinkin' it probly won't happen at all, 'cause guess what! Some police officers showed up at our place not but two hours ago, and they told him he has to surrender himself first thing Monday mornin'!"

Ketch felt like he imagined he might if he'd grabbed onto a live wire. Was he dreaming? He considered asking Kari to pinch him. "So that's why he told me I might have to stand in line," he said.

"Huh?" Joette said.

"Wow! Hey, do you know if you'll still have a job?" Kari broke in, saving Ketch from having to explain his remark. Thank you Kari, he thought; she must have remembered his desire to avoid spreading that part of his story around.

"Well I don't know, I hope so," Joette said. "Maybe I should start lookin' around."

"Hey y'all!" the Captain's voice blared at them from behind a nearby waitress, who almost lost the tray she was carrying. "Hey, foxy lady, how you been?" he said to Joette. Seeing that all the chairs were taken, he swiped an empty one from another table without asking and dragged it over. "Am I late? What did I miss – besides the beer?" He regained the attention of the startled waitress and bellowed, "Ahoy there darlin', bring us two more a whatever he's got, if you please!"

"Joette was just tellin' us that Bob Ingram is gettin' arrested," Kari informed him.

"You don't say! I heard somethin' 'bout that just this mornin'. So they're really gonna retry him, huh? I'll be damned... Ain't that somethin', Ketch?" he said, casting Ketch a sly look. "Gimme the scoop, Jo, and don't leave nothin' out!"

While Joette repeated her tale, Ketch excused himself to go to the rest room, and almost chose the wrong door. He thought he might be in a mild state of shock. The extent of the relief he suddenly felt made him realize just how much of a strain he'd been under lately. Were his troubles really over at last? It seemed too good to be true – but being the optimist that he was (not), he figured he'd still better hedge his bets. If anything, investigating the contents of that salvage drum now seemed even more urgent to him. If there was any doubt about how that retrial might turn out, he could erase that doubt if he was right.

When he returned to the table, Joette was gone. "Well, how 'bout that?" the Captain said to Ketch. "Between this and nailin' him for dumpin' toxic waste, sounds like you might be out a the woods after all."

"We'll see," Ketch said. "Let me show you the reason why I asked you to come here." He set his laptop on the table and started to fill the Captain in while it booted up. Kari sipped silently at her wine while he showed the Captain the picture and explained his theory, including what he thought it might all mean in light of Joette's news.

"Well," the Captain ruminated, "seems like a stretch to me – but it could be, who knows? It's as good a theory as anybody else ever come up with. You gonna call the Guard?"

"No, not right away. I don't want to embarrass myself and waste their time if it turns out to be nothing," Ketch said. "Captain, I know you're busy tomorrow, so I want to hire your boat on Sunday. I want to go out there and raise that drum and see what's in it. If it's what I think it is, then I'll radio the Coast Guard."

"You and who else?" the Captain asked. "I don't dive – and I wouldn't leave my boat unmanned even if I did, unlike this other dang fool I know."

Kari finally spoke. "I can go. I usually close the shop around noon on Sundays. We can go after that."

"Are you sure?" Ketch said, carefully watching her. This was a rhetorical question to him; she had to go, and he would have tried to make her see that if she hadn't seen it on her own. She seemed to be reacting to all this better so far than she had at the shop earlier – unless that truly had been due to some kind of illness. "That would be a big help. I don't have much experience with lift bags."

"That's right, you don't," she said. "And you also haven't taken that class yet, mister solo diver, so you're not gonna do that again on my watch," she sternly added, but with a tempering smile. "I think you should come to the shop tomorrow mornin' so we can do some plannin'. If we have to shop for somethin', it'd be better to do that tomorrow since the day after is Sunday."

"Well okay, I'm game," the Captain said. "And don't be talkin' 'bout hirin' the boat, just chip in for the gas and let me do some fishin' on the way back and I'll be happy. And oh, hey – what you gonna do with them floats now?"

Ketch had already decided about that, so this answer was easy. "I'm going to install them anyway. Who knows what'll end up happening? I don't want to count my chickens. That way, I'll be covered if Ingram is still able to go on somehow, and if another one just like him comes along someday. Besides, what else would I do with them? I doubt I can return them, and I'd have to sell them dirt cheap on eBay or whatever."

"That's what I like most about this character," the Captain laughed. "He's the most optimistic fella I know!"

It had been long enough since he'd had anything to really celebrate that Ketch couldn't help insisting on treating them all to dinner again, and then buying Kari what he thought was a rather fetching sundress at the gift shop. Though she'd still seemed a little edgy partway through dinner, the mood appeared to have dissipated by the end of it.

When he and Kari arrived back at the house, they let the dog out and decided to relax on the deck for a while with a couple of beers – and another of Ketch's joints, at her suggestion. He didn't mind; he had no other use for them and wasn't saving them for anything, and he didn't intend to make it a habit. When they were gone, they were gone, that's all.

They hadn't lit the tiki torches, but had left all the lights off except for one back in the kitchen, to hopefully avoid attracting insects; and maybe the ganja had also helped with that. Not that either of them would have noticed them much unless they got really bad – he was somewhat buzzed, and she seriously so. After Ketch had fed the dog the dinner scraps he'd saved for him, the dog got bored with the two of them and Ketch let him go inside.

"Thanks again for the new dress," Kari said, removing it from the bag, "I like it a lot. It's nice to know you're not about to stop spoilin' me," she beamed.

"You should try it on and make sure it fits."

"Yeah? Okay," she giggled, and starting stripping off her top.

"I didn't mean right here," he said, glancing around apprehensively.

"Relax, it's dark and there's nobody around. Here, hold these for me," she said, and flung her undergarments at him. "Fits just fine," she declared as she slipped the dress on. She pirouetted in front of him. "So what do you think? No, never mind, I know exactly what you think, or at least what you were thinkin' when you showed it to me at the gift shop. You were thinkin' it looked like somethin' you'd like to do me in, right?" Ketch was struck dumb. "Well hey, you ever tried doin' it in a hammock?" He mutely shook his head. "Me neither! So come on around here." She took his hand and pulled him toward the side deck.

He finally found his voice. "You truly are something else," he said. He might not have gone along with this under normal circumstances; but between the beer and the weed, he was not currently normal. "This is crazy, this is crazy..." he started to intone.

"*Vacation!*" she gleefully responded. "We should go see a movie sometime, we hadn't done that yet." She stretched out on her back in the hammock. "So," she challenged him in her best Christie Brinkley voice, "are you gonna go for it?" He slipped his shorts off and cautiously climbed on top of her. "Just don't get too wild and dump us out, Sparky. Careful now..."

~ Seventeen ~

The best way to learn whether you can trust someone is to trust her.

So he wouldn't be taking the dog hiking in Buxton Woods this morning after all. Kari was right, it would be best to inventory and assemble their gear today, rather than risk being stuck needing some essential and possibly hard-to-get item on a Sunday morning. He didn't know if the dog would remember him mentioning going to the woods last night; and to be honest, his own memory of last night was a bit hazy and he wasn't sure he had in fact mentioned it. But he tried to apologize anyway.

"I'm sorry, boy, no walk in the woods today," he said to the dog. "We'll do that some other time. But you like to go see Kari, right? Let's get ready to go for a ride and go see Kari!" The dog responded with enthusiasm as he always did, which made Ketch feel better.

He re-provisioned his backpack again, this time with biscuits, a fresh bone, the leash, and the dog's water dish in place of that Hardy Boys detective kit he'd cobbled together earlier in the week. Who had he thought he was when he'd done that? Still, he decided to toss in his notebook and a couple of water bottles just in case, though he didn't anticipate needing them. Better safe than sorry. And his phone was just about fully charged, good. As an afterthought, he added the dog's football and frisbee to the backpack. Maybe they could play out in back of the shop later on.

Kari had left for the shop a while ago, wanting to get an early start she'd said. His work crew should be here soon. Mario had surprised Ketch by phoning him to say he and Len were on their way, and it had only been seven-thirty or so – amazing. He heard the rattle of Henry's bike outside, and shortly thereafter the rumble of the truck. He grabbed the backpack and he and the dog went out to greet everyone.

"Mornin', Mister Ketchum," Henry said. "Hey, Ketch!" the other two called. "Bet you're surprised to see us this early," Len grinned.

"I am indeed, and thank you again. Good morning, Henry. I have to go out this morning, but you boys just go on and get started. I'm leaving the front door unlocked, and you know where the drinks and the bathroom are, so feel free. Henry, that goes for you as well, so don't be shy. I'll bring some pizza back with me for lunch." Gidget's, to be specific – the best in town in his opinion, and surprisingly some of the best he'd ever had anywhere, including his city's Italian neighborhood back north.

"Thanks, Ketch, we appreciate that," Mario said. "Don't worry, man, we got things under control here. Hey, where you headed? You goin' out with Don today?"

"No, just running some errands."

When Ketch arrived at the shop, Kari was ready for him. "Hey there, Clark!" she said with a wink. "And hey, Jacky, how you doin'?" She started talking business while she was still hugging the dog.

"I wish I had more in case one springs a leak, but I've only got two hundred-pound lift bags on hand, which ought to be enough though – but just in case, I also have two fifty-pounders we could carry with us. If all that isn't enough, then there's somethin' else in that drum other than what you're thinkin'. Don had a stern line on his boat last I knew, but I don't know if it's long enough, so I threw in a coil of anchor line I had layin' around. I'm pilin' it all up over there in the back," she said, pointing. "I stuck a couple of good lights and some heavy-duty hooks and clips in there too, and I set aside some tanks though they're not all filled yet, two rental regulators for fillin' the bags, and some extra weights. Except for the lift bags, that all might be twice as much stuff as we'll need, but it's good to plan that way in case somethin' breaks or somethin' else goes wrong. I did some calculatin', and we shouldn't need more than one tank for the bags..."

"Whoa there, slow down," Ketch laughed. "Seriously, thank you for doing all that already, I'm impressed. I hope you're keeping track of how much this is costing you, so I can make that right." The dog was nosing around looking for something to do, so Ketch gave him the bone he'd brought.

"We'll figure that all out later," she said, waving him off. "And me and you'll talk out how we're gonna do the job later on, that's important too. I don't want either of us gettin' hurt, and there's ways that could happen. I was thinkin' about how to fasten the bags and the line to the drum and keep the whole mess stable, and I thought about a fish net, maybe a five-hundred-pound-test knotted lift net, but then I thought a chain sling might be the way to go. Since you said it's a metal drum, that should work, since it'd be rimmed on both ends."

"What's a chain sling?"

"Here, I'll draw it for you." She started rummaging around for a blank piece of paper, and Ketch saved the day with his trusty notebook. "Oh good, thanks. Like they say, a picture's worth a thousand words," she smiled, finally starting to lighten up a little. "We tip the drum on its side, see, and the grab hooks attach to each end, and the horizontal drum and the sling make a triangle. It's made of steel chain so it can handle a load, but it's not too heavy and it's adjustable. But I don't have any of those."

"No problem, I'll run down to Hatteras and see if I can find one." It would have to be Hatteras, as there were no other marine supply outlets anywhere else on this island.

"Two," she said. "Remember, redundancy is part of a good dive plan, especially when you're playin' at tec divin'. You can take one back later if we don't use it. The grab hooks are the most important part – if you could find a couple of those and some chain, we could make our own sling."

"Okay, I'll go do that now. Mind if I leave Jack here? I don't like to leave him in the truck on a hot day."

"Course not! We'll be all right, won't we boy?" she said to the dog, who was lying on a throw rug behind the counter and happily gnawing away. "Oh, and see if you can get one more hundred-pound lift bag. They might have one down at Outer Banks Divin', since you're goin' to Hatteras. I hate sendin' you to a competitor, but I'd feel better if we had one more just in case."

Ketch was able to find everything he was looking for in Hatteras, which was a good thing as he'd otherwise have had to drive up to Nag's Head or Roanoke. It wasn't lunchtime yet, so he couldn't make the most efficient use of his time and gas and stop at Gidget's which was on the way back, but that kind of thing bothered him only a little now.

Kari was satisfied with his purchases and decided the gear collection for the following day was essentially complete, except for packing their individual gear bags. "And except for goin' over the dive plan," she further qualified. "Pull up a chair here by me and take some notes in that handy-dandy little notebook of yours. By the way, is that your detective notebook? I saw some cute scribblin's in there."

"Oh, you thought they were cute, did you? Well, I guess you're easily amused," he said, though in a friendly tone. "Go ahead and make fun of me if you must, I don't mind."

"Nah, I'm good for now, thanks anyway. Hey, I had the weather on the marine radio before. They said there might be another tropical storm brewin'. We'll still be okay tomorrow, though, it's nowhere near here."

"I wonder what they'll name this one if it gets big

enough?"

"I think 'Ernesto' is the next one up on this year's list. Yeah, I've got the lists up on the wall here. Ernesto is what it'd be."

What 'it' would be, no longer what 'she' would be. Ketch knew that the World Meteorological Organization mandates names for Atlantic tropical storms and hurricanes in the form of six annual lists of names, which are used in rotation and recycled every six years. They also have similar lists for storms in other parts of the world. If a storm is deemed to be of historic import and severity, its name is retired and another is designated in its place. When they'd first started naming Atlantic storms back in the Fifties, they'd only used familiar female names; but now there were both male and female names in the lists, including some Jewish ones mixed in with the Christian ones, and there were English, Spanish, and French names, and some from other parts of Europe. Ketch thought a hurricane should have a strong name – and yes, a female one at that, and preferably mythological if he could have his way; 'Hurricane Fred', for example, which was actually on one of those lists, sounded just plain ridiculous to him.

When they finished discussing Kari's dive plan, it was time for Ketch to call in his pizza order. He decided he'd leave the dog here at the shop again, drop off two of the pies back at the house for the guys, and then bring the third one back here. He'd miss that Yankee game even though he wasn't diving today after all, but that was okay and it was being recorded. He could fill the tanks that needed filling and load the pile of gear into the back of his truck, whose bed was capped and lockable. Not the tanks, though; they'd get too hot in there, so he'd just rig them today and load them tomorrow. Then maybe he could play with the dog and let him cool off in the canal behind the shop, and go pay off his helpers at the house before dinner – at home for a change? – and then maybe she'd watch the game with him tonight. Maybe he'd pick up something to cook at Risky Business, his favorite local seafood market; it was pretty much fresh off the boat there.

The rest of the day played out mostly as he'd planned, except for the typical daily (at least!) wrestling match with Kari, which occurred after another joint (the last one) and some more of his fancy wine. They stayed away from the hammock this time, thankfully, but it was the first time he'd done anything like that while watching the Yankees – which didn't seem right, but he'd enjoyed it nonetheless. As well as the quickie encore at bedtime. She seemed almost compulsive about the sex, he thought, and maybe also with the substance abuse lately, more so than he'd ever been aware of before albeit from a greater distance. Maybe she was just wilder than he'd known, maybe she just had a strong sex drive; or maybe she was trying to escape from something, which he still suspected might turn out to be the case. He wasn't about to complain just yet, though.

He woke before she did on Sunday morning and was able to leave the bedroom without being asked to perform for a change. He fed the dog on the side deck (the one with no hammock) and let the dog explore out back along the waterfront while he relaxed at the table with a hot buttered bagel, a glass of juice, and the Sunday paper. The stacks of foam blocks in the back yard were more depleted than he'd anticipated; the boys had managed to put up twelve of them yesterday, considerably more than he'd expected. They were all taking the day off today.

And today was the day, finally. Joette's news flash Friday night had relieved him of some of the pressure and urgency he'd been feeling, but he was still anxious to get out to the dump site and wrap up that particular mystery at least – and maybe help put Ingram away for good in the process. The weather looked decent enough so far and the forecast was favorable, that developing storm notwithstanding. If it amounted to anything, and if it ended up coming this way, it wouldn't get here for a few days at least. So all the omens looked good – unless one considered the thirteen blocks that were now installed on the underside of his house. Thirteen... It's a good thing he wasn't superstitious.

Kari came out the back door with a cup of coffee and joined him at the table. "Hey," she said, "I wondered where you went. I missed you when I woke up." She nonchalantly appropriated half of his bagel without asking.

"Jack wanted to go out. Guess who's on the front page of the newspaper?" He showed her the headline with Ingram's picture below it.

"Huh. Well, he *is* the kind that likes gettin' his picture in the paper, right?" She seemed subdued this morning; maybe the previous night's activities had something to do with that. A protracted yawn supported that impression.

"So I guess I'll get my gear together and then join you at the shop later and load up the tanks," he said. "I'll give the Captain a call as well, and make sure we're still on for this afternoon."

"Sounds good," she said. "Well, I think I'll go jump in the shower. I should get over to the shop after that." She quickly finished off the bagel and the coffee, then padded back inside. He noticed she hadn't asked him to join her in the shower this time; but that was all right with him as he was tired, too.

He confirmed with the Captain when he'd finished skimming the newspaper, then called the dog in and got himself cleaned up. He methodically packed his scuba gear as usual and his backpack, which today would contain the dog's boating paraphernalia as it typically did for a charter. He went to Village Grocery to load his cooler with deli sandwiches, drinks, and ice for later, drove back to the house to pick up the dog, and made it to the shop more than an hour before Kari's noon closing time. The parking lot was empty.

"Hello," he called when he and the dog entered the shop. "Did you get much action here this morning? Were you able to pack your gear?"

"Hey, Jacky! Yeah, I got a little action – but nowhere near as much as I got last night," she said with a tight smile. "I'm packed. Let's load the tanks and take off, there's nothin' happenin' here."

When they got to the boatyard, the Captain's arrant voice started assaulting their ears before they'd even killed the truck's engine. "Ahoy there swabbies, top a the day! Y'all need a hand with your gear? If you do, I got a number you can call!" he cackled from the deck of the *Minnow*.

The Captain's good humor roused Mario, who'd apparently been puttering around on his boat. "Hey, Ketch! Hey, Kari!" he called. "You guys goin' divin'? Hang on, I'll be right over." Ketch put the dog's life jacket on for him and got him squared away aboard the boat while Mario threaded his way to the truck.

"So where you guys headed?" Mario asked as he helped them haul their equipment out to the *Minnow*. "You got a lotta gear here, you goin' wreckin'? Find a new U-boat or somethin' like that?"

"No, just one of the known wrecks," Ketch answered, thinking fast. Keying off Mario's 'wrecking' inquiry and relying on him knowing, as everyone around here did, that salvaging artifacts from shipwrecks in U.S. waters without permission was illegal, he elaborated in a lower voice, "No offense, but I don't want to say which one. I saw some odds and ends there that I'd like to bring home, you know, portholes and such."

"Say no more, man," Mario demurred. "Your secret is safe with me." When he finished helping them get everything loaded, he called, "Have a good trip!" as he retreated back to his boat.

"Well, that was smooth," Kari commented when

Mario was out of earshot. "Damn right," the Captain said. "Where'd you learn how to fib like that? You're almost as good as me!"

"It's not something I'm proud of," Ketch said. "Come on, let's cast off and get this thing done." He was seriously starting to taste the prize now, and he wanted to get going.

While the Captain piloted them north up the sound toward Oregon Inlet, Kari sat Ketch down at the table in the cabin and went over the dive plan again with him. Though he listened attentively enough, knowing what was at stake, he also kept an eye on the dog, who was reclining out on the aft deck. The dog looked relaxed, but his nose was constantly twitching as he savored the rich olfactory treat the sea breeze was providing him. Shades of salt and fish seasoned with a tinge of death, Ketch thought; he liked it, too.

Kari would dive with a dual-tank rig, one tank for her to breathe from and the other for filling the lift bags, each tank with its own regulator. Controlling a lift bag was tricky business due to the fact that the pressurized air it had been fed from the tank would expand inside the bag as the depth and ambient pressure decreased on ascent, like a balloon being inflated, making a runaway ascent a distinct and dangerous possibility. Since she'd had some previous experience doing it, she'd be the one to fill the bags, manipulate their dump valves as necessary, and control the ascent of the drum.

Ketch would use a similar rig; he'd be able to

breathe from both tanks if necessary, and they could use air from his second tank for the lift bags if needed. He'd be the first to descend on the anchor line and the one to locate the drum, using his wreck reel to reprise his circular search until he found it, while Kari hovered at a shallower depth to conserve her air, but keeping him in her sight. She'd drag the chain sling, previously attached to the free end of the boat's stern line topside and with two empty lift bags clipped to it, with her on her way down, along with a third empty bag clipped to her BC just in case. When Ketch signaled that he'd found the drum, Kari would complete her descent and he'd back away from the drum and ditch his reel. She'd try to tip the drum, and if she couldn't do it on her own, Ketch would approach and help. If they both had to tip the drum, they'd stay together only for the time it took to do that, and then Ketch would back off again.

They were to maintain neutral buoyancy throughout and avoid touching or even finning near the bottom, to minimize silting and preserve visibility. Kari would secure the sling to the drum and then start releasing short bursts of air from her second regulator into both of the lift bags as evenly as possible. At all other times except in the event they had to use some of Ketch's air for the lift bags, they'd remain in constant sight of each other but stay well clear of each other to avoid entanglement and injury. Neither of them would be physically attached to the drum, and they'd both avoid lingering directly above or below the drum as much as possible.

Ketch would provide lighting during the setup and ascent as needed, and the Captain would keep the stern line taut topside and take up the slack during the ascent, again to prevent entanglements; and he'd also keep the engines idling in case he had to nudge the boat closer to wherever the drum was located. When the drum reached the surface, the Captain would cleat the stern line, and Ketch and Kari would re-board the boat, doff their gear, and help haul the drum aboard. The five-minute safety stop at fifteen feet would be omitted today, but that shouldn't be a problem at the relatively shallow depth they'd be diving. Sometime later, Kari would make a bounce dive to recover the reel and free the anchor if necessary.

She was certainly all business today, he thought, and she seemed tense as well – to a degree that he wondered if she was deriving any pleasure at all from this trip, despite her assertion a few days ago that she'd enjoy diving without students for a change. This wasn't really a recreational dive, though, and its goal was admittedly less than uplifting. Regardless, the most important thing for now was that she seemed to have thought of everything. But he knew things could still go wrong; what if she needed more or less weight, or he couldn't find the drum, or they couldn't tip it, or they needed a replacement bag or a third bag, or the grab hooks didn't hold, or the drum got away from her during the ascent, or there was too much current for her to stay with it, or they got tangled somehow, or someone got injured, and so on? What if Eleanor

Roosevelt could fly, he thought, recalling one of his favorite old *Saturday Night Live* skits. They'd just stick to the plan and do the best they could; they had a redundant set of tanks and they could revise the plan if they had to try again, if it came to that.

They soon passed through Oregon Inlet and headed out to sea. With the *Minnow*'s powerful twin inboards smoothly plowing a path through the water at a faster clip than Ketch's *TBD* could have safely managed, it didn't take much longer for them to reach the target area. They anchored at about the same spot Ketch had earlier in the week. After he'd tethered the dog to a table leg in the cabin and Kari had run up the dive flag (which she'd insisted on doing for safety), they set up their rigs, suited up, and began their descent.

So far so good, he thought as he glanced back up at her along the anchor line. She didn't seem to be having any trouble descending, and she was signaling 'OK'. The visibility was at least as good as it had been the last time he'd been here, and there was hardly any current so far. He clipped his reel line to the anchor when he got close enough to the bottom and started his search, periodically verifying that she was still in sight above him and still signaling 'OK'.

He found a couple of groupings of drums and shined his dive light on every one of them, even the ones that didn't overtly look like salvage drums, so he'd be sure to spot the telltale swatch of brightly colored fabric – but no luck so far. When he found a third grouping about fifteen minutes into the dive and struck out again, he looked up at her and shrugged his shoulders. She signaled 'OK' again and motioned for him to continue searching – which he knew they still had plenty of time and air to do.

He finally hit pay dirt a few minutes later in the next grouping he found. He had to make a conscious effort to control his breathing as he excitedly signaled to her that he'd located the drum and she should descend, which she slowly did. Before he backed away from the drum as planned, she got close enough for him to see the expression on her face behind the mask and regulator. Knowing her more intimately as he now did, it seemed to him that she looked surprised, and possibly also a bit upset for some reason.

But it didn't seem to matter. He watched her work at freeing the drum, gently rocking it back and forth while she hovered upside-down so her fins wouldn't stir up any more silt than necessary. Excellent buoyancy control, he thought. She was finally able to tip it onto its side. A small silt cloud rose up around the drum as it re-settled onto the bottom, but not enough to completely obscure his view. He moved a little closer and shined his dive light on the drum to help her see what she was doing, and watched as she successfully attached the chain sling to the drum and began squirting air into the lift bags.

Everything was proceeding according to plan so far, with nary a glitch. Maybe he'd been mistaken about what he thought he'd seen on her face; maybe she was just concentrating on her designated tasks. He followed below her at a safe distance, being careful to not drift beneath the drum, as she alternated between adding small amounts of air to the bags and dumping air from them, waiting for what seemed like an inordinate amount of time after each action in order to gauge the reaction. But what she was doing made perfect sense; it was somewhat analogous to avoiding oversteering while handling a boat.

It turned out the amount of air in her second tank was more than sufficient for the lift bags, the grab hooks were holding, and the stern line wasn't getting in the way. When the bags at last broke the surface and he heard the boat's engines cut off, Ketch was both relieved and amazed. Their plan had worked flawlessly so far, something he knew didn't often happen in the real world. Of course, they literally weren't quite out of the water yet, so something could still go wrong. For example, they'd have to be careful when they hauled the drum aboard; after all this effort, it wouldn't do to dislodge a grab hook and send the drum plummeting back to the bottom of the ocean.

Kari surfaced ahead of Ketch and swam to the stern and handed her fins up. When he was about to do the same himself, he thought he could hear the dog barking – but not the way he did when he was happy about seeing someone. As soon as his head popped above the surface, Ketch saw the reason for the dog's apparent distress.

"Gimme your fins," the Captain directed him, squatting on the stern platform. "And then get your ass up here. As you can see, we got company, and neither me nor your dog's much likin' it."

~ Eighteen ~

Anyone can behave poorly if given the chance.

*K*etch obeyed and passed his fins to the Captain. He could see that there was another boat tied up alongside the *Minnow* – Mario's boat – and he heard voices drifting down from the flying bridge. Kari for sure, and who else? He looked up and shaded his eyes. Mick. It sounded like they were arguing, though they were keeping their voices down and he couldn't make out what they were saying. "Jack, settle!" he commanded the dog, who stopped barking but kept a low rumble going in his throat.

"They snuck up on me when I was mindin' the stern line, didn't notice 'em at first with the engines runnin'," the Captain explained, keeping his voice low as well as he helped Ketch wriggle out of his rig. "Said their head was busted and could they use mine, Mario said he really had to go."

"I figured Mario was here. Anyone else besides Mick?" Mario would have to be involved, Ketch knew, since it was his boat and Mick didn't know much about boats. Nor did Mick dive or know much about that either, nor was he educated in anything at all that Ketch knew of. He wondered what Kari had ever seen in that wastrel.

"Nope, just them two."

"What are they doing out here in the first place?"

"That's what I wanna know. I'm guessin' we'll find out shortly."

"Hey Ketch," Mario called, emerging from somewhere below, not from the head. "Could you make sure I don't get attacked? I don't think ole Jack here likes me much today, acted like he might want to nail me before."

Ketch went into the cabin and held onto the dog's collar while Mario passed. "So you couldn't find a bush, eh?" he said.

Mario laughed at that. "Ketch, my man – and you too, Don – I want you to know this ain't personal, it's just business. Mick heard you guys were makin' a score and we just decided to get in on the action, you know? And I'm real sorry about not finishin' the work on your house, Ketch, but I figure you probably won't be wantin' me around after today anyway, am I right?"

"What kind of score? What are you talking about?" Ketch said.

"You know – treasure, man! What'd you do, find some old Spanish ship? Or maybe a load of coke or grouper somebody had to dump? Whatever we can sell, it's all fine with me." Mario called up to Mick, "Hey, come on down from there, let's get whatever this is outta the water and check it out!"

"Ha!" the Captain said to Ketch, "I wish 'em luck tryin' to sell what you-all brung up! So that's what they're after? Well, the joke's on them. What a couple a idiots!"

But Ketch knew it wasn't that simple. Mario apparently believed a story that Mick had probably fed him to gain the use of his boat, which Mick had done because Kari had apparently tipped him off; and she knew there was no treasure, so that wasn't really what they were here for. But if Mick and Kari were in this together, then why were they arguing?

The two collaborators climbed down from the flying bridge and joined Mario on the aft deck, Kari doing her best to avoid Ketch's penetrating stare. Yes, she was definitely involved. He should have known better, he thought; and though he was sad about losing the best thing he'd had in his life in a long time, his predominant emotion was anger. Why hadn't he trusted his instincts and followed up on *all* of his suspicions? Why had he allowed it to come to this? Well, he knew why – he'd let himself degenerate into a besotted poon hound, that was why, and he'd gotten bamboozled because of it. She was to blame, for sure; but so was he.

"So, Mario told y'all what's happenin' here? Good. Okay now, I want you and you," Mick said, pointing to Ketch and the Captain, "to stay in the cabin and set down there at that table. And make sure that dog stays tied up so I don't have to hurt him, hear?" The dog was snarling now, and in a very convincing manner.

"Oh, so you think we're gonna just set back and let you-all do whatever you want?" the Captain retorted, taking down a gaffing hook he happened to be standing near. "Who do you think you are, the ree-tard pirates a the Caribbean? Kari, Ketch, get on over here, I got more stuff we can use. It's three against two, we can take 'em!"

A smirk grew on Mick's face. "Wrong, old man, she's on our side," he spat. "And it don't matter how many sticks you got," he declared, extracting a small handgun from a pocket of his cargo shorts. "This here is the only thing that matters."

"Hey, what the hell, man?" Mario said. "What'd you bring that for? We don't need that!" Ketch noticed that Kari looked like she might upchuck at any moment.

"Shut up and start haulin'," Mick snapped. "Kari, you give him a hand if he needs one, and watch out he don't drop the damn thing. Go on, get on over there. Don't make me tell you twice, bitch, you know what happens then!" When she complied, Mick turned and trained the gun on the Captain, who silently re-mounted the gaff and retreated into the cabin.

"What in hell does she have to do with all this?" the Captain asked Ketch when they were both seated at the table. "I never figured her for a floozy. Oh, hey, I'm sorry buddy, I really am. I know you were sweet on her." Ketch got up and stood in the doorway of the cabin, and watched his femme fatale and her hooligans raise the drum and stand it upright on the deck.

"This just looks like one of those drums we been dumpin'," Mario remarked, disappointment evident in his voice. "Is there somethin' we can use inside? I don't get it."

"This ole coot," Mick said, motioning toward Ketch, "reported us to the feds for dumpin' them drums, so we gotta move this one to deeper water."

"Ketch did that? Why'd you go and do that, man?" Mario said. Incredibly to Ketch, given that he'd been ready to steal from him, Mario actually sounded hurt.

Oddly, Kari tried to cover for Ketch. "He just found the drums and reported them, he didn't give any names, he didn't know it was you," she started to explain.

"Shut up," Mick said. "I don't care about all that, he still went and done it."

"But why do we have to move this one?" Mario asked. "Why not all of 'em?"

"Because there's something special in that one," Ketch answered from the doorway. "Something that could put people away for the rest of their lives." But who, exactly? Was one of them, or both of them, working for Ingram? Did Kari have some kind of connection with Ingram? Was Mick just a flunky, or was he the killer?

"Get out!" Mario said. "What, is there, like, a *body* in there or somethin'?"

"You can ask her about that while the two of you get them other drums off your boat and onto this one," Mick said. "She can tell you all about it. You, get back in there and set down!" he commanded, waving the gun at Ketch. The dog's snarling increased in volume. "And shut that damn dog up or I'll shoot him, I swear!"

"Huh? I thought we were just gonna dump those other drums out here like usual. I thought we were just dumpin' garbage. What's in those other two drums, more bodies?" Mario persisted.

"No, not yet, but there will be soon," Ketch said.

"Shut up!" Mick said. "I told you to get back in there!" He aimed the gun above Ketch's head and fired a shot into the air. Ketch sat down, the dog howled, and Kari cringed.

"Hey man, I didn't sign up for this!" Mario protested. "Look, why don't you gimme that gun, we can find a better way to work things out here."

"No way! Look, you're in it now, like it or not, so just... What the -"

Mick ducked and dodged, and the fish knife the Captain had just thrown at him sailed through the air over his shoulder, missing it by at least a good foot – or as the Captain might put it later if he lived to tell the tale, by a hair. A split-second later, the dog, who'd slipped his collar, skidded out onto the deck through the cabin doorway, leapt onto Mick, and sunk his teeth deeply enough into Mick's free arm to draw blood. Mick screamed and, staggering backward, tried to bring the gun to bear on the dog, who refused to let go; but Mario grabbed that arm with both hands and managed to divert it, and the shot went wild.

"Jack!" Ketch yelled as he ran out onto the deck. He lowered his shoulders and dived at Mick's legs, meaning to tackle him; however, his momentum made Mick topple over backward, with Mario on one arm, the dog on the other, and Ketch's arms wrapped around his feet. The gun went off one more time, the dog yelped, and they all fell off the stern platform into the water.

The Captain hustled to the stern. "Ketch, you

okay?" he called as Kari jumped into the water beside him. Ketch was conscious but appeared groggy, and there was blood on his forehead. Fortunately, they were both still wearing their wetsuits, so they were positively buoyant. Kari turned him onto his back and dragged him to the stern, and the Captain helped her get him up onto the platform.

"I'm okay, I think," Ketch said. "I think I hit my head, that's all. Where's Jack?" A bark from the port side answered that question. The dog paddled to the platform and Kari dropped back into the water to boost him up onto it. He had a bloody snout, but the blood wasn't his. He let out a joyous yelp and started licking Ketch's head.

"Holy Mary mother a God!" the Captain exclaimed, leaning on the gunwale and holding a hand over his heart. "You sure you guys are okay?" He watched as Kari turned and swam out farther, toward where Mick was floating away half-submerged face-down in a pool of bloody water, then helped Ketch up and sat him on a portside bench on deck. Surveying the scene again, he noticed that Kari hadn't bothered to turn Mick face-up as she had with Ketch – while over on the starboard side of the *Minnow*, a sodden Mario was busy wrangling one of the drums from his boat over both gunwales of the conjoined boats. He succeeded, and immediately started working on the second one.

"Well, I guess you're okay too," the Captain called to him, "not that anybody cares. What the hell you doin' with them drums?"

"Hey, this ain't my fault, man. Like I said, I didn't

sign up for any of this, and I want nothin' to do with these things." When he'd gotten the second one onto the *Minnow*, he started hastily undoing his ends of the lines that tied the boats together. "I'm sorry, but I'm outta here. I can't be involved in all this. Nice knowin' y'all." When he'd gotten his lines freed from the *Minnow*, he quickly started his engine, throttled up, and took off.

The Captain saw that Kari had made it back to the stern with Mick's body, so he helped her pull it up onto the platform. "Well, I'm sorry this had to happen," he said, "but if somebody had to bite the bullet, so to speak, it's only fair it was him. Rest in peace, you worthless bastard. Where's the gun?"

"I don't know, probably on the bottom by now," she said.

"Okay then. There's one more thing we gotta do." He spun one of Mario's drums over to the platform. "Like Ketch said, I bet there's nothin' in here yet but some chain for ballast," he said as he unclamped the lid. "There, just like I thought. Help me stuff him in here."

"What? Are you serious? You want to put him in there?"

"Why the hell not? He's beyond carin'. We can't go sailin' in to port with a dead guy hangin' off our ass end, and I don't want him on deck or in the cabin and stinkin' up the joint on the way back. Come on now, before he stiffens up." She reluctantly acquiesced and assisted him with his gruesome task, and helped him move the drum out of the way after it had been resealed. Then she hurried to the starboard side, bent over the gunwale, and threw up into the water.

With an unsympathetic nod in her direction, the captain declared, "That reminds me, I'm starvin'." He dragged Ketch's cooler into the cabin, popped the lid, and set the food and some soft drinks out on the table. "I'm gonna drain the lizard and go get myself a beer or three. Get on in here in the meantime, you two. We got some talkin' to do."

Ketch still felt shaky, largely because he was cold, he realized. The water that gets inside a wetsuit during a dive helps insulate and warm the diver beneath the surface, but has the opposite effect topside after. He removed his, toweled himself off, and put his shirt back on. His bathing suit was still damp, but the hot sun was already starting to do its job and he felt a little better. He didn't speak to Kari, who was still hanging over the starboard gunwale, but he did toss a dry towel toward her. He made his way into the cabin with the dog in tow and again leashed the dog to a table leg, then removed the dog's life jacket so that both he and it could dry out. He poured some fresh water into the dog's dish and opened a can of pop for himself.

"Well, that's better," the Captain said, returning with a can and a half of beer, the other half-can having already been consumed. He sat down at the table and unwrapped a sandwich. Kari shuffled in soon after, minus her wetsuit as well, with the towel wrapped around her bathing suit. She took a seat with her head down, and didn't speak or make a move to eat or drink anything.

"Come on, you got to at least drink somethin'," the Captain admonished her. "A little pop'll do you good, settle your stomach. Here, drink up," he said, sliding a can over to her. She wordlessly opened it and took a sip.

"So," the Captain said between bites of his sandwich, "now it's you that's got some splainin' to do. Start talkin', Lucy."

"Well," she started. She was quite pale and still looked like she might be sick, Ketch saw. Too bad. He started nibbling on a sandwich. "I guess you'll be turnin' me in when we get back to the boatyard, right?" she said.

"Maybe so. But why exactly would we want to do that?" the Captain asked. "Because you're a dang pirate wench?"

"Because I killed her. Bob's wife," she replied in a monotone. Both Ketch and the Captain nearly choked on their food. "That's why I told Mick about what we were gonna do today. When they autopsy that body, they'll probably find my DNA on it somewhere, maybe under her fingernails since she scratched me, and Mick's too. He was supposed to move it yesterday, but he said he couldn't find anybody to help him, that he could trust."

"Whoa now, slow down!" the Captain said. More gently he added, "Start at the beginnin', darlin'."

"Okay," she said, then chugged the rest of her drink. "Can I have another one of those? I'm really thirsty." Ketch passed her another can.

"Well, just before she disappeared, before I killed her I mean, Bob signed up for private scuba lessons. He wanted me to come out to the house and do it in his pool. The first time I went there, he wasn't home yet, he'd said he'd probably be late, so I went out back to scout out the pool area, to see where I wanted to set up and all. And she came out and started yellin' at me." She stopped to take another drink. "She thought we were havin' an affair, I guess because he'd done that to her before. She was drunk. She got real nasty and she started tryin' to shove me around. I shoved her back one time, and she slipped and fell and hit her head on the edge of a concrete step. And I mean hard, there was blood all over. I didn't know what to do." The Captain mutely offered her a sandwich, but she shook her head and pushed it away.

"Mick pulled in right about then, 'cause I'd asked him to bring me some fast food, since I figured Bob would be late and I hadn't had a chance to eat. He told me I'd go to jail. I know it was a dumb thing to do, but I panicked, I didn't know what else to do at the time. Mick wrapped her up in a tarp and stuck her in the back of his truck, and he found some bleach and cleaned up around the pool. He said he'd take care of the body. I didn't know what he'd actually done with her 'til later on."

"So you knew he was dumping those drums all along?" Ketch finally spoke up.

"Yeah, I did, and I hate myself for that too. It's an awful thing to do to the environment – but I couldn't tell anybody, could I? I started to get worried when you found some of 'em, but I didn't know if they were ones from Mick or somebody else, or if that was the spot he'd dumped her at. I tried not to think about it much, 'til you showed me that picture."

What she'd said so far cleared up a lot of things, Ketch thought, but not quite everything. "So what happened with Mick after that?"

"Well, he dumped me a while back, quite a while actually – I told you the truth about that – and I figured I'd never see him again, which was okay by me, considerin'. But then he started comin' around now and again and hittin' me up for money."

"He blackmailed you?"

"Not exactly. He knew he'd go down right along with me if he turned me in, and I knew he wouldn't do that."

"So why did he think you'd give him money?"

She hesitated before answering, then blew out a long breath. "He told me he'd beat up on me and break stuff if I didn't cooperate."

"And did he?"

"Yeah, a couple times. He got mad at me one time last week 'cause I didn't have as much as he decided he wanted that time. That's how I got that bruise you were wonderin' about."

"God damn!" the Captain exploded. "A piss-ant protection racket. I'd like to kill that son of a bitch, if he weren't dead already!"

And that explained the rest, Ketch thought; but wait, not quite. "So why did you play along with all this and let me drag you all out here today, if you thought the drum wouldn't be here anymore?"

"Well, I had to, didn't I? What else could I do? Well, I guess I could have told you about it. I should have done, I know that now." She wiped at her eyes. "But I didn't want to be at home alone, and I thought you'd hate me!"

"I'll be damned," the Captain said. "Ketch, what do you make out a all this?"

"I don't know, I don't know what to think," Ketch tiredly replied. He did feel sorry for her, and he'd maybe like to put that hillbilly jerk out of his misery as well if it hadn't already been done. But he was still angry with her – for today, for deceiving him, for not trusting him. For almost getting him killed.

A couple of tears escaped from her eyes then. "I am so sorry, Ketch, I really am. I should have told you. I really do care about you, you know, I wasn't just usin' you. I didn't know you'd found her 'til Friday. I didn't know he'd be here today, and I didn't know about those other drums!" She covered her face with her hands and quietly sobbed into them.

The Captain got up and put his hands on her shoulders. "Hey, I think that's enough for now. How 'bout if you go below and lay out for a while? Come on now, let's go." She let him herd her to his bunk, and then he returned to the table and sat back down.

"So now what?" he asked Ketch. "What do you think we should do?"

"I don't know, call the Coast Guard? I don't know," he repeated.

"Oh yeah? Well, I think I know what I wanna do.

We still got a few hours a daylight left. I'd like to sail on further out, locate a good deep hole with the depth finder, and drop all a them drums in it."

Ketch perked up at that. "Are you being serious? You are? I see. So you'd let her get away with murder? And what about Ingram? I can't stand the man, you know that, but he's about to be retried for this, and he's innocent. The evidence in that drum could help his case – as could a confession from her, of course."

"Oh, he ain't innocent. He might not a done this one in, but I still bet he done the first one. And he's a cheater and a damn crook, you said so yourself, and who knows what else he done. If they convict him this time, it likely won't be nothin' he don't deserve for one thing or another. There's the law, you know, and then there's justice, and they ain't always the same. I say justice'll be done. If they don't convict him, they'll keep him busy long enough so he'll be out a your hair that way too."

"Okay," Ketch said after a moment's thought, "I might be able to live with that. I still think it's wrong, but you're right, he deserves some kind of punishment regardless. Maybe they won't convict him – they shouldn't, anyway, if the legal system does its job. And that isn't my problem, so okay. But what about her being a murderer?"

"She ain't no murderer, that was just an accident! Maybe she didn't handle it right, and it sure wouldn't look good in court, but she didn't set out to kill nobody."

"All right then, what about you? And what about

me? If all this ever comes out, we'll be considered accessories, and that'll mean prison for us, too."

"It ain't gonna come out. Mario don't know who's in that drum, and he won't be talkin' about what happened here today. He'd be an accessory too, or worse – he's the one made the gun go off. Besides, I'd lay money that ole Mexican bandit's finally gonna get to see his homeland. Anyway, we ain't ever gonna see him again around here. As for myself – ain't we best friends, me'n you? And you know what they say about that – friends help you move, best friends help you move the body. As for you, you ought to be willin' to do the same for her. Mick was, and you're a damn sight better man than him."

"You *are* my best friend, I have no doubts about that," Ketch hoarsely responded. There was something caught in his throat, so he took a drink. "I don't know if I'll ever be able to look at her the same way, though. Regardless of what we do here today, I think she and I might have to be over."

"Well, that's just plain stupid," the Captain pronounced. "Look, you might not want to hear this, but this is the love a your life you're talkin' about, anybody can see that. You know, everybody has secrets, I bet you do too. Hers is just a little bigger'n some, that's all. I say get over yourself and move on."

The Captain got up from the table. "Tell you what," he said, "I'm gonna go take in Mario's lines and haul up the anchor. If your reel comes up with it, fine, otherwise the hell with it – and if the anchor won't come, the hell with that too. Neither one a you's in good enough shape for a bounce dive. Then I'm gonna head east. And then you're gonna explain things to her when she wakes up, whether you want to or not. I done enough talkin'." He left the cabin to head for the bow.

"I'll tell you one more thing," he said through the cabin window as he passed by it. "If you're too dumb to know life's too short to pass on a good thing like that one down below, then the hell with you too!"

Ketch said nothing and remained seated at the table, lost in thought. After a while he gave the dog a hug, stood up, and headed below. He was exhausted, and he thought it might do him good to go lay with her for a spell, as they would say hereabouts.

~ N i n e t e e n ~

The weather in the hurricane months is the finest of the year, when there are no hurricanes.

*I*t was Tuesday now, and Ketch couldn't recall when there'd been a more beautiful morning. After taking care of some business on his computer, on a whim he'd walked the dog down to the boatyard to speak with the Captain, instead of calling him on the phone. He and the dog were out in the back yard now, playing frisbee. After the dog had his dip in the sound, Ketch would take him back inside and get to work.

Henry would be along soon; Ketch had called him to come over and mow again, and he could maybe use his help getting the *TBD* onto its trailer and pulling it far enough up the launch to hitch it to the truck. He probably didn't really need the boy for either task; but he still wanted to help him reach his goal, whatever it was he'd said he was saving up for.

Red sky at morning, sailors take warning... The beauty of this morning was a false one, he knew. The storm they'd first heard about on Saturday had intensified to tropical storm status, and it looked like it was going to bypass the Caribbean and head directly for the East Coast. Landfall was projected for sometime around the end of the week, and it might be a full-blown hurricane by then.

Kari had been right – 'Ernesto' was indeed its

name. Not a name Ketch would have chosen, but not bad, not one of the more ludicrous ones on those WMO lists. Where had they dug up some of those god-awful names? What kind of people had they hired to do that, and how much had they been paid for their efforts? Not much, he hoped. Where the storm would make landfall was uncertain at this point, probably somewhere between Georgia and Virginia was all they knew so far, but Ketch wasn't going to hang around to find out first-hand – he'd be migrating inland for the duration.

Which was a shame in a way. He'd always found storms exhilarating, maybe because of the lowered barometric pressure or the surplus of ozone or magnetic field disturbances or something like that, who knew? And if he stayed here he might possibly be able to see some rare and dramatic atmospheric phenomena he'd only read about, like the sundog, a parhelic illusion of two suns in the sky created when sunlight encountered ice crystals in the upper atmosphere; or Saint Elmo's fire, visible electrical discharges from ships' masts and church spires that used to strike terror into the hearts of superstitious souls who believed these were portents relayed to them from above. But that wasn't reason enough for him to stay here and ride it out and risk bodily harm; he could see those things on the computer if he wanted to.

There were still just as many foam blocks stacked behind the house as there had been on Sunday. With Mario gone, Ingram no longer a threat for the time being, and now this storm to deal with, Ketch hadn't pressed Len about finishing the job right away. The bedraggled crew of the *Minnow* had all professed ignorance Sunday night at the boatyard when Len had wandered over and inquired about Mario's whereabouts, and Ketch had done it again when he'd spoken with Len earlier this morning after seeing the Captain. Maybe Mario was out somewhere scoring something or other with his boat, or maybe he'd gotten himself in some kind of trouble and left town in a hurry, who could tell? He was just gone for some indeterminate amount of time, which wasn't all that unusual with transients like him. They'd agreed to leave Mario's kicker truck right where it was; it would be there if he ever came back, and if he never did then the authorities could deal with it sometime later on. Mick's truck wasn't at the boatyard, so Mario must have picked him up somewhere else; which was good, one less thing for them to have to explain.

"Hey, Mister Ketchum! You out back there?" Ketch whipped the frisbee into the water for the dog and walked back up to the driveway. Henry must have heard the dog barking at the flying disk.

"Good morning, Henry. Thanks for coming."

"No problem, sir. Want me to get the mower out?"

"Not just yet. If you don't mind, could you help me with the boat first? I need to get it onto the trailer so I can tow it, and we need to put the cover on it."

"You leavin' town on account of the storm? Mama said we are too, probably tomorrow or the day after."

"Yes, I am. Tomorrow is the day for me." The

sooner the better, just in case. Route 12 was the only way off this island by land, and if they were told to evacuate it would soon be choked with barely crawling traffic. And if the road washed out up around Rodanthe, as it occasionally had before even during less severe storms, those on the wrong side of the washout would be stranded.

After letting the dog greet Henry, Ketch put the dog in the house so he wouldn't be underfoot when they moved the boat. It didn't take the two of them long to get the *TBD* squared away. Ketch got Henry started with the mower and went in the house to pack, giving the dog a new bone to keep him occupied. It was a good thing he bought those bones by the bagful, he thought, and a good thing he'd just bought another one at the Food Lion.

There wasn't much to be done as far as storm-proofing the house went, as it was supposedly built to be hurricane-resistant, so he didn't intend to go to much trouble that way. He'd just leave a couple of windows cracked and brace them to stay that way, so the air pressure gradient between the inside and the outside would hopefully not reach a level where windows would blow out and the roof would try to lift off.

He'd picked up the laundry yesterday, so they didn't have to worry about having enough clean clothes; taking advantage of the laundry service had turned out to be a fortuitous move. Still, he wished they'd had enough energy to do more chores yesterday. But yesterday had been busy enough, he guessed, considering.

They'd slept in until being awakened by the phone. He'd fielded a call from the NRC, telling him they wouldn't start investigating his report on illegal ocean dumping until sometime after the storm had passed – which made sense, as he knew if it landed anywhere around here the Coast Guard and other agencies would have their hands full for a while; and yes, he was to e-mail them his pictures, which he'd done this morning. Then they'd unloaded the truck and rinsed their gear, which they'd neglected to do Sunday night; returned the tanks to the shop, which they'd kept open for a couple of hours until she got tired of hanging around there; eaten some seafood (delicious as always) along with a couple of beers each at the Mad Crabber; and gone home and crashed again, like they had immediately after their showers on Sunday night.

Since returning from Sunday's adventure, they'd tallied more hours sleeping than they had doing everything else; but they seemed to be finally getting back on an even keel today – as evidenced by an exceptionally satisfying encounter at sunrise this morning in the bedroom, which until then hadn't happened since their return. He hadn't at the beginning been at all sure about what he was doing – it had made him feel like the bottom of his stomach was about to drop out at first, when he tried to think much about it – but he guessed he'd just needed to get used to the idea of being an outlaw. He hadn't talked with her much about the whole thing yet, but he didn't really feel like he needed to, not urgently anyway. They'd do that later, after they'd gotten some more distance from it.

He decided now that the Captain had definitely been right – he'd been crazy to think about turning her in and giving her up. Life was indeed short, especially at his age; the drums they'd dumped would never again be seen by anyone; and Ingram had plenty of both money and lawyers. So no apologies, after all – rest in peace and let the crooked bastard fend for himself, that's the way it was going to be. Ketch knew now that she was no femme fatale, not really; and though it made him a little wistful to lose that last vestige of his little noir detective fantasy, he was glad of it.

Today was her usual day off, but she'd gone to the shop earlier to make sure everything was shipshape there, and to call the customers who'd signed up for her Open Water class, which was supposed to have started tomorrow and which was now canceled. The shop would remain closed for at least the rest of the week. She'd also wanted to call her mother and her sister, to make sure they'd be okay and find out what their plans were. She was probably at her apartment in Buxton by now, loading her car with important documents and whatever else she needed to save.

He packed a large duffel with the clothing and toiletries he thought he'd need, and set it in the living room by the front door, where his guitar, fireproof file box, dive gear, and the backpack with his laptop and a single photo album in it were already piled. He packed a smaller duffel with a leash, some food, treats, and some toys for the dog and added that to the pile, reminding himself to also toss in the dog's bed and dishes tomorrow morning. As an afterthought he also added the dog's life jacket; you never know. He tried to visualize other things he might have forgotten to pack, and concluded that everything else he owned was either replaceable or relatively unimportant.

Thinking that, since she wasn't back yet, he could help her by packing indisposable sundries of hers that she'd kept here, he opened a suitcase (he was out of duffels) and set it on the bed. But when he started trying to guess what she might consider indisposable, beyond the obvious such as a toothbrush, he realized he was out of his depth. He settled on laying the sundress he'd bought her across the suitcase and called it quits.

He noticed the sound of the mower had ceased, and he heard voices out in the yard. When he got to the front door the dog was already there of course, wagging and begging to be let out. "All done, Mister Ketchum," Henry called up to him. Ketch opened the screen door and let the dog out. The dog went first to Kari, and then to Henry, and then wandered off to patrol the yard and check out Henry's work.

"Henry told me he helped you get the boat ready," Kari said. "He's a handy guy to have around, isn't he? You better give him a good tip!"

"Don't worry, I most certainly will," Ketch said, getting his wallet out. "Here you go, Henry."

"Wow!" Henry exclaimed, glancing quickly at the

bills before stuffing them in a pocket. "Thanks, Mister Ketchum!"

"No, thank *you*, Henry. Come see us when you get back to town."

"Will do, sir." Henry got on his bike. "I have to go, my mama called and said I better get back and start packin'. Bye!"

"Good luck! See you on the other side!" Ketch called as the bike rattled off down the road.

"He really is a great kid," Kari said.

"I know, and I hope we see more of him once everything finally settles down around here – if it ever does, that is." Doing a passable Eugene Levy he added, "What a week I'm having!"

"*Splash*!" she laughed. "You know, we really do need to watch some movies. Maybe we'll be able to do that some while we're in exile, you think?"

"I knew I was forgetting something! I had the same thought earlier, and I wanted to pack some of my DVDs. I wouldn't mind watching *Captain Ron* again. Kurt Russell might not agree, but I personally think that's the finest performance of his career. By the way, I reserved us a two-bedroom suite at a Residence Inn in Raleigh. That should be far enough inland, and Adriana says it should take about five hours to get there, not counting pit stops." He'd been pleased to find they'd allow pets there (for an extra fee, of course) and they didn't have to stay at some trashy motel on account of the dog. They'd caravan there tomorrow, Kari's car following his truck with the boat.

"Two bedrooms?" she queried with one eyebrow

raised. "You gettin' tired of me already? I knew you would. And who's Adriana, pray tell?"

"Adriana? That's what I named the voice on the Google GPS I use on my phone. She needed a name." He shrugged. "I just wanted to make sure we had enough space, that's all. I don't like to be cramped."

"Uh huh, okay, if you say so. Hey, you said you talked to Don, right? Where's he goin'?"

"He has family on the Pasquotank River, I think that's what he said, off Albemarle Sound up by Elizabeth City. He'll stay with them, and they have a place he can dock the boat. He's sailing in the morning, and if he gets tired he says he'll stop over around Kitty Hawk. He'll call us when he gets there."

"It's too bad he has to sail alone. I wish we could go with him. What about his truck? Does he have somebody to drive it for him?"

"No. His condo in Hatteras has carport parking, so he's just going to leave it there. He says the *Minnow* is worth a lot more than the truck, so he'll chance the truck. It'll be safer there than at the boatyard, at least. Len will pick him up there at first light and drop him off at the boatyard on his way out to Tar Heel."

"I hope that works out for him. Course the storm might not even hit us directly here anyway. Guess we'll see. Well!" she said, looking suddenly tired again. "I got everythin' else done, now I guess I should go pack some of my stuff from here."

"I already started doing that for you," Ketch said as they all went back inside the house, keeping a straight face. "You'll see."

He went to where his DVDs were stored, she went to the bedroom, and the dog settled in front of the wood stove for a nap. As he fanned through the cases and started making some selections, he heard an exclamation from the bedroom. "Yeah, that's some packin' job you did there," she laughed.

It didn't take her long to finish packing, and he had the DVDs he wanted. He added them to his backpack, then carried her suitcase out from the bedroom. "I think we have everything now," he said, waving at the pile by the front door. "I'll load it all in my truck in the morning and we'll take off. Why don't we go out for an early dinner, and then make it an early night? I don't have much food left here. I needed to go shopping again to begin with, plus I threw out the perishables this morning."

"Okay, and a shower and nap before? I could go for that."

They ended up in the pub at the Froggy Dog again. What the heck, Ketch had thought, it's her favorite place – and that's where they'd gone on their first official date as well, he remembered. It seemed like that was such a long time ago, but in reality it was just shy of a week. How could so much have happened in such a short time? He wouldn't have believed it was possible if it hadn't happened to him. It was unnatural for things to happen to folks constantly, one right after another, in his opinion; there should always be at least some time between major events. Someone should speak to someone about that.

While they enjoyed another fine meal, along with

another bottle of fine wine, Ketch decided to broach an idea that had occurred to him just this morning. Well, he guessed he'd daydreamed about it a few days ago as well, and dismissed it at that time; and then a couple of days ago he'd wondered if he'd ever be able to stand the sight of her again; and now he'd come full circle, and this time he intended to stay there.

"I was thinking about something," he said.

"Should I alert the media?" she innocently asked.

"No, seriously. I know you've had a hard time making a go of it with the shop, and I'd like to do more to help. I'd like to become your partner."

"Really? That's an interestin' idea. How would that work?"

"Well, I'd buy into the business – I don't know how much money that would take, we'd work that out – and I'd get more involved in the daily operations, help more with the classes, help out in the shop, and so on. I'd take a cut of the profits – I don't know how much of a cut, it would depend on whether I was a full partner or something less, we'd work that out, too – but you'd get a cash infusion to expand and advertise more, which would mean more revenue and more profit..."

"I don't know about that, I'm not feelin' as confident about that as you are," she started to interrupt.

"Now hang on, hear me out. You'd also have fewer expenses, because you'd get to use my boat, and you'd get free web programming, not to mention no hoodlums extorting money from you..." He faltered for a second, then soldiered on. "And you wouldn't have to pay rent anymore, because I'm asking you to move in with me permanently." He went on before she could object. "You've been camping out with me already every day for the past week, and we're about to do it again in Raleigh. It's not like we wouldn't have any practice at it." She didn't respond immediately, so he tried to backtrack and save face with a little humor. "But I know, what we've been doing hasn't been quite the same as dealing with you throwing out all my stuff to make room for your shoe collection, your furniture, and so on. And we haven't been together that long, so maybe it's too soon to be thinking like that."

"Well, there's that," she finally said, with a hint of a smile. "Though I feel like we've lived about a year in the last week or so. Really, it seems like we've been together forever already. But there's also the other thing, which we hadn't talked about all that much yet."

"I assume you mean what happened on Sunday," he said, "and the things that happened before that, right? Well, that's a done deal as far as I'm concerned. There's no going back anyway, after what we did on Sunday, and I've obviously forgiven you or we wouldn't be here right now."

"I guess," she said. "But are you really sure? Are you sure you won't change your mind and think less of me and hold it against me, down the road?"

"I won't hold it against you until we get home," he said, reprising one of her own jests. That got a broader smile. "Look, I know what you mean, and we can talk about it all you like, whenever you like. I know you might need to from time to time, and who knows, I might, too. But I want you to be clear on this – I see you as nothing more than a victim of circumstances, plain and simple, and I don't see my mind ever changing on that."

"Huh. Well, thank you for that. Really, it does make me feel better." She finished off the wine and said, "Let's go home. We can think on it all some more this week while we're away. But I have to warn you, your idea's awful temptin'. You might be sorry you brought it up, you might never be able to get rid of me!"

When they got back to the house, they decided to take the dog for a walk. They stopped by the boatyard, but the Captain was already gone for the day. When it was time to go to bed, Ketch went out to the living room to take one last look at the pile by the door. The dog's dishes were there now, and he'd add the dog bed in the morning. Had he forgotten anything important? He didn't think so, but there was something nagging at the back of his mind that held him there nonetheless.

Finally, he opened the door, went down the steps, and removed the life preserver from the nail it had been hanging on since shortly after he'd moved into the house. He carried it inside, deposited it on the pile, and went to bed.

~ Twenty ~

*He'd asked too much and loved too much,
and he'd worn it all out.*

This was the first Outer Banks hurricane Ketch had ever experienced in person, despite all the time he'd spent vacationing in Avon over the years, and despite having lived there full-time for the last three. More than forty hurricanes had assaulted this coast over the past hundred years, with on occasion more than one in a given year and several in one particular year, and they'd never gone without one for more than a few years in a row. So they'd been lucky so far during his tenure, but now he supposed they were probably due.

Hurricane Ernesto had made landfall at Cape Lookout, the southernmost extent of the Banks, on Saturday night, the fourth of their stay in Raleigh, and the city of Beaufort had been severely pummeled by Ernesto's punishing winds and storm surge. Born of a tropical wave off the coast of Africa, Ernesto had skirted the eastern Caribbean as a category 1 hurricane on the Saffir-Simpson Hurricane Wind Scale and then shifted northward, inflicting some damage most notably on Puerto Rico.

It had grown in strength to a category 3 storm over the warm waters of the Bahamas, and had weakened to a category 2, but still with sustained winds of over a hundred miles per hour, by the time it slammed into the North Carolina coast. It quickly weakened further as it tracked north through eastern North Carolina and into Virginia before turning east into the Atlantic off the coast of Virginia, departing as a marginal category 1 storm.

Winds of tropical storm force had extended over a hundred miles out from the center of the storm, and Ketch and Kari had weathered those winds in Raleigh, along with the occasional hurricane-force gust and copious rainfall. They and the dog hadn't been able to go outside very often since Saturday and Ketch thought the dog especially was developing a serious case of cabin fever, but they were pretty much okay otherwise.

The Residence Inn had lost some roof tiles and there were branches down, but they still had power, and there'd been no flooding and no leaks in their suite. They'd done some shopping locally upon their arrival, and the staff had also made sure there was food and water available right at the Inn, so they hadn't had to venture out into the storm for staples.

It was now Monday evening, and the weather here at least was finally starting to improve. They'd managed to watch a couple of movies early on, but since Friday night they'd kept their TV tuned to news and weather. A few small tornados had been reported across the state, but none where they were and none in Avon that they knew of.

The Banks however had been hit with some hurricane-force winds, and there'd been isolated reports of power outages and structural damage in several locations. Most of the damage, though, appeared to have been done by rain and storm tides, especially in Pamlico Sound, where the winds had blown the sound water westward, causing creeks and rivers to flood; as the storm had passed, those waters had receded eastward and piled up against parts of the eastern shore of the sound, that is, the westward side of Hatteras Island. Eight-foot tides had been reported in some places, and some docks had been smashed, some boats sunk, and some homes flooded. The water had surged across the island at Rodanthe, as Ketch had feared, and Route 12 had been breached there.

They'd been in periodic contact with the Captain throughout, and Kari had spoken with her family. Everyone seemed to be doing all right. The Captain, though, hadn't chosen the best refuge as it turned out, as there'd been similar though less damaging problems in Albemarle Sound; but though he and his family had had to contend with hurricane-force gusts of wind and some overfilling of the river, they'd come through it with only some minor damage. The Captain had said part of the dock had lifted and the *Minnow* had gotten slammed around some, but he thought she was still seaworthy. They were speaking with him now on Ketch's cell phone.

"We're itchin' to get on down there and check things out," Kari was saying. "We know there was some damage, but we hadn't been able to get a lot of details."

"Well, the road's washed out, you know, though I

hear it ain't so bad they have to put up one a them temporary steel bridges again, like they did the last time. It might only take 'em a few days to make it passable this time."

"I wonder if the looters will wait that long," Ketch said.

"That's the spirit!" the Captain laughed. "That's the thing I like most about you, you're a positive thinker! First you worry 'bout gettin' mugged, and now looters. This ain't Jersey, folks around here help each other out."

"Yes, well, we still have people like Mario, and I imagine we have vacationers from Jersey. Anyway, I'm thinking about seeing if I can find us somewhere to stay closer, and then taking my boat to the public launch at Pea Island. If I keep her speed down some, I know I could almost make it to Avon and back on one tank, but I'll bring a couple more gas cans with me. We could at least check on the house and the shop that way, though we won't be able to get to your place or Kari's."

"That's all right, I ain't real worried, it is what it is. But you better keep your speed down, some a the shoals have probably shifted, though you should be okay with your draft. I'd offer to take you myself, but I got some repairs to do, and when I go down I'm gonna have to crawl all the way there."

"We could come to you and drop one of us off to sail with you when you're ready, so you don't have to do it all by yourself," Kari offered.

"Well that's right nice a you, darlin'. See what I

mean, Ketch, you ole sad sack? Don't worry 'bout it right now, though, I ain't comin' back 'til they fix the road at least. Hey, if you can't find a place to stay, y'all could come here, we could put you up for a spell. We still got another guest bedroom here we ain't usin'."

"Thanks, Captain, we'll keep that in mind," Ketch said. They hung up shortly, and Ketch fired up his laptop. There were no Residence Inns around Nags Head and not many other pet-friendly hotels to choose from, and the ones he found looked to be on the unsavory side and didn't have good reviews. They might have been damaged by the storm anyway, so he didn't bother to call any of them. There may have been some options around Elizabeth City, but if they went there then they might as well stay with the Captain. They decided to take him up on his offer and called him back.

They reloaded the car and the truck, checked out Tuesday morning, and arrived at the Captain's place in the afternoon. The Captain's family went out of their way to make them feel welcome, which they were grateful for and Ketch was humbled by. Southern hospitality wasn't just a fable, at least not among the old guard. With very few exceptions, if any (he couldn't think of any at the moment), the ones he'd met on and around the Banks all seemed to be standup folks who'd have your back if you needed them to.

There was some property, which pleased the dog, around the surprisingly spacious house which sat on a knoll above the river, and the fact that it was riverfront pleased the dog even more. He was pretty adaptable for a dog, Ketch had to admiringly acknowledge, and he seemed comfortable here.

Which was good, since he'd decided against subjecting the dog to another long drive and probably equally long ride on a small boat. Counting the drive from here to Pea Island and back, and sailing the boat from Pea Island to Avon and back, it could be at least a ten-hour trip overall.

After getting settled into their room, they passed some time socializing with their generous hosts. When dinner was over, Ketch and the Captain went to town to stock the cooler for the trip.

"So, who-all's gonna be goin' on this little junket?" the Captain asked. "I need to know, so I can make sure we get the right kind a beer."

"Well, I thought me and Kari," Ketch said. "But then I wondered if leaving Jack here might be imposing too much."

"Nah, it'll be okay. You two are the ones that should go. I might could tag along, but I got work to do, and you'd burn more gas with the extra weight. Jack knows me. He can hang out with me, I'll keep a good eye on 'im."

After a comfortable (and respectfully quiet) night, Ketch and Kari met the Captain out on the back porch shortly after sunrise. They shared a quick breakfast with him, then loaded their cooler onto the boat. Before he got in the truck, Ketch had a word with the dog, who was looking nervous and concerned. He explained the situation as best he could, using words he knew the dog would understand, and hugged the dog, though not excessively. You can't make too big a deal out of arrivals and departures if you don't want to have a neurotic pet. When he started the truck, he saw that the dog was calmer, if resigned, and sitting next to the Captain. He called to the dog, "Jack, be good, I'll see you later!"

"Bon voyage!" the Captain said. "If y'all come across any a them dang looters, give 'em a kick in the pants for me!"

The drive to Pea Island was uneventful, though tedious, as they had to first stop for ice and gas – for the truck, the boat, and the extra gas cans – and then skirt the perimeter of Albemarle Sound on a maddeningly tortuous route before finally making it onto the Banks via the bridge above Kitty Hawk. Of course, it didn't help that they were both anxious to get the boat in the water. But at least there were no breaches in the road and no significant delays, and once they got off 158 and onto 12 below Nags Head they felt like they were on the home stretch – which they were.

When they shortly crossed the Bonner Bridge over Oregon Inlet, still intact and passable, under a finally blue sky, Ketch was again struck by the beauty of this confluence of the Atlantic Ocean and Pamlico Sound – the multifarious blue-green hues of the inlet, the sound, and the sea; and the waving cordgrass in the marshes... The postcard views from the elevated bridge made his breath catch in his throat every time he drove across this bridge, without fail. He had to slow down and force himself to pay attention to the road; it was a wonder he'd never accidentally driven right off it.

Once they crossed the bridge, it wasn't much longer before they reached the Pea Island refuge. They found the public boat launch functional and open, but busy, and they had to wait their turn. When they finally had the boat in the water and were underway, they both felt a sense of great relief. Kari cracked open the cooler and extracted two pint bottles of beer from it, which she or the Captain must have stuck in there, as Ketch had not.

"I know you have to watch out for the shoals," she said at a skeptical look from Ketch, "but one won't hurt."

He didn't argue, and in fact had to admit it was going down quite well. He wasn't sure why, but although he felt trepidatious about what they might find later, he also felt good, and happy. He was glad he'd remembered to pack his tarp hat and bring it along today; though he still had hair, it wasn't quite as thick as it used to be, and on this finally sunny day he could burn without it. Maybe it was just being out on the water again making him feel so good, or maybe it was who he was sailing with; maybe both. No longer having to worry about his house being seized might be another reason.

He'd been gradually accelerating since they started and was now going faster than he ordinarily might have under these circumstances, but he didn't want to waste time; and though not strictly necessary, it would also be nice to make it back to the Captain's place tonight before full dark. He'd have to get very unlucky to have a problem with shoals with his nine-inch draft – but if he did, things wouldn't end well for the boat at this speed; and there might also be some storm debris here and there, so he'd still keep a careful eye out ahead. No more beer for him until maybe on the way back later.

"Hey, do you think we might have time to dock and go inside for a few minutes when we get there? You know, to check and see if the bedroom's still okay?" she called over the engine with a mischievous look on her face.

"There might not be a dock anymore," he called back.

"Well, we could still pull the boat up onto the shore though, right?"

"I don't know." They were approaching the outskirts of Rodanthe now, and he could see there'd been some soundside flooding there. There was debris considerably above the normal high tide line, and some of the elevated houses looked like they still had water under them. They both saw where the road had been breached at the same time.

"Wow, look at that," she said. "It's not as bad as it could be, though. If we only got it this bad, we'll be doin' okay." Ketch didn't reply, and just kept watching the water ahead with only an occasional glance to the side. Waves and Salvo looked about the same as what they'd seen in Rodanthe, minus the road breach.

"We'll find out soon," he finally said. Next stop

Avon. She was right, what they'd seen so far wasn't that bad, considering. And *Port Starbird* had enough freeboard to park a car under the deck, which was more than twice as much as was mandated for his area; so although his dock might have washed out and there might have been water under the house, at least there shouldn't be any inside it. He hoped. If all he had to do was get a new lawn mower and a new bike and rebuild his dock, that wouldn't be so bad. Though maybe there'd also be some roofing to be done, depending on how the winds had been. Well, he had flood insurance.

They didn't talk after that, both of them lost in probably similar thoughts. When he could see that they were approaching the north end of town, he slowed down and steered the boat closer to shore, as close as he dared to get without risking running aground. There appeared to be a lot of debris along the shore here as well, more so than in the other towns.

"I don't know if we should chance the canals to check on the shop," Ketch said. "I'm afraid there might be too much junk in the water. We could get marooned if we foul the prop."

"That's okay. We can drive down as soon as the road opens, I can wait 'til then," she said. "Can't do much about it now anyway, and if we can't get there, maybe your pirates or looters or whatever can't either. Let's check out the boatyard, though, it's on the way."

They proceeded slowly and cautiously to the entrance to the boatyard. Ketch throttled back when they got close enough to see, not wanting to advance much further.

"Oh wow," Kari said. There'd been flooding here as well, and many of the docks were buckled and splintered. The boats that had remained here were in a state of disarray; some had apparently collided with one another, and two of the houseboats were partly beached sideways on the shore. Ketch backed out in silence and steered them around the bend.

Again, more flooding; here most of the houses were missing roof tiles, and there was water in every back yard and under some of the houses. The debris line, and water marks on the pilings, indicated the water had risen even farther and then receded. The pilings of one house looked to have given way, and the formerly elevated house now rested directly on the soggy ground; it was one of the old ones, so maybe the wood had been rotting and weakened. And then there was the house in the water.

In the water? Ketch steered closer and throttled back again. He rubbed his eyes to make sure they were clear and scanned the neighboring properties to be certain he had his landmarks straight and wasn't making a mistake. There was no mistake – that was his house, that was *Port Starbird*. Or what was left of it anyway.

"Oh, Ketch," Kari softly moaned. "Oh God, what happened?"

The house appeared to have settled approximately where the dock had been. Whether the dock had washed out first or been crushed by the house was impossible to tell. The house had apparently been knocked off its pilings, by hurricane winds or the receding water from the opposite shore of the sound slamming into it, or both, and either floated or slid down the back yard. Maybe a tornado had touched down here? He doubted it could have floated much or for very long, as only half of the foam blocks he'd ordered had been installed; they might have instead been smashed on impact. But the blocks were probably what had allowed the house to migrate as far as it had, one way or another, both the ones that had been installed and the others stacked behind the house.

But why? He'd had the house inspected before he'd bought it, and one more time since, and he'd been assured that the pilings and superstructure were in good shape. Len and Mario had installed most of the blocks on the same half of the house – maybe the extra weight was too much, maybe it was the imbalance that had tipped the scales.

"So, do you still want to go inside and see if the bedroom's okay?" Ketch rhetorically asked with a mirthless laugh. The house wasn't level, and the impact must have loosened joints; the entire structure was out of square and leaning like some old barns he'd seen that looked like they were about to fall over. And because of that and probably also the wind, the roof had started to collapse. All of the windows looked to have been shattered.

Just a few years ago, an event like this would have completely derailed him for sure, no doubt about it.

He might have had to check himself into a mental hospital. But though he was of course still devastated nonetheless, things were different now. *He* was different now, finally. Kari watched him in silence, trying to read his face.

"Looks totaled to me," he said. "Can't just bang out the dents on this baby, frame's bent." He cut the engine and dropped the anchor. One of his favorite John Prine songs inexplicably popped into his head, and he drummed on a gunwale with his hands and sang a twist on a bit of it. "Looks like... someone knocked you into the sea... same thing... same thing happened to me!" He got himself another beer from the cooler, opened it, and gulped some down.

"Hey, are you okay?" Kari asked with a worried frown on her face.

"I'm just fine! Here, I'll tell you why," he said, and broke into song again:

"Any day you're not six feet under is a good day,
Any day that big old world's still spinning around,
Let the small stuff go and the good stuff will make things okay,
Don't let that goofy old world start bringing you down."

"I don't recognize that one, is it one of your own?" she nervously asked.

He stopped singing and looked at her. "I'm scaring you, aren't I?" he said. "I'm sorry, I didn't mean to do that. I'm okay, really." He took another sip of his beer. "That is indeed one of mine. It's called *Have a Good Day.*"

"Huh, so you do have more than just that one you

played at the house that time." Ketch saw that she was looking a little more relaxed now. "You'll have to play all your songs for me sometime. When you're not writin' your book."

"When I'm not working with you and helping you grow your business," he corrected her. "I'm still serious about that offer I made you. I'm afraid, though, I might have to rescind the invitation to live at my house. How would you feel about a houseboat?"

"A houseboat? Where? The boatyard's wrecked."

"Well, I still have my lot. We could just park it out back. No, wait, there's something in the way there."

"Anywhere is fine by me. I'll go wherever we need to go," she said with a smile. "Which for a while might mean my apartment, if it's still standin'. Do you think you'll rebuild?"

"I don't know, we'll see. We'll figure it all out eventually."

She moved closer to him and enveloped him in a hug. "Are you sure you're okay?"

"Yes, I think so. Though I do feel kind of like Santiago."

"Santiago who?"

"You know, the old fisherman, in *The Old Man and the Sea*. All that struggle, all that effort, the ordeal he went through trying to land that giant marlin, and by the time the sharks were done all he had left was a pile of bones."

"And the boy."

"Right, and the boy. And I have you." He gave her one more squeeze and went back to the cooler. He got out another beer for her and the food they'd brought, and started laying it all out on one of the seats.

"Damn that Hemingway," he chuckled. "But I'm better off than Santiago in one way – I don't have to eat raw fish to survive. That's something."

He mock-bowed and beckoned her to join him. "Milady, luncheon is served!"

About the Author

Garrett lives in upstate New York, where he and his wife serve as the housekeeping staff for two rather spoiled dogs. He has degrees in biology and computer science. After a career that ranged from testing experimental drugs (not on himself!) to developing computer operating system software, he decided to retire from the real world and try his hand at writing fiction.

Garrett lived in coastal North Carolina for a while some years back, and the current focus of his writing is a place that's very special to him, the Outer Banks region of North Carolina. PORT STARBIRD is his first novel.

In addition to being a writer, Garrett is a so-so tennis player and sometime scuba diver. He also plays guitar and writes songs from time to time. If you'd like to hear some bad recordings of original music that's untainted by success, visit his web site at:

www.GarrettDennis.com

You can also visit Garrett Dennis on **Facebook** at:

www.facebook.com/garrdenn

You can also follow him on **Twitter:**

Garrett Dennis @PortStarbird

If you have comments, or if you want to be placed on

his mailing list for news and future releases, you can reach him via e-mail at:

garrettdennis.author@gmail.com

If you enjoyed this book, you might also enjoy Ketch's next adventure:

Port of Refuge

Thanks for reading this book! If you have time, please consider taking a few minutes to log a review at Amazon and/or Goodreads. Reviews help increase an independently published book's visibility, and the author would greatly appreciate it.

Made in the USA
Middletown, DE
17 May 2015